A PLAY OF LIGHT

20p

Also by Henrietta Soames

At the Hall

A PLAY
OF LIGHT

Henrietta Soames

HEADLINE
REVIEW

First published in 1996
by HEADLINE BOOK PUBLISHING

A HEADLINE REVIEW hardback

10 9 8 7 6 5 4 3 2 1

British Library Cataloguing in Publication Data

Soames, Henrietta, 1958–
  A state of grace
  1. English fiction – 20th century
  I. Title
  823.9'14 [F]

ISBN 0 7472 1809 9

Typeset by Palimpsest Book Production Limited,
Polmont, Stirlingshire
Printed in England by Clays Ltd, St Ives plc

HEADLINE BOOK PUBLISHING
A division of Hodder Headline PLC
338 Euston Road
London NW1 3BH

I would like to remember my father, the late H. W. Soames.
And the late Ronnie Ferguson, a brief but important friend,
whose observations contributed to this book.

I am very grateful to Sonia Davenport for advice on ancient
Greek, Michael Grossbard for illuminating phone calls and, as
ever, my brother and sisters for their perennial support.

I am old now and the skin on my hands is wrinkled like the jam test for setting point. My face has shivered into deltas of dry lines and crevices.

It is strange to be old. I find that I am invisible, that people's eyes glaze over my corner of the sitting room by the window. Sometimes a child will glance at me, then stare full on for a moment before asking in a high, loud voice, 'Who's that? Isn't she *old* . . .' Until the parents, with an embarrassed and apologetic murmur, hush the child and pull him away. One afternoon at tea there was a pair of boys – twins? – dressed identically in summer shorts and cartoon-printed T-shirts, giggling as they watched me reaching for my cup with my crabbed fingers. When their parents noticed, the boys were strictly admonished and sent out of the room. But I hadn't minded. I wouldn't have minded even if they'd come right up to me and asked why my hands were curved and knobbled as old tree trunks, my fingers locked into my palms. I would like to have spoken to them, and I know I could have entertained them for a little while, long enough maybe for their parents to have had a break, an hour to themselves in bed.

But this does not happen, nobody approaches me here. The old have a moat around them which the young do not cross. We are living fossils, no longer human – an alien species. I can only sit and watch those bright children leaping through the hotel like sparks from a fire, smiling at them while they giggle and look away, bold and shy, defiant and timorous simultaneously. I, who have never had children, now study them with a curious hunger.

They are kind to me here in the hotel. They light a fire every day, even now when it is high summer. The fire is comforting, alive, company through the long day. They keep this sitting room

1

private for me in the mornings so that I am undisturbed, but after lunch it is open to the other guests and I sit here observing their lives, their histories, their unspoken communications. People give away so much of themselves in tiny movements – the fraction of a hesitation before a wife greets her husband, the glance of a father to his tall grown son, his hand slapping a little too heavily on the taut, burly shoulder.

It is quiet. I listen to the fire softly crackling, to the gulls crying as they fly over the lake towards the sea. Later, in autumn, the geese will migrate, huge arrows of them fired into the sky. On the mountain opposite, the ewes are grazing, nibbling determinedly around the thick stems of bracken. They are no longer bleating for their lambs, as they did in the spring, when I first came here – most of those lambs have gone to the abattoir now and sheep have short memories. I hear the sweep of clouds, the hissing of the sun, a voice calls, someone laughs, crockery is laid out. Little waves of sound lapping over me.

Peace? That is harder to find. Oh, I know that when they look at me – the young looking at the old sitting with a magazine or knitting, whittling away their stick of time until it is broken into tiny pieces – they think that we are at peace, when really we are imprisoned in bodies which will no longer obey our will, no longer allow us to be active. The old either sink into apathy, shocked at the approach of death, or we fritter and fret our hours away. How much more difficult it is to keep one's mind and not allow it to warp. I think about death, I think about old age, seditious subjects no one wants to discuss.

Often I doze in the afternoons. When the guests leave the dining room after lunch and come in here for their coffee, they see a white-haired old lady sitting upright in her armchair, her ugly hands tucked away beneath her shawl and her face smoothed shut. They stop for a moment and whisper, 'She's sleeping, doesn't she look peaceful . . .'

They do not see the snakes writhing in her mind like Medusa turning her to stone.

'You're sure you wouldn't like the telly moved in here for company, Miss Mair?' Annie said when I first came. 'I could easily set it up for you, and I'm pretty sure you'd get a good reception in this room. Of course,' she added quickly, 'I'd still make sure you had the room to yourself in the mornings. Would you like that?'

'It's kind of you,' I said. 'But I prefer the quiet.'

She frowned. 'I just don't like to think of you sitting here on your own – some folks wouldn't take to it at all.'

'I'm used to it,' I said. 'It's what I want. The last few months . . . I haven't seen people much—'

'Oh, I heard all about that,' she broke in. 'My word, but you were lucky, Miss Mair. Someone was looking after you.'

'You could say that.'

'And without a scratch on you too.' She was shaking her head. 'I don't know how you can be so calm. I admire you, really I do. If it'd been me – well, I'd still be shaking like a leaf just thinking about it.'

I smiled. She was so earnest, so innocent. 'It's Annie, isn't it? Your name? I'm afraid I'm not very good with names these days.'

She hesitated. 'That's what I like to be called.'

'But it isn't your name?'

'My mam had me christened . . . differently.'

'What did she christen you?'

She flushed poppy red and mumbled, 'Anastasia.'

'But that's a lovely name. Why don't you like it?'

'It's showy,' she said firmly. 'My mam, she'd read this book about Russia just before I was born. My dad used to say it was lucky she hadn't been reading about China or Japan, or heaven knows what I'd be called now.'

'Well, I think it's a very pretty name. I'll call you Anastasia in future.'

'Oh, no!' She looked horrified. 'Please, Miss Mair, I don't want folks to know. It's – well, it's a secret, really.' She bit her lip. 'You won't tell anyone, will you?'

A secret pressed into my palm like a small bead.

'No – no, of course not,' I said humbly. 'I promise I won't breathe a word.'

'Oh, I'm sorry, Miss Mair.' She came up to me and shyly brushed my arm. 'I know I shouldn't be so touchy about it. It's my own fault.'

'It's forgotten already.'

She smiled. 'Well, I'll just go and fetch your coffee in for you. And you're sure you don't want the telly? Or the radio? I could bring in the tape machine from the kitchen and you could listen to music . . .'

She's a dear girl, a kind girl, but she doesn't understand. In her smooth cheeks, in her dextrous fingers there are no ancient conversations trapped as in the bole of a tree. There are no excrescences, no knots or warts. I am full of dialogues, of looks that have yet to be untangled, words to be unravelled, my fingers searching for the end of the thread, the clue, the beginning.

Gregory visits every few days. Father Gregory, he'd probably like me to call him, but I'm not about to bow my head to that old cant. He's a waste of a young man, tall, dark-haired, good-looking, fit. 'You should be married and raising a family, not hiding in black skirts,' I told him when he first came. 'What is it with men like you – are you afraid of women? Afraid of having children?'

But he just laughed. 'You don't beat about the bush, do you, Miss Mair?'

'Your Father Superior – or Abbot, or whatever he's called – should have warned you before he sent you to check up on me,' I said sharply. 'He and I have had our brushes in the past. You ask him.'

'You don't seem to have a very good opinion of our Order, Miss Mair,' he said after a moment. 'May I ask why?'

I looked at him. 'Do you really need to ask? After what your Order has done?'

He held my gaze. 'It wasn't our doing, Miss Mair. Surely you can see that?'

'Oh, yes.' I gave a bitter laugh. 'You just begged *not* to be given the estate – "Let this cup pass us by . . ."'

There was a pause. Then he said quietly, 'You're not religious at all, are you, Miss Mair?'

I took his measure for a moment, then replied in an even voice, 'Teddy took me to meet one of your lot once to discuss conversion – it was before the Dowager died. I had what I believe is called a "Preliminary Catechism". This "priest" –' I spoke the word with disgust – 'spent the whole time looking at my legs –

4

rather fine in those days for my age, I admit – and at the end of the hour asked me, very *sotto voce*, whether I wore stockings or tights.'

He looked away. 'I'm sorry.'

'Don't apologize – it was very amusing.'

'It was most unfortunate.'

'Not good PR for your lot, I agree.' I gave a mock sigh. 'You certainly missed your chance with me.'

'You wouldn't be willing to give us a second one?'

'I'm too old for that now. I don't like all that mumbo-jumbo and dressing up in women's clothes and making an exhibition of yourselves. I've been an actress myself, Gregory, I know the excitement of having an audience.'

Unexpectedly, he laughed. 'Is that what you think it is? Just a craving for adulation?' His blue eyes were very clear. 'Well, it's a hard way of getting that, I can tell you. If that was all *I* was after—'

'So, you *do* find it hard, then?' I broke in. 'And do you have doubts too, about your "vocation"?'

'Didn't you ever have doubts about yours?' he countered.

I shrugged. 'Acting was never really a vocation for me. And it was a lot easier in those days – not so many rules, one could slip into a company without all the union nonsense they have now. Of course, I enjoyed it, loved it even, but—' I stopped.

'Would I have seen you perform?' he asked politely.

'Not unless you were in very short trousers,' I replied tersely. 'It was all a long time ago. I gave it up when I went to live with Teddy in Belle House. Anyway – ' I looked at him – 'you're not going to get me to reminisce all misty-eyed about "the good old days" if that's what you think.'

'Why not? It's what I'm here for.'

'Is it? So you're here to shrive me of my sins, are you? Some sort of religious shrink, waiting to hear my confession?' I could feel myself becoming angry. 'Think you can wipe the slate clean so that when I die – which won't be too long, I hope – I can go and meet my maker all kitted out in a clean, fresh soul and you can kneel in your chapel at night and feel satisfied that you've done a good job, saved another sinner from the flames of damnation? No, thank you.'

I took a breath, then went on in a lighter tone, 'But the doubts about your "vocation" – well, now, I'd much rather talk about that.'

'And I'd much rather not,' he retorted sharply.

I raised one eyebrow. It is a trick I learned early in my career. I've always thought that it would have been most useful on television, but as I did very little screen work the impact of my eyebrow has largely been lost. Now, however, its effect was most gratifying.

'Oh, forgive me,' he said humbly. 'That was a very unChristian response.'

'Human, though,' I replied. 'And therefore infinitely preferable. Teddy used to tell me that I could be really very provoking.'

'It's not that I have doubts,' he struggled. 'Not doubts exactly, but—'

'Regrets?'

He frowned. 'For a faith to be strong – to be secure, to have solid foundations – it must be able to withstand a great deal of questioning.'

'And that's what you're doing?'

'Miss Mair—' He looked away, colouring. 'This is not something . . . I am used to talking about freely.'

Another little bead.

'I understand.'

'Honestly,' he went on after a moment, 'I'm not here to "save your soul", you know.'

'You'd have a job trying.'

'I know.'

'Ah,' I put in quickly, 'so that's your strategy, is it? Lull me into a false sense of security—'

'Miss Mair!'

'—and then whip out the chalice and the holy oil and all the rest of the props.'

'Miss Mair, really—'

'Lavinia,' I interrupted him. 'If you're going to be visiting me on a regular basis, I'd prefer you to call me Lavinia.'

He looked at me with surprise. 'You want me to visit again? You're sure?'

'Don't play the ingénu with me, Gregory,' I said tartly. 'In fact, don't play any sort of role. I can see straight through most of them.'

'You don't leave me much scope – Lavinia,' he said uncomfortably.

'Just be yourself, Gregory,' I said. 'Is that so difficult?'

And so the visits began.

Because of my hands, it is hard for me to cut up my food and someone – Annie probably – has noticed this, so now I find that my food is served already cut up into small portions. It is done so tactfully, so discreetly, that I cannot remark on it, and whatever I order from the menu – fish, steak and kidney, salad – is presented in such a way that I can eat it with just a fork and spoon.

Even so, I do not eat a lot. I got out of the habit at the Dower House. Annie asks when she removes my still-full plate, 'Is there anything else you'd like instead, Miss Mair? We've a lovely bit of local soft cheese and I made the biscuits for it myself this morning – or a little apple turnover? Have something, Miss Mair, please.' She looks so keen, so young. I want to reach out and smooth the thick lock of chestnut hair that falls across her peaches and cream face that is so shockingly fresh and unlined. It has grown very strong in me, this need to touch youth, to wonder at the softness of new skin when my own is so terribly haggard and dry. And so to please her, to see her smile, I agree to have one of the turnovers, or a slice of cheese, and she whisks my plate away and happily bustles into the kitchen.

But like sleep, which I no longer seem able to achieve easily, my body does not want food. As if it is emptying, paring itself down in preparation for death. I would like to be one of those plants that live suspended in the rain forests, existing only on mist and air.

It is such a mystery, this death. More and more as I anticipate, I wonder about it. More and more, I turn it over in my mind, trying to understand it. But it is as if I am trying to peer over a huge door that towers above me. And it is such a lonely investigation. Oh, most people can tolerate with smothered yawns and glazed eyes an old person talking about her life, her past, but talk about death – that looming cliff which overshadows everything – no, they don't want you to talk about that.

And yet I suppose it is a natural process – getting old, the body breaking down, dissolving. Natural as giving birth. And maybe, as in birth, there is some natural physical preparation. Maybe there is a drill which locks us into old age and dying as inexorably as the one which locks us into being born. Maybe it is all programmed like a rocket, each stage leading to the next until we are released.

'Why is it,' I asked Gregory one morning, 'that there are so many euphemisms for death? "Passing away", "falling asleep", "going over". You know, all of that?'

'People are afraid,' he said. 'We're all afraid of the unknown.'

'Even you, with your angels and your God and your heavenly harps?'

'Even me, Lavinia.'

'I thought religion was meant to sort all that out for you?'

'It's not a cure-all.'

'Some people seem to think it is. It's certainly packaged as such.'

He looked down at his hands. 'I haven't found that it answers *all* the questions,' he said slowly.

'But you joined up nevertheless.'

He smiled. 'One has to be a little humble – not expect all the answers at once.'

'Strikes me as a pretty poor deal,' I said crisply. 'Put that in a contract and no actor worth his salt would sign. We like to know what to expect.'

'And you've never taken something on trust? Never suspended your judgement?'

I took a quick breath but didn't answer. Looked out of the window, where a spring storm was darkening the sky. I could see rain approaching over the mountain.

'I don't know how your God can stand it,' I said eventually. 'If I was him, I'd wash my hands of us mortals altogether.'

He didn't reply. I didn't want him to. The first heavy drops struck the window and we watched together in silence.

I came to this hotel to be serene, thinking I would glide gracefully into death. And though I sit here with my shawls and my white hair and my stillness which deceives everybody, I am not deceived. I cannot accept this extinction. Cannot accept that I will be wiped out of life as carelessly as a fly is swatted or a pigeon shot down. I am like a horse stopped at a fence, refusing to move. There is a bridge and I will not cross it. Death and I face each other, implacable as poker players.

'I feel very indulgent, sitting here with a fire at the height of summer,' I said to Annie as I watched her brushing the hearth this morning. 'I suppose I could do without it – save you all this bother.'

'Nonsense,' she said briskly, her accent scrunching up her words like crisp autumn leaves. 'We can always do with a fire. It can be right chilly here, summer or no summer.' She glanced over her shoulder to the window. 'See those clouds building up? May not be so fine for the races this weekend if the wind's up too high. They had to call them off one year – said it was too dangerous for the youngsters. Well—' She stood up. 'I'll fetch your coffee in at eleven, Miss Mair.'

'Oh, call me Lavinia, Annie, please. Everyone else does.'

But she drew herself up. 'It wouldn't be right,' she said firmly. 'You're an old lady, Miss Mair, and you deserve respect. Now, you just ring the bell if you need anything . . .'

After lunch the room filled up with guests talking quietly as they bent over their maps and guidebooks. It is interesting to watch them all, the families with their tensions held in check by a thin skin of holiday cheer. I listen to the silences between people, the dull looks of a couple who have run out of conversation, each paddling separate boats that have become becalmed, the glances that shoot beyond the recipient and land wide of the mark, the little pebbles of talk that do not skim over the water but are swallowed up and sink beneath the surface.

Yesterday evening at dinner a couple came over to ask if they might share my table – the room was full, naturally I agreed. They did not try to include me in their conversation but talked animatedly, loudly, the woman darting covert glances from time to time, checking to see if I was watching. She needed an audience – they both did. But this morning when I glanced in at the empty dining room, they were both sitting in silence – the man determinedly eating his way through egg and bacon and sausage, the woman picking at toast. They had nothing to say to each other without a witness.

*　　*　　*

9

Growing old, as Teddy used to say, has no future. I never thought that I would grow old. I had always been so young, so active, so energetic. I never thought that I would experience life as the old experience it, that my body would become weak, frail, tired – though I do nothing to exercise it. That I cannot open the lid of a new jar of jam, cannot move quickly, or manage stairs, or go for a long, exhilarating walk. Yet instead of falling into a dull drowse as I edge towards death, I find that I have become more alert, as if the skin of my self is thinner, the world brighter, more poignant. And I see my mind growing ragged and wild as uncut hair, ranging too widely, peering into dark corners, lifting slabs of memory which should remain untouched.

Oh, it is a cruel thing, this age. Teddy did well to escape it. And yet with him, though I was old – we both were – I never *felt* old. Maybe if he was with me still, I would not now have aged so quickly.

I look at the young, at the new couple who have just now come into the room after their day by the lake, and I see them as ignorant – no, *innocent* creatures. They do not believe that this can ever happen to them. And if they see me at all, it is as an old thing. Not a woman, not even a person, but a *thing*.

Babies cry unceasingly when they are born, but when one is old the tears no longer flow and instead there is a protest, sharp and hard-hammering – why me? why in this way? why life and death and the whole cruel joke of it all?

And when – as these two now settled into their chairs, touching and smiling, counting the minutes till they can respectably leave for bed – when they look at me and see my wrinkles and my tired flesh that has folded up and resigned itself to ugliness, they do not think that I was young once as they will be old one day. They do not imagine that I too held a lover in my arms tight as an oyster clutching its pearl. No, I am of another breed to them, I did not come to this state gradually in the daily breakdown of my body, my skin drying, my hair thinning, my bones weakening – no, to them I have always been old. But I have been a person too. I have been young. I too have held the flame of life so close that it has burned my fingers.

So many of the people I knew and cared about are dead now – other actors, producers, directors. Or I've lost touch with them, like Bernard, disappeared into his hideout in the Highlands. All those people, all that gaiety.

It is one of those jokes in life that you are not told when you are young but have to find out for yourself. As you get older, you sit at the top of a tree and watch the branches leading up to your perch being lopped off one after another until you are alone up there with that high, wonderful view and no one to share it with. A cruel joke that life plays: Here, it says, spread out like a tree in the sun, spread out, make friends, companions, lovers, and live long, long enough to watch them being plucked away one by one. Long enough to realize that death is no respecter of age, that it will take the young – those in the very prime of life – with the same zest with which it culls the old. And too, live long enough to lose your ease of movement, so that your days become an ordeal of trivia – washing, dressing, going from room to room – little molehills made into mountains. And yet – and this is the cream of the joke – retain absolutely your clarity of mind, so that you can observe each stage of this dissolution with a pitiless lucidity.

It is cold today for all that it is summer. The wind has freshened and the surface of the lake is covered in little ruffles like a lace sleeve.

'Is this a good time?' Gregory was standing in the doorway. 'I'll come back later if you're busy.'

'Do I look busy?'

'Well, I—'

'Do I look as though I'm up to my ears in something terribly important?'

'Lavinia, I only wanted to make sure—'

'Oh, for heaven's sake, come in and sit down.'

He sat, spreading his habit carefully beneath him. 'How are you today, Lavinia?' he began.

I studied him. 'I'll say one thing for you, Gregory, you know how to wear your costume. Goes a long way in our profession – but then, you're probably aware of that already.'

'Oh, well—' He tried to laugh. 'I don't quite know what to say to that.'

'Stumbling over your lines, however, is not to be recommended.'

11

'Lavinia, I—'

'Nor is drying, corpsing, making the wrong entrance, or upstaging another actor – though in your case I imagine that means another performer taking the stage – the Bishop, maybe, or God.' I stopped. He was waiting for me to continue, his face wearing a patient, politely indulgent look that I find particularly nauseating. 'Unless,' I added, 'these "mistakes" are tricks of your performance. In which case, of course, they can be very effective indeed.'

After a moment he said evenly, 'I don't understand what you're trying to tell me, Lavinia. I'm sorry—'

'Don't apologize – I don't like apologies.'

'I still don't understand.'

'No.' I looked away, back out over the lake to the boats with their bright sails. 'How am I today, Gregory? I'm full of poison, that's how I am.'

'Poison can be drawn.'

'Oh, don't give me that pseudo-symbolic claptrap.' I turned back to him angrily. 'If that's all you've come here for, you should know better by now.'

'I came to tell you that work's begun on the Dower House,' he said. 'I thought you'd like to know.'

'I don't see why. I'm not going back there – I've said so.'

He shrugged. 'The work will take a while anyway – most of the summer we think. We hadn't realized the state it was in. It practically needs demolishing to be rebuilt properly.' He paused, then added, 'We were thinking of adding on an extra room or two, and making the windows larger. What do you think?'

'Do what you like with it, I don't care. It's your property.'

I turned back to the window. A pair of butterflies hopped and danced in the garden. At the corner I could see Annie pegging out washing – sheets billowing in the wind. She was laughing, calling out to someone I couldn't see.

'You can go if you like,' I said after a while. 'Duty done.'

'No, I'll stay a little longer.'

'Hoping to gather some gleanings of my soul to pick over in your cell?'

'I just thought I'd keep you company, that's all.'

I looked at him. 'Gregory-the-poultice?'

He smiled and gave a little shrug but didn't reply.

'It gets rather wearing, fighting.'

'Do you have to fight?'

'I don't know anything else. It's what I've always done.'

'But you don't have to fight alone.'

'Oh, Gregory,' I cried. 'What do you know? You're so young. You know nothing – *nothing*.'

He looked down at his hands. 'You're probably right.'

'You can't help that, though.'

'But I'd like to help, really.' He leaned forward, eager as a puppy.

I shook my head and turned back to the window, where the shadows were chasing each other over the fells, a play of light and dark ancient as stone.

I can see the boats from here. They have been lining up all week and sometimes one breaks out and sweeps across the lake like a skater. It looks warm outside, sun shining, a soft breeze. But I feel cold. I am often cold. I suppose one's blood thins as one gets older. I watch children running about on the lawn, their faces red as poppies, while I sit with the shawls wrapped tight around my shoulders, my feet so cold they might already be dangling over my grave.

Is this what happens, then? That gradually one gets frozen out of life? Like a planet dying, with all the warmth slowly sucked away? Or is it that I do not want the flames of my life to be fanned up out of the ashes? I do not want to be warm, to be attached, to love and be loved again. I want to untie the knots and slip into the dark painlessly so that the loss of this bright life should not tear me open, so that death will not come as a shock, so that I can say, I don't care, I didn't want to go on living anyway.

Lies. Deceit. If I am honest, I rage against death. I rage as a child rages against life when it is brought into this world howling. I rage against the indignity, the cruel sport of it, that I should be pushed from this world into God knows what darkness just when I have become accustomed to life and accepted that it is good. I want to defy the boat, defy the wind and sail against the current anyway.

Soon it will be time for tea. Annie will bring in the tray and fuss as she does with the cups and milk. She will bank up the fire and straighten the chairs, while through the open door I will hear the hum of guests in the hall as they stamp their boots and shed their shiny green jackets. Soon the room will be dotted with people, all cutting into their scones and lifting the fine china to their lips. They will be talking about their day, about the coming races, about the weather, their walks, what they might do tomorrow. And their faces, so fresh and clear, will shine too brightly, shocking me who wants to get used to the dimming of the light, who does not want life to still grab me by the throat and twist me with its utter and unbelievable and eternal loveliness.

'It might be fine for the races, after all,' Annie said as she shut the door behind her.

The children were still clamouring for her in the hall. 'Magic up something with your magic wand, Annie,' they cried.

'You're very popular,' I said.

'Oh—' She smiled, blushing a little. 'They fair wear me out, they do.'

'But you still love them.'

I watched as she neatened the magazines and polished the tables, flourishing her pink and yellow feather duster. The room plumped up like a cushion. Oh, but she was so young, so pliant and resilient, her energy crackling all around her like a crisp new petticoat.

'Why are you smiling at me like that, Miss Mair?' she asked, straightening up for a moment. 'Got soot on my nose, have I?'

'I was just thinking—'

'Thinking what?'

'I was just thinking how pretty you looked. There,' I said as she blushed again deep crimson, 'that's what comes of fishing for compliments.'

'Oh, Miss Mair, I never—'

'Soon it'll be time for you to have children of your own,' I went on. 'Hasn't your John asked you yet? Because if he doesn't hurry up, I'm sure there are plenty of others who won't take so long to pop the question.'

'Oh, Miss Mair!'

'I could have a word with him, if you like. You know, giddy him on a bit.'

'Miss Mair, you wouldn't – you mustn't – I wouldn't want—'

I smiled. 'It's all right, Annie. I'm only teasing.'

'Really, Miss Mair.' She shook her head in mock reproof. But then stood there for a moment, twisting the feather duster in her hands. 'Miss Mair, there *is* something I'd like to ask you,' she said hesitantly.

'Oh? What is it, Annie?'

She pulled a few feathers from the duster unconsciously. 'It's – well, it was John's idea really, but I think it's a good one – I told him I'd ask you and see if—' She broke off, glancing at me uncertainly.

'Go on. I'm intrigued.'

She took a breath. 'You see, I told him about you being resident here and how you sit looking out of the window all day, and he said – well, he said—'

'Yes?' I prompted. 'John said?'

The speech came out all in a rush while the feather duster fluttered in her hands. 'You see, Miss Mair, he said – well, what with the races coming up, wouldn't you like to see them properly, from the lakeside? He said he could come up in his car and we'd take you down – he'd drive ever so carefully. There's a nice quiet spot we know where we could all sit and watch everything. And I'd make up a nice picnic – the turnovers you like, and some gingerbread, and John's mam's still got some strawberries left in her garden. And we'd take great care of you and bring you back whenever you wanted, but you'd get some good sun and fresh air and it would all – we could all – we could have such a nice time . . .'

Her face was so keen it almost hurt to look at. What have I done, I thought, to provoke such loyalty?

'Annie, my dear, it's very kind of you,' I said as gently as I could. 'But—'

'Oh, Miss Mair, don't say no,' she broke in. 'Not straight away – not immediately all at once like that. I know you think it'd be an upheaval and that, but we'd make it ever so easy for you, really we would.'

'I know.'

'Then think about it,' she pleaded. 'Say you'll turn it over in your mind at least. You don't have to decide yet – there's plenty of time. Promise you'll think about it. Promise us that much.'

Never refuse a kindness, Teddy used to say. You don't always receive a second offer.

'All right, Annie, I'll think about it.'

The feather duster waved jubilantly. 'Oh, thank you, Miss Mair.'

'But I'm not promising any more than that, though.'

'Oh, yes, that's fine enough.' She gathered up her things, her face shining as the sun. 'I'll bring in your coffee.' She beamed as she left.

And suddenly I remembered Edna.

Edna closing the door of my dressing room when I staggered in exhausted. Edna examining my reflection dispassionately in the mirror – my red eyes, the new deep lines by my mouth – and calmly laying out the darker sticks of make-up. Edna standing behind me, combing out my hair, twisting it into a neat bun that would fit beneath the wig.

'At this rate I won't need any wigs,' I said, touching the broad new streaks of white in my hair.

'I can give you a rinse for that, madam,' she replied evenly.

'They say Marie Antoinette turned white overnight from shock,' I said, trying to make a joke of it.

She caught my eye in the mirror. 'That was because she didn't have her rinse, madam.' And placing the wig tightly over my forehead, she pulled, and with one deft movement it was fitted snugly back and over my scalp.

I looked at my reflection – there, an old crone . . .

Thin, sallow, seemingly locked for ever in an indeterminate middle age, Edna was completely self-effacing. I hardly noticed her at first except that she was reliable, that my costumes were cleaned and pressed, ready for me when I needed them, that my make-up was laid out as I liked, my coffee prepared when I came off-stage.

I remember, I had a silk scarf that I had torn badly and thrown away. Edna brought it back to me one evening beautifully mended with tiny stitches. 'I think you should be able to wear this again now, madam.' I looked but couldn't see any trace of the tear at all. 'No, you keep it, Edna – you deserve it.' And she wore that flamboyant red silk every day with her fawn raincoat and her lace-up shoes.

I didn't know it then, but that was to be the last time I worked.

A Play of Light

It was a long, potentially arduous, American tour. Unfamiliar theatres to work in, unknown cities to find one's way around and a company which, though warm and close-knit to begin with, I knew from long experience would probably splinter into little cliques and petty rivalries. But I didn't care, nothing mattered, I was happy – too happy. Because as we waited for planes and trains and coaches, as we crossed the prairies and trundled up the long coastlines, as we smiled for photographs and gave publicity interviews to impertinent journalists, I was only thinking: Oh, Teddy, we are going to be so happy, you and I . . . As if I was a young girl instead of a middle-aged woman. And not even the memory of the Dowager and her malevolent stare prickling over me as I walked down the long hall at Belle House to greet her, the clusters of diamonds winking on her taloned fingers as she gripped her black cane, the curl of her lip – 'Edward tells me you are an *actress* . . .' – no, nothing could stop my heart singing. '. . . And of course you will take instruction in the Faith . . . ?' Yes, yes, anything, whatever she wanted. Teddy had said that we would be married as soon as my tour was over. The Dowager would have got used to the idea by then. We would be married and live happily ever after . . .

A month from the end of the tour, Teddy's letter arrived.

I'd been at a party the night before and had got to the theatre late, cutting it rather fine for the matinée performance. I propped the letter up against the mirror and smiled at it as I made up. I would read it during the second act, when I had a decent long break. Teddy was not a good correspondent but this envelope with his embossed crest on the back felt thick with the promise of many pages.

I hurried rather sketchily through my performance and, off-stage at last, dispatched Edna on some errand, settled down in the armchair and broke the seal.

My dear Lavinia

Not 'Dearest'? Not 'Vinny'?

This is a very difficult letter for me to write but I'll make the best of it.

The Dowager died three months ago.

17

Well, that'll make our lives easier . . .

Of course, she was a great age and though strong, as you could see when you met her, she had been unwell since Christmas. It has been very cold here. I am grateful that my mother did not suffer. She passed away peacefully in her sleep after receiving the sacraments and has been laid to rest, as she wished, in the family vault here on the estate.
However,

I could feel him pause here, turning the pen over and over in his hands.

unbeknownst to me, or to anyone other than her solicitors, shortly before her death the Dowager changed her will. As I say, I was completely unaware of this.

Now I was reading quickly, my heart clenched inside.

Belle House and the whole of the estate, with all the income, rents, land sales and revenues, have been left not to myself but to an Order of monks to which my mother had become deeply attached over the last few years. As soon as probate has been granted, the Order will have the running of the estate completely. I have already had meetings with them to discuss the practicalities and they are being extremely generous.
I know you might jump to conclusions, Vinny, but please believe me that my mother's decision *had nothing to do with you personally*. The fact is, unfortunately she became aware of our 'affair', of which, as you know, for all these years she knew nothing. Realizing that I had continued to take the sacraments even though, because I was still married to Eve, I was not in a fit spiritual state to receive them, the Dowager felt deeply wounded and shocked that I had betrayed her highest principles.
I admit that my own conscience troubled me greatly, but I was not brave enough to be truthful either to my mother or to the Church. Consequently, I see my disinheritance now

18

as a penance to be accepted humbly. Please, Vinny, my love, believe that never, at any time, have I doubted the validity of my relationship with you. You are my rock.

How did the Dowager come to hear of us? By an extraordinary mischance. Your niece, Helen, has written a play which has caused some stir in the papers here. The play, *A State of Grace*, is, according to the gossip columnists, based on you and me and our relationship. What started as a speculative paragraph in the evening paper ended as a half-page article in one of the tabloids and a friend of my mother's sent her the clipping. Of course, I'm sure that Helen was quite unaware that her play would prompt this kind of distasteful publicity or would be anything other than a repeat of her previous success. For myself, the outcome is simply unfortunate.

In the meantime, because of the media interest which this play has caused – and which will die down very soon – I am so very relieved that you are out of the country. I wish I could get away myself, but there is a lot of business to discuss with the Order.

Vinny, my love, by the time you return all this stir will be yesterday's news and I do not want you to be worried. I hesitated and thought deeply before writing you this letter, but I felt I had to let you know what has happened. Please, please, do not be distressed on my account.

I hope you have enjoyed your tour and that it has been a success.

My love, Teddy.

I don't remember getting on stage for the final act. I remember returning to my dressing room after only one curtain call. Edna was waiting with my gown, coffee steaming in a jug, and the pages of his letter picked up off the floor and replaced in the envelope. Edna wouldn't have read the letter, but she didn't need to. She knew. Night after night she cleared away the brandy glasses, laid ice-packs on my puffed eyes, smoothed thick make-up on my face. Every day she posted my furious letters to Helen that went unanswered. Every day when I asked her to buy me an English newspaper she looked me straight in the eye and said there were none left.

And through it all, having to give performances both on-stage and off, my stomach awash with acid, my voice tight with fury. I had to laugh, speak my lines archly, masterfully, whether I was addressing my fellow actors in the theatre or in the hotel, where some members of the company, laying aside their newspapers, looked at me askance.

Only Edna, shutting the dressing-room door, handing me my gown, peeling the wig from my head and, when I was too exhausted even to lift my hands, gently stripping the false colour from my cheeks with cotton wool. Only Edna . . .

'I don't know what I'd have done without you, Edna,' I said when finally the tour was over and I stood on the platform in England, waiting for the train that would take me to him. 'I'll never forget you.' But I did. Somewhere on the journey to Belle House, Edna, invisible as her stitching, simply slipped from my mind.

Teddy was sitting in the library when I arrived. It was raining, a cold, dark spring, the house damp and forbidding. He looked distant, weary. There was a black armband on the sleeve of his jacket.

'But you must fight this,' I kept saying to him. 'You can't just take it lying down.'

'Vinny, there's nothing I can do,' he repeated. 'The Dowager had a perfect right to leave the estate to whomever she wanted – it wasn't entailed – there were no guarantees that I'd have inherited it even without—' He broke off abruptly.

'I'll bloody murder Helen,' I growled. 'Why? That's what I want to know – why write such a play?'

'Oh, leave it, Vinny. It's too late now.'

'Well, I hope you've told her to pack her bags and get out of the Annexe. That's one thing you *can* do.'

'Vinny, please – leave it.'

'But what are you going to do?' I cried. 'Where will you go? What will you live on?'

'Oh, I can stay here at Belle House – for my lifetime,' he replied. 'The Order will give me an allowance. I might even be able to help with the estate—'

'Help?'

'If they'll let me,' he added mildly.

'Jesus, Teddy—' I turned away.

20

'And we can still be married, Vinny,' he spoke humbly to my back. 'If you'll still have me?'

'Of *course* I'd have you, Teddy – I'd have you despite anything, you know that.' I paused, gathering myself, then looked straight at him. 'But I'm not getting married.'

'But, Vinny—'

'I'll live here with you, but I won't get married.'

'But why?'

'Because it's the only protest I can make,' I said defiantly. 'Because I know full well that it'll upset those narrow-minded little half-men to have me "living in sin" here with you. Because it's a matter of principle, Teddy. I'm making a stand . . .'

But maybe that came between us. Because it strikes me now that my wilfulness cost him dearly. And maybe for all my fine words I was afraid to marry, afraid to be a wife, afraid that with that legal binding I would no longer be a distinct individual but would melt away as ice melts into the water which surrounds it.

Sometimes I can feel him under my hands so vividly it is as if I have his body here in front of me and I am sculpting it. He had a little dip in the centre of his chest that I could fit my cheek to. Still now I can feel the weight of him pressed down on me, the softness of the dark hairs under his arms. I can smell his sharp herringbone sweat that arrowed into my breasts, my belly. I can feel his hands, the strong fingers and clipped nails, the callouses dragging slightly over my skin. I can taste the dark strawberry stains of his wide nipples puckering in my mouth. But his face – his face, that I can only see as if it is way down beneath water, his features shifting and dissolving, moving and blending and never staying still long enough for me to scoop it up, keep it, hold it.

Oh, if I could resurrect him out of all those parts he would be here with me. My Teddy, my love, who looked at me and saw not the flamboyant actress with her scarves and her jewellery and her busy confidence, but Lavinia before the make-up was put on, Lavinia tired, bad-tempered, pushing at the wrinkled skin on her neck, Lavinia reading a book and dozing with her mouth open, Lavinia sprawled on the bed in the Annexe, giggling as he made love to her.

I had never really believed that I might find him. I had accepted, become resigned. It is too late now, I told myself as I passed my fortieth birthday, I am beyond grand passion, I said coolly when I was forty-five, I am used to being alone, I thought as my fifties loomed, I've had my share of love and lovers, I have my work, my friends, I need nothing else, I am content . . .

I acted so well I almost believed myself. And then I met Teddy.

'Do you think,' I asked Gregory this morning, 'that your God has a sense of humour?'

'*My* God?' he questioned.

I waved my hand impatiently. 'Don't quibble, Gregory. Your God – the God – any God – you know what I mean.'

'A sense of humour?' He thought for a moment. 'It's hard to say exactly. I don't know—'

'Well, you ought to know,' I broke in. 'You've dedicated your life to this – this *being*. At the very least you ought to know something about it – him – her. Don't you agree?'

He frowned. 'The things I do know,' he said slowly, 'and the questions you're asking . . . You see, we don't necessarily share the same language, Lavinia.'

'That's a very garbled answer,' I said. 'You really ought to do better than that. We mortals below your pulpit don't want uncertainties and ambiguities. We like a nice clear message with no nonsense.'

'Lavinia, I didn't mean—'

'And,' I went on, 'if you want to recruit more members, these little homilies of yours will have to get snappier. And don't tell me you're indifferent to the recruiting drive. Every cult I've ever heard of wants to rule the world and I doubt yours is any different.'

'Well, I wouldn't say—'

But I was getting into my stride. 'Actually, I think Joy had the right idea.'

'Joy?'

'My sister. You see, she thought—'

'You have a sister?' He was looking at me in surprise.

'Had,' I replied shortly. 'She's dead now.'

'Oh, I'm sorry.'

'Don't be. It happened years ago. Tragic at the time, though – she was still a young woman.'

'You were close?'

I frowned. 'Gregory, you're trying to sidetrack me. But in answer to your question, yes, you could say we were close, though there was a great difference in our ages. Joy was ten years older than I. As a child, I remember her always out of my reach, being able to do things I wasn't allowed to – very frustrating. But later the difference wasn't so apparent – twenty and thirty aren't as far apart as ten and twenty. Anyway – ' I held him back with a look – 'the reason I mentioned Joy was that I think she had the right idea with her gods—'

'Gods?' His voice rose. 'Your sister was – she believed in—'

'Joy was a classics scholar, Gregory, not a pagan cult member, so you don't have to look shocked,' I said. 'Quite a brilliant scholar too, but she gave up her degree course during the war and volunteered to drive a bus and she never took it up again afterwards. She went off and married a fellow Graecophile . . . But what I *wanted* to say about Joy before you diverted me,' I continued, 'was that she had the right idea. From what I understand, those ancient Greeks were *very* clear about their gods. Knew what they liked and disliked, their foibles, their habits – *and* whether they had a sense of humour,' I challenged.

'Well, what do you think, Lavinia?' he asked after a moment.

'Me? I wouldn't presume to have an opinion. God isn't my field. And don't give me your little smile, Gregory,' I added quickly. 'For one thing it's fatuous and for another it's extremely patronizing.'

The smile was wiped off immediately. 'I'm sorry. God knows, I don't want you to feel patronized.'

I raised my eyebrow. 'Oh, so God knows that, does he?'

Teddy said it was what God intended. He said it couldn't be wrong, that God was too generous, too good to make our relationship unlawful.

'Even though you're married, darling?' I said. 'Teddy, come on, you know very well that your Church wouldn't approve of us at all.'

23

'God approves,' he said firmly, holding me very tight, very close in the hard horsehair bed.

The Annexe shook slightly as a train went past, then it was quiet again. I could hear an owl hoot. Hard to believe that this little house was in London.

'I *know* God approves,' he said again. 'Trust me, Vinny, it will all work out.'

'"All shall be well, and all manner of thing shall be well,"' I quoted.

I could feel him smiling in the dark. 'Now how on earth do you know about that?'

'I'm not completely ignorant, Teddy. I do know a thing or two. Anyway, I did a play about Dame Julian once.'

He laughed.

'That's what comes of bedding an actress,' I went on. 'Especially an old warhorse like myself. I know a very little about a very great deal, and nearly all of it gleaned from the theatre in one form or another. Tinsel knowledge – most of it quite useless.'

'Not *all* useless.' He ran his hands over my breasts, cupping their soft weight delicately. 'Is it hard learning lines?'

'Not really.'

'Photographic memory?'

'No, just discipline. You get used to it. One's memory will retain an awful lot if it's trained . . .'

But it will not supply his face turning to me, smiling at me, taking me again, covering my mouth with his.

No, I have to glimpse him in the shifting of the sun over the mountain, in the scurrying of the sheep over the fells, in the grey and purple of the scree rearing up from the lakeside, in the tweed mistiness of the heather. He is in this landscape, though we never came here together for all that it is close by the estate. If I call his name, the lake ripples. In the long summer evenings when the sun is slowly pulled down, the water darkens, becoming almost solid, and I think I see him striding over the surface – or swimming, a small white pebble in the water – but never his face. Always his back to me, never his face . . .

'Lavinia?'

I look. 'Oh, you're here, Gregory.'

'You were miles away.'

'Yes.'

He lets the silence rest.

There is an art to silences. On stage they are a technique – the pause, the look, the hesitation – all manufactured, a tool of control. But in life it is not so easy to be with another person in silence. With Teddy, I could sit in a rich fertile silence for a whole evening – reading, learning lines – his leg pressed lightly against mine maintaining contact. With Gregory, the silence has a watchful quality as if he treads around me, pressing upon panels looking for a way in. Cunning monk – they train them young, I suppose. And yet he is not uncomfortable with silence, he has skill enough to let them be.

'I was thinking about Teddy,' I say after a while.

'Is that what you think about when you're on your own?'

I don't answer.

'It's just that I imagine you must get lonely.'

'It's the human condition, Gregory,' I say drily. 'You'd better get used to it.'

They say you go towards a very bright light. They say you travel towards it at great speed, that you are drawn there inexorably. They say there is a feeling of great peace and love and that it is a homecoming, that your self is sloughed off, burned away, jettisoned like the unnecessary casing of a rocket.

But what of those who fight against it? What of those who are not ready for the journey? What of those who are unwilling – for whom it is a voyage into the dark?

It is not possible to find out in advance. We know nothing – *nothing*. Oh, there are those fantasies concocted by religions, those unconvincing fairy-tales of happily ever after and good and evil justly repaid, but to me those fables are just make-up, padding, a false bottom in a suitcase, scenery made of paint and plasterboard. People have to have some fiction to pacify themselves as they balance on this cliff edge we call living.

And I? I stand here at the very edge and cannot move. I am petrified. I look out at the lake, I watch the guests – and I wait and wonder about death. Now it is no longer a homecoming, the reunion I longed for with Teddy when all I wanted was to die and follow him, when death hovered tantalizingly out of my reach like a bauble on a Christmas tree. Now it is more terrible. I see myself squeezed through an opening as narrow as the one through which I squeezed into life. I imagine a crushing pain as the life is pressed out of me. And then – what? Is it some secret, some joke so huge and clever that no one yet has ever broken ranks to come back and tell us the punchline? Or is death a two-way mirror through which the dead can watch and hear us but cannot influence us as we blunder through our lives? And are they, too, frustrated by their impotence? I don't know. *I don't know.* This is a part I cannot learn in advance, I will have to improvise – and I have never felt comfortable with improvisation.

Sometimes I am certain that it would be a blessing to have this consciousness erased, to have no memory or awareness of who I am or what I've done. To shut out life altogether, as I tried to do during those months at the Dower House.

But then I see the sunlight shifting over the fells. I see the flare of bracken, the sear of heather. I see a child on the lawn look up and run towards his mother, beaming, crowing as he is picked up and swung high over her head. And I feel life hooking its fingers into my heart and pulling hard at the strings, playing them like an instrument.

What would Teddy have made of old age? Would he have given in gracefully? I mean real old age – this condition that I have embraced like a lover in the months since he died. This is not the old age we laughed about when he pointed out my white hair and I made him get his eyes tested for his new, shyly worn half-moon spectacles. What would he have made of this long-drawn-out approach to death?

'Out like a light – that's how I want to go,' he declared. 'Here one minute, gone the next.'

Do we prescribe our own death, then? And did he know? Was he aware when he stood for that one moment with the startled look on his face, his arm still tangled in the sleeve of his dressing gown? Did he know when he cast that look out to me – that look which hooked me like a fish as he choked, slipped, fell – did he know that was his last look? His last moment? Was he ready, or did he fight against it?

And I, with that look streaking past, I, wanting to run to

him, but everything slow as if in a dream, my movements stiff, uncoordinated, going towards him even as he was going away, seeing his hands sliding off the bed, losing hold, slipping into death. And then sitting there on the floor cradling his head, his shoulders, rocking him as if I could coax him back to life, as if his spirit had just loosened for a moment and I could tease it back into his body. How could he be gone? How? He was just there. He had been just *there*. But now he was not there. He was gone and what I held was an empty chest, an egg that had been blown out. Give him back to me, I bargained with God. Give him back just for an hour, a minute – just to say goodbye. Oh, let me have him back . . .

It is almost impossible to realize people dead. All those cold months in the Dower House I waited for him to return, looked for him as if he had simply been mislaid, like an odd sock or a single glove – surely the other would turn up? The mean, damp Dower House that the dead Dowager haunted, greening the walls of every room with her icy breath, slamming doors behind her in the draughts. Through my brandy I could even hear her keening, as Teddy had told me she'd keened for Christian, his older brother, killed in the war. She too had shut herself in here to mourn, though when she'd emerged it had been into the arms of priests. I kept my door locked when the Order tried to visit. The village shop delivered my brandy and sometimes I ate the bread they sent, mostly I didn't. Sometimes there was a fire lit, other times the place was so cold I simply stayed in bed. I drew the curtains so that I shouldn't see out. I watched the shadows crossing the walls. I heard the clink of my glass against the bottle. And felt my body cracking, shrivelling, the spiteful Dowager breathing old age into me like a poison seeping into my bones, swelling my joints and twisting my hands into claws. And I *welcomed* it, wanted to become gnarled as an old tree, to be as cold as he was, lying out there in the family plot, stiff and empty.

He wanted to be buried. He said he wanted his body to decompose slowly and merge with the soil.

'But you'll be lying there,' I protested. 'Just under the ground—'

'Not *just* under, Vinny,' he replied with a smile. 'A good six feet at least.'

'Lying there,' I repeated. 'Where I'd know you were – *rotting.*'

'Vinny, it's just the body breaking down, darling. You must know what it's like when someone dies. What about with your sister?'

'It was different with Joy.' I twined my fingers around his, feeling the warm, living flesh. 'I wasn't there when she died – and anyway, the Professor had her cremated and her ashes scattered – a classical custom probably.'

'Must have been hard for Helen, though.'

I dropped his hand. 'Why must you always go on about Helen? She was only a little girl. It didn't make any difference to her.'

He looked at me.

'All right, all right,' I conceded. 'But don't go on about her, Teddy, please. I don't want to get into a row about Helen.'

'It doesn't have to be a row.'

'If Helen's in it, it *will* be a row.'

'Vinny, if you could just forgive her. If *I* can feel forgiveness for her, surely you can?'

'I'll make a pact with you about your funeral arrangements,' I broke in, heading him off. 'If I die first, you can do whatever you like with yourself – join the Dowager in the vault if you want, it won't make any difference to me. But if I'm the one who's left – ' I looked at him, pressed his hand – 'then it'll be up to me to do what *I* want, all right?'

He smiled. 'Keep my ashes on the mantelpiece?'

'If I like.'

'I'll haunt you, Vinny . . .'

But you have done that anyway, my love. Bone of my bone, flesh of my flesh, and his body laid in the earth just as he'd wanted, though I refused either to witness the interment or to ever visit his grave afterwards. Even so, his voice sounded in my head: There, Vinny, my brave darling, I knew you'd come round in the end and it's not so bad, is it . . .

But it was bad, worse than I could have imagined. The trees and the hedges and the fields all spoke of him, remembered him. I sat in the dark, but still he called to me from every corner of the estate, in every gust of wind, in every bird that sang with such blithe indifference. He called even in the voices of his dogs as they whined, searching for him.

He had always wanted dogs but the Dowager had forbidden them. After I moved to Belle House, I didn't have the heart to deny him them as well. He'd lost everything else, how could I refuse him this?

We had to live quite simply. Teddy's 'allowance' was not generous by my standards, but he wouldn't complain. I sold my old sports car, but even so the few savings I had were soon gone. Money had always slipped easily through my fingers, I'd never really thought about it, never worried. But Belle House ate money and now, however, I had to learn to be more careful, to housekeep. Because we couldn't afford staff, other than an occasional cleaning woman, I learned to cook – a skill I had previously never bothered to develop. I made bread, jam even. I polished brass fenders and arranged flowers and kept the dogs strictly out of the few main rooms we'd left open – we'd shut down most of them, along with many of the bedrooms, rattling in that place like peas in a drum. I'm having enough trouble keeping this house marginally civilized as it is, I told Teddy, I don't want your dogs making it worse. He acquiesced without protest.

He took such pleasure in those stupid, great-hearted animals and such care to keep them out of my way. They lived mainly in the shabby gunroom, where Teddy sat on the evenings he wrote his reports for the Order.

'I think it's appalling that they should make you do these reports,' I told him as I stood in the doorway, looking in. 'I mean, it isn't as though you don't know how to run the estate. Don't they trust you?'

'Well, I haven't been as efficient as I might have been,' he said mildly, rubbing his eyes. 'I can see that now. The estate *is* somewhat run down, not really what it could be.'

'I think they should just leave you alone.'

'Do you?' He looked up at me. 'Actually, Vinny, I'm finding these reports are rather a good discipline – makes me attend to the minor details that would otherwise get lost. And I'm building up a record of the estate for them. I think they're going to find it very useful.'

I turned to leave. 'Your goodwill to those grasping monks is sickening, Teddy. I thank God I'm not that charitable.'

The dogs were curled by his feet, glancing at me, gazing up

at him, waiting for us to finish so that they could continue their silent communion with their master uninterrupted. As Teddy looked back down at his report, the bitch raised her head and laid it tenderly over his feet, and without taking his eyes off the page he leaned down to fondle her ears with exactly the same gesture which he used to stroke my head when we sat together.

God, I was jealous of those dogs. Jealous of the love that shone out of their eyes when they saw him – their tails beating eagerly, their muzzles pushing against his hands, his legs. And though he tried to keep his voice strict, he betrayed himself with every caress he gave them, the laugh with which he let them out in the mornings, the pride when they had their litters. Yet they all tried so hard to hide this love from me.

But after he died I wouldn't give the dogs to the monks. They had everything else – Belle House, the land – they weren't getting his dogs as well. 'They can stay with me at the Dower House,' I said.

But they were a man's dogs – his dogs. They kept escaping, leaping over the straggling hedges and sniffing up old trails, running back to Belle House to search for him. And when I kept them indoors, they yelped and whimpered, pressing themselves against the door, scampering out of my way when I shouted, flinching when I raised my arm.

The gamekeeper took them in the end. 'I'll look after them for you, madam,' he said. 'For his lordship's sake. They'll keep out of trouble with me.'

And though I was relieved to see the back of them, to be freed of their slavering and their smell, I was aware that once again I had let Teddy down, I had failed, I had not done what he would have wanted. So I closed the curtains, I reached for the brandy and alone in that dark, dank cottage I shouted for death to come and get me too.

No, I have decided that I won't go to the races. If I am honest I would say that I never seriously contemplated doing so. All that fuss and bother, no, I've passed the age for distractions.

Annie will be disappointed. This morning I pretended to be asleep when she came in. She was expecting my answer and spent rather longer than usual cleaning and setting the room to rights. Maybe she knew I was pretending. At one moment she stood right in front of me. I could feel her shadow on my face. 'Miss Mair?' she said softly, but loud enough. 'Miss Mair?' I kept my face absolutely impassive, my breathing regular, noticing with all my old training how I appeared completely oblivious. 'Miss Mair?' she tried again, but it was a half-hearted attempt and she gave up with a sigh. Poor Annie, but what can she expect? I was an actress, after all.

But after she left I felt foolish – foolish and cowardly, my mind making whiney little excuses: I'd slept badly, I didn't want a scene, I just wanted to be left alone . . . Plywood excuses, Teddy would have called them.

'If you've got a difficult thing to say, far better to just spit it out than to tie yourself up in knots trying to make it sound smoother.'

It was early in our relationship. We were at the Annexe, lying in bed, the covers pulled tight around us, the late winter sun dipping in the sky.

'Oh, and I suppose that's what you told yourself when you met me?' I teased. 'I certainly don't remember you beating round the bush.'

He chuckled. 'Nor you either, my love.'

'I should have been more coquettish,' I said with a mock frown. 'More – you know, led you a dance.'

'Life's too short.' He spread his hand over my breasts.

'But really, Teddy, aren't we rather too old for this? I mean, for heaven's sake, I'm nearly fifty and you're already—'

'Speak for yourself, Vinny.' His fingers tiptoed over my nipples. 'I don't think of myself as old – I probably never will.'

'And what about Eve?'

'What about her?'

'Well—' I propped myself up on one elbow. 'Don't you think about her at all? Worry about her? She is your wife, after all.'

'In name only.' He pulled himself up to look at me. 'I told you when we met, Vinny, I was quite honest.'

'Oh, I'm not disputing that.'

'Eve has wanted nothing from me for the last twenty-odd years but her own house and her allowance. As far as I know, she's perfectly happy. Really, I don't think she should ever have got married at all. She told me on our honeymoon that in fact she'd always wanted to be a nun.'

'On your honeymoon?'

'Please, Vinny, you mustn't laugh. I shouldn't have told you.'

'Well,' I said, still giggling, 'I bet that made for a good start. But why haven't you got divorced?'

He shook his head. 'The Church doesn't recognize divorce and we haven't any grounds for an annulment. Eve's content with the situation – she likes having a title, she wouldn't want to give up being Lady Gowan, and she has her porcelain collection.'

'And children?'

He shrugged. 'Once we gave up trying to have children it all became a lot easier.'

'But surely one of the aims of this alliance was to beget a son and heir? What does the terrible Dowager say?'

'She says that if it's God's will that our line dies out, then so be it. She won't countenance divorce,' he added.

'But couldn't you just divorce Eve and get married anyway?'

'Now, is that a proposal?'

'Don't be ridiculous, Teddy. You won't catch me walking down the aisle – I like my freedom.'

'But I'd like to take you out,' he said with a sudden fierceness. 'I want to show you off – not do all this cloak and dagger stuff.'

'Cloak and dagger is my stock in trade, darling.'

'But it's so – cowardly.' He forced the word out. 'Oh, I know I should be able to say, "To hell with the Dowager," and just walk away from Belle House and the estate. I know you must think I'm beneath contempt, tied to the Dowager's purse strings at my age—'

'Teddy, no.'

'But you see, Vinny,' he rushed on, 'I've lived and breathed the estate for as long as I can remember. It's in my bones, in my blood. After Christian died and I realized that if only *I* could survive the war it would all come to me – I tell you, Vinny, that's what got me through that POW camp, imagining the estate, working the fields in my mind, the rotations, the crops. Oh, Vinny—' He flung out his arms. 'I can't explain. I *am* that place. I love every part of it – the land, the cottages, the

32

tenants and workers under my care – and I couldn't give it up, I couldn't bear to lose it, not for anything.'

'It's all right,' I soothed. 'I understand.'

'That's more than I deserve.'

I ran my fingers over his shoulders, pressing out the knots until they loosened and relaxed. A train went past.

'Does this house belong to the estate too?' I asked after a moment.

'The Annexe?' He smiled. 'No. This "conveniently secluded cottage-in-the-town", as he used to call it, belonged to my father. It was his only piece of property. His was an empty title – no land, nothing – but my mother very much wanted a title and had Belle House and her estate to offer for it. So – ' he gestured – 'a tidy business. She became Lady Gowan, and later the Dowager, and he became lord of the manor. Satisfaction all round. But,' he added wryly, 'he kept this little London nest for his own private use, and on his death it came to me.'

I laughed. 'Like father like son, eh?'

'Vinny, believe me, you're my first lapse.'

'Oh, I'm honoured, my lord,' I joked. 'But doesn't the dread Dowager get suspicious at your frequent trips up to town?'

He shook his head firmly. 'I doubt she even notices. We lead fairly separate lives. I'm out on the estate most of the time and she stays in her rooms with her maid and her confessor. She never much cared for me anyway, it was always Christian she adored.'

'Teddy!'

'No, it's true,' he said simply. 'I don't mind. Anyway, sometimes I won't see her for several days. She long ago gave up all interest in the estate. Of course, we meet for Mass on Sundays—' He broke off abruptly.

'So, you don't think she'd appreciate your little sidetrack with me?' I went on, teasing.

But he seemed no longer in a joking mood. 'I'm sorry, Vinny – believe me, I'm sorry I can't offer more.'

'Oh, stop apologizing, Teddy. I tell you, this situation suits me down to the ground . . .'

But how was I to know that he would burrow beneath my skin and pierce my heart? How was I to know with my much flaunted freedom and independence that there would be evenings when, sitting alone in my mansion flat, I longed to speak to him, to lie in his arms, to have him there beside me? How was I to know how much I would come to love that shuttered, secret little house with the trains rattling past and where I saw the magnolia in the front garden burst into blossom for five, six, seven springs? How was I to know that all the time creeping under my heart like moss between panes of glass, like weed spreading over a pond, was this longing for him, this hunger which would no longer be assuaged by snatched nights and brief meetings?

Not until Eve's unexpected death did I admit to myself how much I wanted him. Suddenly now I could drop my indifference and allow my excitement, my hope, to burst out. Foolish Lavinia, who'd never wanted to give up her freedom. Stupid Lavinia, green as a virgin with her first love affair. Mad, happy Lavinia – I would marry him, I would live the rest of my life with him. Never again would we be separated. Everything was going to be so—

No. I will not think about it.

The clouds are pulling over, there is a strong wind and the boats are being tugged back and forth over the choppy water. The scree on the mountain opposite has darkened to gunmetal grey – sometimes it is mauve, sometimes a sulphurous yellow. It is dangerous and people are warned not to walk across it.

On the top of the mountain is a little cairn. Climbers place pebbles there to mark the summit. It is like a beacon in the mist, they say, to show you the way. I don't see how. When the mist falls one sees nothing – a small pile of pebbles won't make any difference. I think it is another fairy-story, another happy ever after that people are told in order to mask the abyss which is waiting for them just there at their feet.

Today it is raining. The fells are covered with mist and the lake is heavy and grey, all the little boats tucked into the shore.

The holidaymakers are frustrated. They will have to go out and spend the day peering through steamed-up windscreens as they drive cautiously down narrow, unfamiliar roads. They will sit in cramped tearooms, shushing the children and giving in to their fractious demands. They will drive miles to visit a dull museum, eat too much, drink too much, and hope that tomorrow will be better, because with every moment the clock of their holiday is ticking away – you should be enjoying yourselves, you should be having a good time.

Even now I can hear them in the hall: Get your boots on . . . Where's your hat? . . . We can look for a present for Grandma . . . No, if the weather clears then we can go for a walk . . . Have you got your cardigan? . . . Where's your hat?

The hotel will be quiet until teatime, when, one by one, they'll return sheepishly early, glad that the day is over. They'll come in here, drawing themselves up close to the fire: We shouldn't have bothered to go out, really. It wasn't worth it. We could have stayed here by the fire all day . . .

And I will sit observing them, envying them their life, their appetite for the scones and cream which Annie brings in. And among their whispers and sighs there will be a moment, maybe when a couple, replete, sweeping the crumbs from their knees, will lean back and light cigarettes and smile. Or when a mother, smoothing the head of her child as he dozes in her arms, bends to kiss the soft nape of his neck. And I, unnoticed, watching without seeming to watch, will scoop up these morsels and hoard them to myself as if they hold the elixir of immortality.

'It has been a good life.'
  'Yes?'
  'I've had what I wanted – success in my profession.'
  'Yes.'
  'Well—' I shifted slightly in my chair. 'Not success as some would call it – one's name in lights and all this film work they do nowadays. But success enough. I have been known – respected in my field. God knows, I wouldn't want to have to start again now, not in today's climate. It's so much harder for them now than it was when I was young.'
  'Yes.' He crossed his legs, straightened his habit.
  'And while I was still working I had the *things* I wanted – the material things. And they are important, you know, whatever your lot might say about renouncing them.'
  'Yes?'
  'It makes life run more smoothly if one has money – not an excessive amount, but enough to buy one's independence, to be able to live as one wants, buy what one wants.'
  'Yes.'

35

'Gregory, I really would prefer you not to say "yes" all the time like that,' I said sharply. 'You sound like a stuck record.'

'But I'm agreeing with you.'

'Really?' I raised my eyebrow. 'You manage to make it sound remarkably like disagreement.'

'Ah.'

'And don't apologize. You know I don't like apologies.'

'Actually – ' he gave a little smile – 'I wasn't going to apologize.'

'Why not? You were being rude.'

The smile became rueful. 'If I seemed rude than I do apologize.'

'Accepted,' I replied promptly. 'Now, where was I?'

'You were telling me how good it's been – your life.' He paused. 'I was waiting for you to get to the "but".'

'Who says there's a "but"?'

'There's always a "but" – in all lives.'

I studied him for a moment. 'So, what's your "but", Gregory?'

'I'll tell you mine if you tell me yours,' he returned.

I smiled. 'Touché.'

He made a gesture of encouragement, but I shook my head. 'Ah, but even so life's hard work,' I sighed. 'I can only say I'm glad I'll be out of it soon. You've still got years left to endure.'

'Oh, I don't know – I could drop down dead tomorrow.'

'Don't be ridiculous, Gregory.'

'I could have an accident driving back, or be struck down by some sort of illness.'

'Yes, and I could suddenly lose twenty years and resurrect the dead,' I snapped.

'I'm only trying to—'

'Well, don't. We may *all* be heading towards death, but some of us are getting there faster than others and I'll thank you not to pretend otherwise – not with me anyway. That brand of saccharine might go down well with your woolly-headed flock, but I'm not one of them.' I stopped, looked out of the window to where the sky was washed clean, the sun stroking the mountain with a soft light. Old people do not cry, our tear ducts are dry as old riverbeds, but there is a wrenching inside.

He leaned forwards. 'Lavinia, what's wrong?'

'Why should something be wrong?'

36

'Because you've been working very hard to tell me nothing is.'

'And you don't believe me?'

'No.'

'How mistrusting of you.' I paused, then said carefully, 'And if there was?'

'I'd like to help.'

'You know,' I said, sitting back and observing him, 'any psychiatrist worth their salt would have some interesting comments to make on why you have this overwhelming – I take it it is overwhelming – need to help people.'

'Isn't it normal human instinct?'

'Not the lengths you've gone to – joining the Order, becoming a monk. I mean, couldn't you have kept it within bounds and simply worked for the social services?'

'Who says being a monk is about helping others?' he said defensively.

I laughed. 'Well, if it isn't, then God help *your* flock.'

'It's also about helping myself. It's the best I can offer to God.'

'How generous of you.'

I looked out of the window again. A pair of gulls was flying over the lake, ducking and diving. Playing, I thought, then realized, no, they were fighting over territory. Swooping, wheeling, bearing down, chasing each other.

'The fighter planes were like that,' I remembered suddenly. 'During the war. I used to watch them when I was a little girl. We could see the dogfights. Of course, at that age – ten, eleven – it was all tremendously exciting. I didn't like the bombers, though,' I added, after a moment. 'I used to shelter with my parents in the cellar and while they were fussing about the silver and their wines, I'd just be thinking of Joy.' I turned to him. 'It must have been one of the few times I actually talked to your God. You know: God, don't let her be killed, keep her safe. Standard *in extremis* prayers.'

'I'm sure very sincerely offered.'

'Well, whatever the motive, God seemed to like it. Unlike thousands – no, millions of others – my sister survived the war.'

'And?'

'Not so much of an "and", Gregory, more your "but".'

'Ah.'

'Ah, indeed.'

'You don't have to tell me anything, Lavinia,' he said after a pause.

'What? Deprive you of "helping"?'

He looked distressed. 'No, Lavinia – really.'

'I know, I know—' I waved my hand wearily. But I wanted to talk. 'Our parents cut Joy off without a shilling – as they used to say. Because as soon as the war was over she married a penniless classics professor – though he wasn't a professor then – and she went off to live with him in suburbia while he completed his doctorate or research or something – ' I waved my hand – 'I don't know what. I do know that he worked for a while in a prep school and that money was very tight, and I know that Joy completely abandoned her own academic career in order to support him in his.' I sighed. 'Such a fool, Joy, in many ways. If she hadn't swept off in such high dudgeon, *of course* our parents would have eventually welcomed her back into the fold.' I gave a wry smile. 'Poor things, they didn't have much luck with either of us really. As soon as I could, I talked my way into drama school and they never recovered from that. One daughter treading the boards, the other making an undistinguished provincial marriage – not something one boasts about at the golf club.'

'Your sister's marriage was unhappy?' he asked.

'Oh, no – far from it. They were *very* happy. I kept in touch with Joy as soon as I left home and went to stay with them once for . . . convalescence—' I hesitated. 'I'd – I'd been ill. Anyway, they were living in a new house near a university where the Professor – he was a professor now – had been given a Chair or a senior post, or whatever they call it. They were very pleased with themselves. They'd been for a long holiday in Greece to celebrate his appointment.' I paused. 'And Joy was pregnant – with Helen.'

He was watching me closely. 'You make it sound . . . as if that wasn't altogether a good thing?' he said delicately.

'It was good for them – at least, they thought so.'

'But?'

I smiled. 'Exactly, Gregory. We've come to my "but".'

*   *   *

In the wash of time, as if on a beach with the waves rolling in and pounding the rocks to sand, all those years have dissolved. All those lines I've learned, all that waiting in the wings with my heart hammering, all those dramas with agents and directors – Bernard and his theatre, his mad Martini matinées – all washed away, with nothing but a suitcase of yellowed programmes to show for it.

These are the times when I feel that it is a useless fight and I am tired of it. Tired of being old and weak, tired of my days beating themselves out as repetitively as the little waves on the shore below. And tired most of all of the past, with its rocks and hidden crevices that, like an unwary climber, I fall into. Tired when I look back and see the crumpled rag I have made of my life, which seems such a small, such a tawdry thing.

Oh, it is an insidious descent, this growing old. I have made it into a shell, a cave, and I sit here hunched in the dark with the weight of all that past above me. Old couples cling together, they don't want to be separated. Suddenly the place by your side is empty and cold. If Teddy was with me now, I would have his arm to hold on to and we could have faced this together. Then maybe I would not be feeling this loneliness, this sail flapping loose in my heart.

But I find that I have become set in my ways. If I drink tea at all, I like it weak not strong as he liked it. If I sleep at all, it is in the middle of the bed. I do not go out. I do not like change. I have become set in a series of little routines and I wonder if really I would be so happy if he were to walk into the room. And that is typical of the old, I realize suddenly. We want stasis, not action. We are like horses in a race with the final fence hurtling towards us and we must stay in stride, in rhythm, before that last great leap.

'You're sure, Miss Mair?' Annie stands before me, dressed in her Sunday best cornflower and daisy sprigged dress. 'Because you can still change your mind. John's just outside. I can have him come in and help you to the car, and we'll all be down by the lake before you can say Jack Robinson.'

I smile. 'You're being very kind, Annie, but I'm sure – quite sure. You go off and enjoy yourself. I'll be quite all right here.'

She stands hesitating. 'I can't change your mind?'

'Go on, now,' I say. 'It's a lovely day and you don't want to miss the start.'

'Well – ' she is suddenly decisive – 'there is one thing I *can* do for you.' And she steps past me and flings the window wide open. 'It's a lovely day, as you say, Miss Mair, so you might as well have a good breath of it.' She brushes her hands and stands looking at me a little defiantly.

One thing I have learned as I've got older is that it is easier to allow the young and active to briskly do whatever they want for what they assume is my benefit. They live their lives so fast, their busy minds switching this way and that, quick as shoals of fish. We old live slow as massive planets edging our way through orbit.

So I smile at Annie, bow my head in mock submission, and she leaves with a laugh.

The hotel is still, quiet, emptied. Through the open window I can hear the cheers of the crowd as the boats skim the lake like butterflies. A breeze lifts the branches of the trees so that the leaves are smoothed and turned and shaken out like hair. Teddy used to watch me brushing my hair as I sat at the dressing table, preparing to leave the Annexe. He'd come up to me and let the soft lengths roll over his bare arms before reaching up to my neck, my face, turning me away from the mirror, taking the brush out of my hand . . .

I am almost dozing when the door opens and I sit up with a start.

'Oh, excuse me.' A young woman stands hesitantly in the doorway, ready to draw back. 'I didn't see anyone at the desk and I thought—'

Maybe it is the sun in my eyes, maybe I am still half asleep, maybe that conversation with Gregory has shaken something loose in me, because there *she* stands. There, in front of me, with her isolation like a moat around her and her eyes full of defiance and denial.

'Helen?' I whisper. So she comes back.

'There wasn't anybody at the desk,' she says again. Her voice is even, melodic, the sounds placed very precisely along the scale. But I am in such shock I can only stare at her. 'Excuse me – ' she leans forward slightly, taking charge – 'but this is a hotel, isn't it?'

'They've all gone to the races,' I manage to say.

'The races?'

'On the lake.' I make a slight gesture with my head. 'The boat races.'

'Oh – oh, I see.'

'They'll be back around teatime.' My voice sounds surprisingly calm, normal. 'Are you expected?'

'No. I didn't book anything. It – it was just an impulse.' She takes a few steps into the room, gestures a little nervously. 'You think they might not have a room, then? It's just – well, it looked such a *private* hotel. I suppose I really ought to try somewhere else . . .'

Now that she stands closer, I can see that she is obviously different. Smaller, for one thing, finer-boned, with none of Helen's sturdiness. And her hair is dark, almost black, not at all like Helen's dull rust red, and it is cut quite short like a boy's. Yet there is a look about her.

'You could sit down and wait,' I say. 'They'll be back before long.'

'If you don't mind.'

I shake my head and she sits.

Now, as the light falls on her face, I can see that she is quite, *quite* different – not at all the same, not even alike. Then why is my heart racing? Why, beneath my shawl, are my hands aching as if a crown of thorns is being tightened around each nerve?

'You've come from far?' I ask.

She nods. 'From town – London. I started this morning. At least I think it was this morning – it could have been last night.' She shivers.

'You must be tired.'

'Yes, I suppose I must be.' She stands up suddenly and moves towards the open window. 'But seeing all this—' She takes a deep breath of fresh air. 'Oh, that's better – that's much, much better.'

I have to watch her standing there in her crumpled blue shirt and her innocuous black leggings and try to understand what it is that makes her burn like Helen.

'Do you live here?' she asks, turning to me.

'Yes – for the time being.'

'Then you are *lucky*.' She smiles, warmer and fuller than

41

Helen. 'God, if *I* lived out here—' She looks out of the window again.

'Couldn't you?'

'What – move here?' She gives a derisive laugh. 'I don't think Victor would like that.'

'Victor?'

'My agent – he manages my career.'

'Ah.'

'And I'm meant to be buying a flat in town,' she goes on. 'At least, I think I'm buying one. A long-term financial investment. Well, that's what Victor says.'

'Flats can be sold.'

'Yes.' She snaps herself tight shut as an oyster and moves away from the window.

Private, I decide. That is like Helen – and the child. Closed up. That unnerving feeling I would get with Helen that she was a long way behind a barricade watching me, watching herself interacting with me but never quite coming forwards and forgetting herself. A critical audience.

She sits down again. 'I won't bring my bag in from the car yet,' she says, 'because then they might *not* have a room.'

'You don't want to tempt fate.'

'That's right.' She looks at me. 'I suppose you think that's silly, really. I mean, it won't make any difference, will it?'

'It's just superstitious,' I say. 'Most performers feel superstitious.'

'How did you know I was a performer?' she asks sharply.

I hesitate. 'I don't know – it just occurred to me. And you did say an agent.'

She looks away. 'I have been.'

'And now?'

'Now?' She goes over to the window again, restless as the wind. 'I can see the boats. Look, there's one with a bright yellow sail.'

'They'll be turning in to shore soon and then everyone will come back for tea,' I say, watching her.

'Won't it go on till the evening?' She sounds disappointed. 'There are hours of daylight left.'

'They stop early because of the children – they're children's races, really,' I explain. 'But you could go down now and catch the last of them if you want.'

'No.' She turns back. 'I'll wait. After all, they might not have a room and then I'd have to go looking elsewhere.'

'I'm sure we'll find you something.'

'I hope so.' She sighs. 'This is just the sort of place I imagined while I was driving.'

'You've been working hard?'

'Victor likes to keep my nose to the grindstone,' she says grimly. 'He's got this huge wallchart up in the office with dates booked in for me right up till the end of next year – and beyond.'

'Sounds exhausting.'

'It's a prison,' she says with sudden vehemence. 'A bloody prison.'

'You sound as if you need a holiday.'

'God, yes.' Now she is exhilarated, excited. She changes moods quickly. Did Helen do that? She giggles. 'I've slipped the leash. Nobody knows where I am. I've left a message on Victor's answerphone so that he shouldn't worry, but I know he'll be going spare. *Nobody* knows where I am – not one soul. I even bought some dark glasses—' She pulls them out of her shirt pocket and puts them on. And suddenly there is Helen staring at me sightlessly when I ran into her by chance in the theatre foyer, her body bloated with the pregnancy, her face blank and absent behind her dark glasses: 'Lavinia, I didn't expect to see you – I didn't expect to see *anyone* I knew . . .'

But now there are voices in the hall, the front door opening and closing, children chattering excitedly.

'They're back.' She whips off the glasses and jumps out of the chair. 'I'd better go and see.' She is half-way to the door before she turns and comes back, holding out her hand. 'Thank you for talking to me,' she says politely.

Her fingers are long, slender, the nails cut neatly short not bitten like Helen's. She wears no rings or jewellery of any kind.

I bring my hand out from beneath my shawl and she doesn't quite manage to control her instinctive withdrawal when she sees my knotted fingers.

'It's all right,' I say. 'It's not catching.'

She touches my fingers briefly and leaves the room.

It has suddenly struck me that when I die there will be all those papers of Helen's left behind.

Death will come unexpectedly. I will be in the middle of something, expecting life to continue – Annie to bring coffee, or Gregory to visit – and suddenly it will all be broken off. The day will not unfold as I anticipated. It will be jarred, twisted away from routine, because you cannot, unless you suicide, be in control of the date, the time of your death. And try as I might, I will not be able to leave life neatly rolled up, there will be ragged ungathered pieces, like a ball of roughly made pastry. There will be no moment at which I can say: It is finished, I am ready, I will leave NOW. And yet after my death, life will roll on over me, just another wave in the sea. The world will not end because I have ended. My death may be recorded in the newspapers, there may be obituaries, mention on television even, but it will all be outside me. I will be like a guest at a party standing in the cold, unable to join in.

So does she stand there, then? Does Helen stand watching, waiting for me? Does she look sidelong from some perch where she sees everything I do?

'You should read this, Vinny,' Teddy said after Helen had died and it was all over.

'Read what?' I asked.

We were sitting in the library at Belle House, it was cold, a meagre autumn fire burning. Teddy was slumped in his chair with a mass of loose paper on his lap and the open carpetbag on the floor beside him. He looked tired and thin – and old.

'You're exhausted, darling,' I said, worried. 'All this – it's been too much for you. Let's go away, have a break. We could visit Bernard at his cottage in the Highlands. What do you say?'

'You should read this,' he said again as if he hadn't even heard me. 'Dr Elspeth gave it to me when I collected Helen's things from Hill House. It's what Helen was writing when I went up to find her at the Annexe. Remember? I told you about it – that she'd been writing and that Dr Elspeth encouraged her as part of the treatment.'

'Teddy, please. I want a break from Helen now. It's very sad, I know, but it's over—'

'Do you know what she called the Annexe?' he broke in. His eyes were red-rimmed, bloodshot. 'She called it "the gingerbread house". Isn't that good? Don't you think? Because the place is like that, if you think about it – a little gingerbread house.'

'Teddy, leave it now, *please*.' I tried to keep my voice even. 'I just don't want to think about her.'

'But Vinny, you must have some pity for her. Think of everything she went through – the child . . .'

And what about what you went through, I thought as I watched him bent over the thick black scrawl of Helen's handwriting. Look where your goodness has left you, your wanting to accommodate and please everyone – Helen, the Dowager, the monks, even the tenants, who could come to you with any hard-luck story and expect you to waive their rents. Is that goodness, I wondered, or is it that you are a weak man?

I pushed the thought away. 'I'm sorry, Teddy,' I said. 'But I've had just about enough of Helen.'

'But you *must* read this, Vinny,' he pleaded. 'Really, you'll see a different person, a vulnerable person—'

'Later, Teddy, not now. There's time enough later . . .'

But there wasn't time – there never is, not when you're counting on it. Time pulls the rug out from under your feet, it snatches the tablecloth away and all the china crashes to the floor.

Has it been a year since he died? A whole *year*? Yes, almost a year – months, many, many months. How has all that time managed to slip away – all those seconds and minutes and interminable days?

I have become aware of time now that I am old in a way that I never was when I was young. Then time served me, I was the master, I gave the orders and time did my bidding. Now I serve time, it grinds over me, crushing me like pepper in a mill.

I sit here, I watch the light seeping, the days shortening. Already there is a hint of autumn in the trees, the leaves curl up like fingers. Soon there will be a mist in the mornings and a chill wind and the bracken will spread the hills with a cloth of gold.

She sits in a chair by the fire. Her hands are folded in her lap but her fingers move constantly – turning a button on her shirt, crimping and unrolling her cuffs. She sits hunched forward, looking into the fire, but from time to time she shifts, leans back, and her hands tap out a rhythm on the chair. If she is aware of my observation, she gives no sign of it. Attention runs off her as water from a duck's back. She is used to being watched and has learned to make herself impenetrable.

But oh, it is like a fist in my stomach doubling me over. She has that look about her, the look that Helen had and the child too, that fiercely independent look which had nothing in it of Joy's bright, easygoing nature. In Helen's child the look burned with a secretiveness fiery as her hair. In Helen, it was like a fist being held up, a stubborn fist that defied everything.

And I thought that I had put it all behind me. I thought that I had let it all go, but I have not. I thought that I would die and then it would all be finished. But Helen will not let me die. She holds my head up as deftly as any well-meaning lifesaver. She grips my throat so tightly that I am afraid to die, afraid to meet her there in the next world.

'You know who she is, don't you?' Gregory said eagerly.

'No. Who is she?'

'She's Celia Carey – the pianist. You must have heard of her.'

I shook my head. 'But no doubt you can tell me.'

'It's been in all the papers. There's been quite a furore. She suddenly cancelled all her concerts and just disappeared, walked off the platform. They've been looking for her. I wonder,' he added more slowly, 'if we shouldn't let them know—'

'Let who know what?'

'Where she is – her family, I mean, so that they're not worried.' He was avoiding my eye.

'It's none of your business. Leave her alone.'

'She's very famous, Lavinia – worldwide.'

I looked at him narrowly. 'You may hanker after fame, Gregory, but I can tell you it's not as pleasant as you might think.'

But he seemed quite oblivious. 'She was a child prodigy,' he explained. 'She's been performing since she was about ten. She's quite astonishingly good. I've heard recordings but I've never heard her play live. I wonder if we couldn't get her to play for us up at Belle House—'

'Gregory, that's enough,' I put in sharply. 'Even if she is who you say—'

'Oh, I'm quite sure of that. I recognized her despite the dark glasses.'

'Then that's all the more reason for leaving her alone. She's come here for a rest, not to be pestered by salacious celebrity hunters. I'm disappointed in you. I think you'd better go.'

He blinked for a moment, stunned. 'But – but – Lavinia, I'm sorry, I didn't mean to offend. I was just—'

'Go now, Gregory.'

'But I wanted to show you the plans for the Dower House. I wanted to discuss our ideas about it with you.'

'Another time.'

'Lavinia, I'm sorry.'

I didn't reply, looked out of the window. The sun went behind a cloud – Helen sitting up on the roof, blotting out the light with her hand.

At lunchtime I told Annie to bring me a brandy. She cleared away my untouched plate and looked at me anxiously. 'Are you all right, Miss Mair? Shall I call the doctor?'

'I'm perfectly all right, thank you, Annie.'

'But you haven't touched the hotpot. Maybe you'd rather have had the fish? We've still got some left, if you want – or I could bring you some cheese and biscuits—'

'Just bring me the brandy, Annie, that's all.'

'Miss Mair, are you really sure you want—'

'Oh, for heaven's sake, Annie, just bring me the bloody brandy.'

She flinched and walked away quickly before I had a chance to apologize.

'So,' I said, 'you're on the run?'

It was very late, just the musician and I in the room with the dying fire. I'd got Annie to give me the brandy bottle and I'd drunk a good part of it.

She looked up startled, her whole body suddenly tense, ready to bolt.

'Oh, it's all right,' I said. 'I'm not going to give you away.'

'How did you know?' she asked, her voice very low.

'You were recognized – not by me, I'm afraid, I'm rather out of the arts world these days. No, by an . . . acquaintance of mine. But it's all right. He's a monk, so I think you can trust him.'

She relaxed slightly.

'So, Celia, what happened?' the brandy asked boldly.

'Oh, please don't call me that,' she cried. 'That's my working name. I can't be that now.'

I took another drink of brandy and said after a moment, 'I never used a stage name, myself. Other performers did, of course, but I never thought of using one. I suppose it must help having some sort of alter ego you can pick up and leave behind at the stage door.'

'You were in the profession?'

I nodded. 'On the stage – I was an actress. Not one of the very bright lights and not any more, obviously. One takes a break and the scene moves on without you pretty quickly.'

'I know.'

'Afraid of young talent coming up behind you?'

She shivered.

'Now, *Helen*,' I went on after another sip, '*she* used another name – my name, actually. She said it was a tribute to me.' I snorted. 'Very useful, my name was to her – opened a lot of doors . . .'

'Helen?' She looked at me questioningly.

'My niece – Helen Mair, she called herself.' The brandy was flowing into my bloodstream like pure gold velvet.

'And she's an actress too?'

'A playwright,' I said shortly. 'Was.'

'Helen Mair—' She turned the name over. 'Sounds familiar. I'm sure I've heard of her.'

'*All Greek to Me*,' I replied. 'She wrote it.'

'Yes, I remember now. I saw it with Victor – oh, a few years ago, just after I'd won my first major competition.'

'What did you think of it?'

She paused, shifting a little uneasily in her chair. 'Oh – of course, it was rather good.'

'Rather good, eh?' I laughed.

'Well, you know, I'm sure it was very interesting, the ancient Greeks and everything.'

I smiled. 'You're a lousy actress. Be honest, you didn't like it.'

She shrugged. 'All right, I thought it was a bit too cutting – too satirical. But I probably just didn't understand it.'

I raised my glass to her. 'A lone dissenter.'

'But it did very well, didn't it? Won an award – and ran for ages.'

I nodded.

'You must be proud of her?'

'She's dead now,' I said baldly.

'Dead?'

'Brain haemorrhage.' I drank some more brandy. 'Last year – quite out of the blue.'

'Oh, I'm so sorry.'

'No need to be.'

'I mean for you.' She looked at me. 'I've never had anyone close to me die. It must be hard – especially when they should be the next generation.'

I drew a breath. If you juggle with knives, Lavinia, you're likely to get cut . . .

'Did she write any more plays?' she asked after a moment.

'There was one more,' I replied neutrally. '*A State of Grace* – and then she stopped. For the last seven or eight years of her life she wrote nothing – no plays anyway.'

'But why? She'd started so well.'

I shut my eyes for a moment. There stood Helen by the round table in the Annexe the night I made my 'peace mission'. '. . . If it's any consolation to you, Lavinia, I haven't been able to write a word since that play – not one word . . .'

I opened my eyes and looked at the musician. 'I think it's called a block,' I said expressionlessly. Or divine intervention – or retribution? 'Helen just couldn't write any more.'

'Oh, like me.'

'How so?'

She suddenly twisted out of her chair and knelt by the fire. 'I can't play any more,' she said bleakly. 'I just . . . can't.'

'You don't know that.'

She didn't answer, broke up some slivers of wood and laid them on the embers.

'I don't think you should do that,' I said gently. 'Use the tongs.'

'What for?' she flared. 'It doesn't matter now, does it?'

'Of course it does. You'll play again if you want to.'

'Your niece didn't write again, though, did she?' Her face glared in the sudden blaze of the fire. 'So why should it be any different for me?'

Two children running on the lawn in front of the hotel. It is a bright windy blue day. They run and run, chasing each other and laughing as they play some mad silly game they make up as they go along. They are keen to get out there on the fells, to stretch their arms and embrace all that infinity, where they will not be bounded by fences or hedges or neat small lawns.

Did Joy and I ever run like that? Yes, there were times, holidays when we went boating, riding, making up games to tease our parents, dressing up in silly clothes – Joy leading, me following, looking up to my clever big sister.

But did the child ever run like that – Helen's child? That secretive little girl who watched me with her large still eyes the night of the 'peace mission'. Did she ever run wild and free like that?

The walls are becoming thinner. Like Japanese screens, I can see figures moving behind, shapes growing larger, shadows spreading like ink on blotting paper.

'I've been speaking to the solicitors.'

We were in the morning room at Belle House. I was looking over a script I'd been sent unexpectedly, Teddy standing by the mantelpiece fingering my collection of silver boxes. Spring, my favourite season. Daffodils thick on the lawns, crocuses clustered beneath the trees. I'd filled all the vases with jonquils and their scent drifted sweetly through the rooms.

'The solicitors? Why?' He didn't answer and I put my script down. 'Teddy, is there something wrong?'

He moved the boxes around, picked up a cigarette case and put it down again.

'Teddy, what is it?'

'I . . . wanted to put things in order,' he said slowly. 'It had to be done.' He went over to stand by the window, where he could have his back to me. 'I wanted to make sure you were provided for.'

'Teddy, darling, you're not feeling ill again, are you?' Alarmed, I went over to him. 'Teddy?'

'There's nothing wrong with me, Vinny.'

'But your heart?'

'My heart will last the course.'

'Then why?'

He took my hand and we sat together on the window-seat. 'I just want to make everything straight, that's all.'

'But you'd tell me if there was something wrong?' I pressed. 'You know I don't like you keeping things from me. If you're not feeling well—'

'Vinny, I'm fine.' He squeezed my hand. 'Now, listen to me. I've arranged with the Order that after my death—'

'Teddy!' I cried. 'Please.'

But he stayed firm. 'If it should come to this, I've arranged that you shall have the Dower House to live in for as long as—'

'But Teddy!'

'No, listen, Vinny,' he said sternly. 'I want you to know that you have a home here on the estate – always. It's the best I can give you. Of course, if things had been different—'

'Teddy, there's no need. Please.'

'But there is a need,' he said staunchly. 'It's best to make all these things quite clear. It's just a bit difficult to talk about, that's all.'

'I'd still rather you didn't,' I said weakly.

But he ignored me. 'The Annexe,' he continued slowly, 'I want to give to Helen.'

'What?'

'She needs somewhere secure for herself and the child.'

'After what she did to you – to us?' I was appalled. 'Don't you think that's taking your Christian charity a little too far?'

'Vinny, listen to me. No, listen—' He turned my face back towards him. 'If there's one thing I learned from the Dowager it is that one must forgive and forgive and forgive.'

'The Dowager was hardly one for forgiving.'

'Exactly, and look at her, look how she was all those years, so mean and bitter. She never got over Christian's death, never forgave me for being alive when he wasn't. Even if Helen hadn't written her play, the Dowager might have willed the estate away purely from spite. She was like that.' He held my hands, pleading. 'Don't grow hard, Vinny, it's not like you. Don't get like the Dowager.'

I drew a deep breath and after a moment managed to say tightly, 'It's your decision, Teddy – it's not up to me.'

He nodded but didn't relax his grip on my hands. 'But there is one thing only *you* can do for me,' he said. And I could see it coming, see it distinctly as one sees a storm cloud filling the sky. 'I want you to go up and tell Helen.'

'No.'

'Explain to her—'

'Teddy, no.'

'—that the Annexe will be hers after my death, that she can live there for as long as she likes with *our* blessing, Vinny – ' he was willing me – 'because she's your only relative and she has an eight-year-old daughter you've never met, and because she's still young and when we're young we all make mistakes—'

As he was speaking I was shaking my head. I would have got up and walked away but that he was holding my hands so tightly. Over the months, the years since I'd broken off completely with Helen and moved into Belle House, he'd gone on and on, wearing me down like a tap dripping: Stay in touch with her, Vinny, don't break off with her . . . I thought of the times I'd seen him receiving instructions from the Order in those thin brown envelopes that spoiled our breakfast. How his lips tightened as he announced the Order's plans to make the estate more profitable – raising the tenants' rents, ploughing up more fallow land, ordering more fertilizers – all in the name of efficiency. How he and I had to manage in the house with unreliable and often disrespectful help. I thought of the humiliation of him being a tenant on his own estate, of the gossip that followed behind him in the villages. All this, I thought, is not the result of a 'mistake' – it's a crime.

'You cannot make me go and see her,' I said heavily.

'No.' He relaxed his grip on my hands. 'No, of course, I can't.'

'You're asking too much.'

He didn't answer, just looked at me.

'Teddy, if you're so keen on reassuring her, then go and see her yourself,' I snapped. 'After all, you've *never* met her. Maybe you'd change your mind about her if you did.'

But he just shook his head. 'It has to be you, Vinny.'

'Why? Why, for heaven's sake?'

'Because you need to make your peace with her – for your own sake as much as hers.'

'And if I don't?'

There was a long pause, then he said, 'You're a bright, brave woman, Lavinia—' He gestured to the silver boxes on the mantelpiece. 'Don't let this one spot tarnish your armour . . .'

Oh, my Teddy . . . Lying in bed at the Annexe, we listen to the trains as they rock the house. He grumbles sometimes because my rings and bracelets dig into his flesh: 'Really, Vinny, do you have to wear all this ironmongery . . .' But he likes it when the bracelets run together, ringing as I move my hands over him.

And in the narrow spartan kitchen he stands looking out at the overgrown garden: 'I really ought to do something about that,' as he says every time it catches his eye. He lays out the picnic he has brought on the round inlaid dining table – crisp rolls and smoked salmon and petits fours and champagne. I wear the heavy satin flowered gown he gave me and, as I eat, wander round the dining room and kitchen, looking at the odd, old pictures on the walls, turning over the damp books on the shelves. It is dim because we keep the shutters on the outside of the house closed to ensure our privacy, but I like this half-dark. I like the sparse furniture and the soft grey dust.

'You're prowling, Vinny,' he says, catching the end of my gown. He pulls me towards him.

And later, when he has taken me there in the kitchen I laugh from sheer joy and exclaim, 'Oh, Teddy, darling Teddy – if we could only have met twenty years ago.'

'We're here now,' he says. 'Aren't you happy with that?'

I put my mouth to his and kiss his wide lips, taking them between my teeth while he sits still, quivering.

'I'm more than happy,' I whisper.

And sometimes when we lie, still panting after making love, our bodies damp, melting together, it is as if there is no division between us. His skin is my skin, his breath is my breath. I lie on his broad chest, tracing his face with my tongue. My Teddy – my love . . .

Of course, I made the 'peace mission', as Teddy called it. 'I knew you would,' he said, closing the door of the Rover and standing back to wave from the steps of Belle House.

But it was very strange to arrive in London and pull the car up to a halt outside the Annexe. Strange to see the shutters swung wide open, though the low eaves still crouched secretively over the upper windows. It was a dark spring evening. The magnolia had finished flowering and was dropping waxy petals on the ground. The holly hedge had grown straggly, uncut, the little blue gate hanging off its hinges. She's not looking after the place properly, I thought primly as I walked up the path and knocked at the door. I'll have to say something to Teddy about it . . .

And then the door opened and, for a second, bracing myself to see Helen, I was taken aback until my eyes dropped and I saw the child.

She leaned against the frame. God, but she was the image of Joy – the same lambent eyes, the same glorious hair. But unlike Joy she stood unsmiling, looking up at me warily.

'You must be Marigold,' I said. 'I'm your great-aunt Lavinia. Can I come in?'

She didn't move. 'I don't like being called Marigold,' she said. 'It's a stupid name. At school they used to tease me and call me Goldilocks.'

'Oh, what name do you like then?'

She cocked her head, considering. 'Sometimes, I like Judith,' she said, 'because then I could be called Judy. But my friend Melissa says Barbara is better, because then she could call me Babs—' She broke off, giggling.

'Well, shall I just call you Judy, then?' I asked.

But before she could reply there was a call from inside. 'That's Mummy,' she said, standing back. 'You'd better come in. Don't say anything about my name, though – it's a secret.' She ran ahead.

The house felt smaller, less mysterious – brighter too, with the colours Helen had chosen. In the hall I recognized the table and the porcelain bowl I'd given her. She'd laid rugs down to cover the worn floorboards, garish patterns woven with rough wool.

I went into the kitchen. Helen was standing by the sink, washing up, and turned when I came in. Her hair had grown and the thick blood-red sheaves kept falling into her face. She had to keep tossing her head like a horse to keep them out of her eyes. She had put on weight but carried it well, I thought, more upright than I remembered, more presence.

'Lavinia.'

'Helen.'

We stood looking at each other, then she picked up a cloth and wiped her hands.

'I was just – you're early – I wasn't expecting—'

'Oh, I thought—'

'It's all right, it's all right—'

All this spoken almost simultaneously, all in a rush.

'You'd like a drink? Tea? No, of course, you don't like tea, do you? Coffee then? Or wine?' She kept wiping her hands on the cloth.

'Wine would be lovely, thank you,' I said.

The child had been dawdling her fingers along the counters and Helen turned to her. 'Marigold, go and fetch the nice glasses from the cabinet for me, will you?'

'The green ones?'

'Yes.'

'Can I have a drink from one – please?'

'We'll see. Be careful, don't run with them,' she called out as the child scampered away.

We stood awkwardly.

'She's a lovely girl,' I said at last.

'Isn't she?' Helen's face was bright with pride.

'She looks very like Joy, you know.'

Her face closed instantly. 'I wouldn't remember.'

'But the photographs—'

'To me Marigold's just herself – one and only. Shall we sit down?' She gestured to the round table, still standing in the dining room, though now the inlay was scratched and scuffed,

the surface covered with exercise books and half-finished draw-
ings. She cleared some papers from a chair.

'It's hard to keep Marigold's things all in one place now she's
out of school,' she said with a half-apologetic laugh.

'Term's finished already?' I said, sitting down. 'Isn't it a
bit early?'

'No—' She moved round, clearing some more papers and
books away from a sofa that was covered in a large knitted
patchwork blanket. 'You misunderstand – I mean, I've taken
Marigold out of school.'

'Why? Was there a problem?'

'Not exactly—' She sat down for a moment on the sofa. 'It's
just that I decided it wasn't doing her any good.' She stood up
abruptly and went back into the kitchen. 'Red all right?' she
asked, opening a cupboard and taking out a bottle.

'Oh, fine, thank you.' I hesitated, then asked, 'But why wasn't
it doing her any good?'

'Oh, you know—' She opened a drawer and groped inside.
'The other children – terrible influence, you should have heard
some of the language Marigold was coming home with—' She
took out a corkscrew and slammed the drawer shut, all her
movements heavy, overemphasized.

'But where will she go now?' I asked.

'Oh – ' she plunged the corkscrew in – 'I'm going to teach her
myself.'

'But are you allowed to? I mean, aren't there regulations?'

'It's perfectly all right, Lavinia.' Her look was suddenly cold.
'I have the best interests of my daughter at heart. I wouldn't do
anything to harm her.'

'But her friends?' I had to persist. 'She'll get lonely—'

'I know what's best for my daughter, Lavinia,' she said tightly.
'It's not your concern.' The warning in her voice was very clear
and I had to give up.

As Helen uncorked the bottle, the child came back with the
glasses and placed them carefully on the counter. Helen smiled
and ruffled her hair. 'We'll have to get this trimmed soon,'
she said.

'Short as a boy?' Marigold asked eagerly.

'We'll see.'

'You always say that . . .'

Helen came towards me with my wine. 'I hope it's all right?'
I tasted it. It was sour. 'Fine,' I said. 'Lovely.'

She sat down on the sofa and the child, carefully balancing
her own glass of juice, sat next to her. They looked completely
unalike. The child, so bright and vibrant one would turn to look
at her in the street, and Helen, dark, brooding, thick-eyebrowed,
a person one would instinctively feel wary of. She kept running
her fingers over her daughter's head and through her hair as
we spoke, the child sitting quite still, measuring me with
her eyes.

'I've brought the papers,' I began haltingly. 'As I explained in
my letter, Teddy wants you to have a lease on the Annexe until
– in case – so that for the time being—'

'Later, not now.' She gestured to the child.

'Oh, I see.'

'So, how are you, Lavinia?' she began brightly. 'You look
well.'

'Older,' I said. 'But fine, thank you. And you?'

She flung her arm around the child. 'I've got my beautiful
darling here,' she said. 'What more could I want?'

'Mummy?' The child wriggled in her grasp. 'Mummy, you
know that programme I told you about? You know, the one
Melissa said was—'

'Yes, I know.'

'Well—' She was twining her fingers in the knitted blanket.
'It's on tonight and – can I go and watch it?'

Helen looked down at her. 'Now, Marigold? When your
great-aunt Lavinia's come all the way to see you? You're sure
you want to do that?'

'Oh, Helen, I really don't mind.'

Helen shot me a glance and then turned back to her daughter.
'Well, you remember what we agreed?'

Marigold held up her finger. 'One thing.'

'And only one, all right?'

The child nodded, watching her mother intently.

Helen sighed. 'Then go on – but give me a kiss first, and a
cuddle . . .

'I don't like her to watch too much television,' she said as Marigold skipped out of the room. 'It's really not good for her.'

I took a mouthful of the acidic wine and murmured some sort

of noncommittal agreement, feeling that there was still a lot of the evening to get through.

'Let me give you some more wine.' She made to get up.

'No – thank you – I'm driving.'

She laughed. 'You never used to be so careful.'

'I was a lot younger then.'

'Not so much, surely?' She thought for a moment. 'Seven – eight years since you brought me here? Have you still got that old sports car you had? I was terribly impressed with that, you know. Do you remember finding me in that theatre foyer when I was so big with Marigold and feeling so ghastly?' She was speaking quickly, with an awkward excitement. 'Remember how pleased I was to see you? And how delighted with this little house and everything?'

'I remember.'

There was a pause. I avoided her gaze and diligently drank some more wine.

'You know, I didn't realize that the play would cause you so much trouble,' she said suddenly.

This was hard, harder than I'd imagined. I had thought that we would ignore it, the subject left camouflaged. I would be offering the olive branch and she would accept it. We weren't meant to be discussing the war.

'You see,' she went on. 'I think you misunderstood the play. I just meant *A State of Grace* to be a lighthearted satire – an exposure of marriage and the Church. I thought you'd approve of it. You know, the hypocrisy being shown up –' she looked at me appealingly but my face remained blank. 'And, well, I just thought if I changed the names and the circumstances – ' she was speaking more haltingly now – 'I never thought that people would – that there'd be all that – but honestly, Lavinia, I was in such a state when I wrote it. Bernard was pressing me, I'd gone way over his deadline, I couldn't write the play I'd tried to write all summer and I just felt I had to come up with *something* – everyone was expecting it. I wasn't myself, Lavinia. You'd gone off on your American tour and I was all alone for those last months of pregnancy. I felt so – it was all so – so . . .' She trailed off with a shrug.

I had to take a deep breath before I could trust myself to speak. I wanted to argue, wanted to shout, You cannot claim innocence.

Ignorance of the law is no defence. You betrayed me. But instead I said in a low voice, 'I don't want to go over all that again, Helen.'

'But I didn't mean it – really,' she cried. 'I'd no idea your Teddy would lose all his—'

I felt a sudden flash of anger: God damn you, Teddy, if it hadn't been for you I'd never have been here. But if it hadn't been for him, I thought, I wouldn't be in this situation at all.

I reached for my bag, my hand trembling. 'Now, I've got the lease here,' I said, cutting her off firmly. I made my voice sound very matter-of-fact. 'I think you'll find it's quite straightforward.'

But she just looked at me. 'If it's any consolation to you, Lavinia, I haven't been able to write a word since that play – not one word. I've tried and tried, but – I suppose you could say it's a sort of penance, I've offended too many gods.'

I said nothing. Yes, I suppose now was the moment to say, I forgive you, it's all right. But I hadn't forgiven her, I couldn't – and she hadn't actually apologized. She had spouted a stream of justifications without taking any responsibility for what she had done. It is enough that I am here, I thought, enough that I am speaking to you – no more.

I stood up. 'I think it would be a good idea for you to have a read through the papers,' I said evenly. 'Make sure it's all quite clear. I'll go and say hallo to Marigold. I haven't had much of a chance to meet her yet . . .'

As I stood for a moment gathering myself in the hall, I gazed around to where Helen and her gaudy colours had swept away all trace of the dim, dusty little retreat that Teddy and I had shared. Now it was like looking at an old friend wearing an ugly dress. I will not come here again whatever Teddy says, I vowed. I will never come back here again.

I could hear the television from the hall – it was on quite loudly. I opened the door of the front room and went in. The room was dark, lit only by the flickering screen. Marigold was sitting in a big armchair, her knees drawn up to her chest. She had been sucking her thumb and I could see it, still wet, snatched out of her mouth.

'It's cold in here,' I said, perching on the arm of her chair. 'Aren't you cold?'

'Mummy says not to have any heat in here to stop me watching television,' she replied. 'But I don't mind it cold – I like television.'

'Is your programme good?'

She looked at me slyly. 'It hasn't actually started yet. There are some cartoons first.'

'Oh, good, I like cartoons.'

She smiled back warmly. 'So do I.'

'I watch them in my house too sometimes.'

'Do you – really?' Her thumb had crept towards her mouth again and was brushing her lip. 'What's your house like?'

'Well, it's very big, though we don't use all the rooms now, and it's in the country—'

'Are there animals there?' she broke in.

'Yes, lots.'

'Lucky you.' She sighed. 'Melissa's going to the country for her holiday. She says they'll see cows and lambs and horses and everything. I've never been to the country.'

'Well,' I said carefully, 'you could come and visit me there one day, if you want?'

'With Mummy?'

'Or without – whichever you'd like.'

She blinked thoughtfully for a moment, seemed about to speak and then turned back to the screen as a fanfare sounded. 'Ooh, look, it's about to start,' she said excitedly. 'It's really good – Melissa told me – it's about this burglar, only he isn't a burglar really, but he always wears a mask and at the end he takes it off and everyone's really surprised.'

Immediately, she became engrossed in the programme. As if unaware of me, her thumb was back in her mouth and as she sucked it she smoothed the soft sleeve of her shirt over her upper lip. Though she sat very self-contained in her chair, there was something elusive and tantalizing in her that made me want to reach out and hold her, keep her. But I sat without moving, instead watching the smile, Joy's smile, lapping over her face, her expressions changing, her eyes widening and crinkling as the silly slapstick played itself out.

And then suddenly the music became even louder and she squealed excitedly, 'Ooh – look – look – he's going to take off his mask.'

I glanced over, and there filling the screen, smiling straight into his daughter's eyes, was Jack. Older, less handsome, but still Jack.

'Ooh – I told you he would, I told you.' Marigold was laughing. 'It's good, isn't it? He's nice, isn't he?'

Suddenly the door was flung open and Helen marched in. 'Marigold, this is *much* too loud—' But then Jack was saying his lines and Helen froze, and for a moment there was that whole little family all in the room together.

Then Helen snapped off the set and switched on the harsh central light. 'Bed, Marigold – now,' she ordered. 'No arguments.'

'But, Mummy—'

'Do as I say.'

'—it hadn't finished.'

'Helen, I think you're being—'

She turned to me. 'You keep out of this, Lavinia,' she spat. '*Now*, Marigold, you heard me.'

'It's not fair,' the child protested, but she got out of her chair and went to the door. 'It's not fair,' she shouted again over her shoulder as she went out.

'And don't let me catch you sucking your thumb again, madam,' Helen shouted after her. 'I saw you.'

I stood up. 'Helen, I think you're being rather hard on her.'

'Really?' She turned to me, her eyes glittering with suspicion. 'And I suppose this was your idea, was it? Your way of getting back at me?'

'Oh, don't be ridiculous.'

'And I suppose you were quite ready to tell her just who it was she was ogling?'

'Helen, he's her father – the child's got a right to know her own father, for heaven's sake.'

'She *doesn't* need to know him,' she said stubbornly. 'And he doesn't need to know her. Marigold's *my* daughter.'

'But don't you think he'd be kind to her? Helen, be reasonable,' I pleaded. 'Jack's just another actor – rather down on his luck, judging by that programme, but he's not an ogre.'

'Oh, yes – sure,' she said acidly. 'He'd charm the spots off a puppy, would Jack. But he's not going to charm my daughter

61

away from me. He doesn't know about her, he's *never* going to know about her, and she's not going to know about him – she doesn't need to.' Her eyes narrowed and her words came in staccato bursts: 'She's *mine* – *I'm* her mother – *I* gave birth to her – she's all I've got – and I'm not going to let him – or anyone else – try and take her away – I'm not . . . I'm not . . .' Her voice trailed away.

'Helen?' I went to her. 'Helen?'

'It's all right.' She pushed my hand away but still stood there as if in a daze. 'I'm all right.'

'But you've gone white as a sheet.'

'I'm all right,' she repeated. 'Just a headache, that's all.'

'But—'

'I'll take some aspirin. I'm fine, really.' She summoned a half-smile. 'That wine wasn't really very good, was it?'

'Not really,' I admitted.

We exchanged a look and a train rumbled past, rocking me with old memories.

'I'd – I'd better go,' I said, looking away uncomfortably. 'I'll just get my bag.'

She was standing in the hall waiting for me when I got back. She still looked very pale and was rubbing her temples.

'You ought to go away,' I said gently. 'Have a holiday. It must be hard work bringing up a child.'

'Yes – maybe,' she replied vaguely.

'Have a proper break,' I urged. 'We'd have Marigold for you.'

'No—' She reared up. 'No one's having her.'

I sighed. 'All right, Helen, all right.' I went to the door. 'You'll say goodnight to her for me?'

She nodded. 'Thank you for coming, Lavinia,' she said formally. 'And,' she added more spontaneously, 'thank your Teddy – he's been very generous to me. Maybe I'll meet him one day . . .'

We didn't attempt an embrace.

As the door closed behind me, I took a deep breath of air in relief. The moon was high, bleaching the last petals of magnolia blossom, glinting the sharp holly. It is done now, I thought, I cannot do any more – I will not do any more. But God help that child.

I walked away.

It is dark this morning. Like one of those mornings when Teddy would say, 'Let's wipe out getting up today,' and we'd stay in our great bed at Belle House, cuddled up, reading, talking, making love and sometimes just lying there watching the sky, listening to the silence . . .

Now the hotel is quiet, there are fewer guests. Soon there will be no guests at all, just myself sitting here for the long empty days, watching the fire, listening to the wind and the cries of the gulls.

I wait for Gregory.

The rain has been thick today. Sheets of it rolling down the window and tossed from one side of the lake to the other by the wind.

Annie came in, stood a little back. 'Miss Mair, would you mind? The other guests really can't go out in this weather and it would be nice for them if they could sit in here this morning. Would that be all right – just for today?'

'Of course, Annie,' I said quietly, my head aching from the brandy. 'I wouldn't mind at all.'

'Thank you, Miss Mair.' She turned to go.

'Annie—'

She looked back. 'Miss Mair?'

'Annie, I'm very sorry – the other day, when I was short with you.'

'Oh, that's all right, Miss Mair.'

'Really?' I looked at her carefully.

'We all have our off days,' she said. 'It's forgotten now.'

But she hasn't forgiven me, not yet. She is wary, a little cautious where there was no caution before. An innocence lost, a trust betrayed. I spiral downwards.

I sighed. 'You can bring me a brandy with my coffee later, Annie,' I said, and turned to the window to avoid her look.

So, I had company this morning. I sipped my brandy and watched the guests reading their newspapers, stretching their hands out to the fire, making conversation. The musician wasn't here – maybe she went out. I like to think of her out in the rain when the rest of us are huddled away from it. I imagine her striding over the fells, sheep darting away from her. Does she hear music as she walks, I wonder? Is her world made up of music?

I sipped my brandy, feeling the warmth of it slipping over my body like a soft shawl – this will make it all better, this medicine cures everything . . . Oh, I remember the seduction of that voice singing to me at the Dower House.

And I watched a couple arguing softly in the corner far from the fire. Both were upset, disappointed – and both trying not to show it. They were sad because it was their last day and here it was thick with rain. They kept glancing over to the window alternately, each wanting not to let the other see, both hoping the rain might stop just with their wishing it.

Though they both wore rings, I do not think they were married to each other. Those rings did not link them together. There was a ferocity, an intensity between them that does not have a place in the quiet stable of a long marriage.

You should go back to bed, I thought. Wipe the day out and just go back to bed. That's what you want to do anyway – why wait for the sanction of evening?

The woman was dark, her hair very black, curled around her throat like a cat's tail. And suddenly I saw how he watched her when they lay in bed, how he saw her blue-black hair spread against the white pillow. How, when he lowered himself on to her – slowly, with such restraint – he saw her eyes looking up at him, lambent, opened wide. How, almost losing control, he kissed her neck where her hair was softest, drawing the length of it out in his hands – great fistfuls of molten night – burying his face in its abundance as with a sob he came and then lay still, breathing the clean scent of her deep into his body. And she, lying beneath him, looked over his shoulder at the little hotel room they had made their own – her things on the chest of drawers, his shirt slung over the chair, their towels still wet on the floor. And she stroked the nape of his neck, her fingers tracing the strong tendons, smoothing them out with her long fingernails as she would the fragile silver wrapper of a chocolate bar . . .

But now they sat stiff in their clothes. '. . . but is that what you want? . . . I don't know . . . Oh, darling . . .'

And I wanted to say to them: Go, go on – *go*. Leave this

room, leave your principles, leave your husband, your wife, your children. Take each other while you still can, grab what you can of life, because life is short and hard and cruel, and look what will happen if you give in to it. You will become old one day. You will be old and ugly and your bodies will be haggard and dry and all the opportunities you missed will be seen as flickers of light in the dark. Look what happens – look at me.

'I want you to do something for me, Gregory,' I said as he sat down.

'Of course, Lavinia,' he replied quickly. 'What is it you'd like?'

'My God, you're keen, aren't you?' I scoffed. 'It's as if I'd picked up a stick and said, "Walkies."'

'That's a bit unfair.'

I shrugged. 'I just don't want you making too much of it, that's all. It's just a simple request.'

'Fine.'

A pause.

Then he said carefully, 'You'll have to tell me what it is, Lavinia.'

'All right, but don't look at me like that,' I snapped.

'Like what?'

'Like you're expecting me to go running up the steps into the nearest church and fling myself at the feet of some plaster and gilt statue.'

'I think I'd have to wait a long time for that,' he said, suppressing a smile.

'Well, not *running* then.'

'Lavinia,' he said patiently. 'You've asked me to do something for you – a simple request, you say.'

'I might just want you to witness a will.'

'Is that it?' He looked at me. 'Your will?'

'No – no. I've nothing to leave and no one to leave it to. I used it all up – best thing to do with possessions. Not that you would know – your lot don't go in for possessions, do they? Not your own anyway, though you don't mind other people's.' I was well aware of being scratchy – I hadn't had any brandy and my head was too awake.

But he didn't react, just said evenly, 'It'll be difficult for me to help if you don't tell me what you want.'

65

'I could ask someone else,' I said, pulling my shawl more tightly around me. 'I'm sure Annie wouldn't mind if I asked her, but she'd make a fuss and I don't want a fuss.' I looked at him hard. 'I don't want a fuss, understand?'

'I understand.'

The sun went in behind a cloud and fingers of shadow tiptoed over the fells. I felt suddenly weary.

'I want you to fetch a bag down for me from the Dower House,' I said. 'It's a carpetbag – about the size of a briefcase. It was up there in the attic, must still be there – I shouldn't think your lot have emptied the place completely.' I looked out of the window. 'You can bring it to me next time you come. There's no hurry.'

'All right.'

The clouds were massing over the lake.

'It's going to rain,' I said.

Now, if I think about it, I wonder if the monks, aware of my dilapidation in the dank Dower House, didn't 'arrange' that roof fall? God knows, they could have climbed on to the roof and drilled a hole at any time, removed a few slates even, I wouldn't have noticed. Maybe they were fed up with the souse living at the end of their nice clean drive, a dark sin they couldn't wash away. And maybe, too, I shouldn't have deserted my post as the croaking raven, the unlucky single magpie at their gates.

But maybe the cold and the damp and my joints swelling and distorting weakened my resolve, so that when I woke stiff in my chair that morning to see the sky directly overhead and the plaster and laths all over the floor, when I watched that trapped bird butting the walls, I had no resistance left for when the monks bustled in and took over, bringing me here, where the warmth and the quiet and Annie's kindness have forced me back to a life I didn't think I wanted any more.

Or maybe it was Helen perched up there on the roof like a child on a high table swinging her legs so that their shadow criss-crossed my windows like a pendulum. Maybe it was Helen playfully snapping the slates and tossing them down, Helen drumming her heels on the rafters and casually punching a hole with her fist so that she could reach in and pull me out.

The Dower House must be dried out, they say. And not just the Dower House either, I think, as I sit in my chair, watching them swirl through the rooms in their skirts. We will arrange alternative accommodation for you while this is being rebuilt, Miss Mair – shocking, shocking, if we'd known it was in such disrepair – like so much of the estate . . .

I refuse to leave my chair, refuse to go up to Belle House. I sit stubbornly, watching a blushing young novice uncover my store of empty bottles I'd hidden in the log basket.

You're so lucky, they say. Someone was looking after you – just look at that. And they step out of the way and I can see through the broken wall the huge heavy bough crashed on to my bed, just where I would have been lying if I hadn't been too drunk to get there last night.

Just my luck, I say bitterly.

And I mean it – though they look at me strangely. Had I been a good homely pigeon instead of a croaking raven, I would have been tucked up safe and warm in my bed with my nice book and my cup of cocoa and a nice fat tree would have smashed my head to pieces, so that at last I would have been wiped out, obliterated. No, no luck at all.

The novice is packing a few things for me. He looks embarrassed as he opens drawers, takes my clothes from the cupboard – dresses I haven't worn in months, what's the use of washing, staying clean? As he moves through the rooms, he stirs the dust and plaster so that his robe is white around the hem. Droppings from the birds which have nested in the eaves fall on our heads like confetti. He stumbles, knocking over a bottle.

Hey, careful of that, I shout. That's good brandy – I'll have some of that – give it here.

He glances at his superior, who says: Yes, medicinal, of course – we'll have some for you in a moment – whisking the bottle away.

And I do not protest, I am too tired to protest, tired of being the crow at the gate, tired of holding my head up.

Here – the novice puts a hot cup in my hand. Drink this, it will help.

Help? I should have been under that branch. They think they should treat me for shock, but I am furious. I had a date with that branch and I missed it – I was late. And now I won't get another chance as good as that. Oh, I know that God of theirs, he won't let me draw the ace twice.

I sip the drink without thinking. Tea, very sweet and only faintly a dash of brandy. I drink it for the brandy – after all, it's my brandy, I paid for it. And there should be another few bottles. Where – in the pantry, under the bookcase? But the pantry is smashed and the bookcase turned over and there is a reek of brandy which mingles unpleasantly with the smell of must and earth.

And then they are either side of me, one of them talking as he helps me to my feet. God knows, I am light enough for him to simply tuck under his arm, but he lets me stand.

Well, but the good Lord must be saving you for something really special, Miss Mair, he says.

Oh, yes, I think, a heart attack? A road accident? And doesn't that good God of yours want people to die, then? But I say nothing, only grip his arm as we make our way forwards.

Clear the way, Brother Peter, he calls. No, take that great lump of plaster out of the way. That's right, that's right, Miss Mair, we'll be there just now.

And suddenly the smell of earth inside the cottage is like being buried alive and I stumble, pressing forward, eager to get out.

There now, Miss Mair, there now – Brother Peter, open that door quickly now, for heaven's sake.

And we are outside. Out in a spring which I hadn't noticed, a spring which seems to have crept over the hedges and fields while I was asleep. Birds sing, the air is soft. I am dazed. The stiff old crow no more than a tired old lady sitting in a car with a blanket tucked over her knees as she is driven away.

'The first time it happened,' the musician began, 'I thought I was just tired. I'd already given two recitals that week, but Victor said that this was only a small lunchtime charity do – he said it would be good for my profile.' She gave a dry laugh. 'God knows, it certainly didn't do *theirs* any good—' She broke off, hunched closer to the fire, cradling the wine glass in her hand.

'And?' I prompted.

'Well, it was so – I mean, it was just so odd – almost a joke.' She turned to face me. 'I'd never imagined – I mean, that's what was so ludicrous about it – I'd never even imagined forgetting like *that*—'

'It can happen to the best of us,' I said gently.

'To others maybe, but me?' She struck her breast. 'I've been performing since I was a child – music's in my very blood. Those études and sonatas are more familiar to me than – than— Well, it's like speaking, it's a language to me, do you understand? A language I've spoken fluently all my life and now suddenly – suddenly – to lose it.'

She coiled herself more tightly in her chair, her hair glinting as she moved, blue-black as the night outside.

'Go on,' I said. 'Tell me – the concert, the next one?'

She sighed, took a sip of wine. 'So, the first time was a shock – quite a bad shock, but I just put it down to feeling very tired, exhausted, in fact. Victor wanted me to do a couple of other lunchtimes straight away – "You've got to get straight back on the horse when it's thrown you," he said. But I really put my foot down.' She gave a sudden wry smile. 'I even went to the office – Victor hates me going to the office.'

'Why?'

'Because Miriam works there now that the children are both at school. She does the books. He's terrified she'll find out—'

'Ah.'

'Oh, it's over now,' she said carelessly. 'And it was only a very brief affair, but it's made him very nervous.'

'Useful, then?'

'Exactly.' We exchanged a look. 'I – well, sort of tease him with it when I need to.'

'But you weren't teasing when you went to the office that time?'

'God, no. I was deadly serious.'

'And he got the point?'

She nodded. 'I'll say one thing for Victor, he's very quick on the uptake.'

She took another drink of her wine, then leaned forward to put a log on the fire.

'So, what happened then?' I asked after a pause. 'At the concert?'

Her face darkened and tightened as if a mask was being stretched over it. For a second there was that absolute lack of expression that presages tears.

'You don't have to tell me,' I said quietly. 'You don't have to tell me anything.'

With a sudden movment she drained her glass and set it down. Then, staring straight at the fire, she began. 'I knew as soon as I got on to the platform. Even beforehand in the Green Room I had an inkling, but I kept pushing it away. I don't know if you've ever had that feeling?' She glanced at me. 'Oh, not the usual nerves – nerves are important, useful, you know, they get you buoyed up – but this, this *dread*, this was different.'

She pulled her fingers through her hair, closed her eyes, then opened them again and stared at the fire. I waited.

'I suppose,' she began again, 'I must have seemed fairly normal. God knows, I've walked on to so many platforms I know how to do it – it's second nature to me. But this time, even as I was crossing the stage, I was thinking of other things – the Green Room, the restaurant where I'd had lunch, the street and the traffic outside – anything, anything, just to get away. And then the piano – ' her voice rose – 'standing there waiting for me – like some *creature* with all those red and gold tongues and teeth yawning open. God! And the audience all lined up in their rows waiting, just waiting – those eager, hungry faces all looking at me—' She broke off, trembling, but immediately started again, her voice tightly restrained. 'Acknowledge the audience, Victor always says. So – I stood by the piano, I made a bow and then as the hall went quiet again I sat down. I sat down,' she repeated. 'I adjusted the stool, I moved it backwards and forwards a little, and then I laid my hands in my lap and waited for the rustles and coughs to die down. I waited. It went quiet. They waited for me – all of them – everyone – waiting. And I – just – *couldn't*. As if my hands were – they wouldn't move. I couldn't hear the music in my head – not a single note. Just this *deafening* silence.' She shuddered. 'Of course, they soon started rustling again. A good performer, Victor says, can always measure the mood of their audience. Well – ' she gave a mocking laugh – 'there was *my* audience slipping through my fingers, while I was just sitting there like a block of wood.'

'So – you left?'

'I had to get off the bloody stage first,' she cried. 'I couldn't just disappear, however much I wanted to—' She took a breath. 'I stood up. I turned to face them. They went quiet for a bit then and I wanted to say something – anything – but I just *couldn't*. And when I just stood there – when the monkey didn't perform, they started up again, whispering and rustling and shifting around. They were humming like a swarming hive – God!' She took another juddering breath. 'I don't know how I managed to get out of there – I don't remember. The next thing I remember is being in my car and driving through the night. I think I stopped in a lay-by somewhere and slept for a few hours.'

'And then you arrived here.'

'At least Victor wasn't at the concert—' Her voice was calmer now. 'He doesn't usually miss the important ones, but he had a gala ballet performance he'd arranged to go to with Miriam – she likes ballet. He'd never have let me disappear like that otherwise.'

'And now?' I asked after a pause.

'Now?' She looked at me for a long moment, then stood up suddenly and began to circle the room, touching the tables and chairs. 'Now there's nothing. I've got nothing – I do nothing – I am nothing.'

'Couldn't you try again?' I ventured, watching her pacing like an angry panther. 'After all, things do change. Maybe you were just exhausted, under too much pressure? Maybe this break will help you to—'

She wheeled round. 'Things didn't change for that niece of yours, did they?' she said fiercely.

'That – that was different.'

'I don't see how. She had a block – I have a block. She never wrote again – I'll never play again.'

'But that whole situation, it's not the same.'

She ignored me, gave a cold laugh. 'Do you know, it's just now struck me that it could actually be quite liberating? After all, I'm free. I can do anything I want – become a builder, or a cleaner, or a traffic warden – a gardener even, without having to wear gloves – or I could join the army—' Suddenly she stopped quite still and a bitter smile spread over her face. 'No, I know what – it'll be perfect for me. I'll become a teacher – a music teacher. Those who can't do . . .'

I could feel the waves of her anger and self-disgust beating at me and I closed my eyes defeated. Why am I encouraging this, I thought wearily? What can I do? I do not want to care. Then I felt her standing in front of me and I opened my eyes.

'I'm sorry.' She spoke softly, looking down at me with

an expression of regret. 'All this – it's nothing to do with you.'

It has everything to do with me, I thought. But I didn't say anything.

The flames lap the log that Annie has just put on the fire. It is dark already, an early dark that has crept over the fells. The room is quiet, the guests not yet returned for coffee. I sit here, watching the flames licking the log with cats' tongues soft and distinct. There is a seductive sense of purpose in watching a fire, I feel something is achieved, something done.

This evening I watched a family in the dining room. A son and his new wife sitting with his parents. They talked little, ate stolidly through the courses, heads bent over their plates. They had dressed formally, not for our small dining room but for each other, to mark some occasion.

The older woman wore a dark wine dress with a string of pearls which mocked a tired skin that was heavily powdered to disguise its crevices. She ate quickly, greedily, taking another roll and spreading it thickly with butter before sinking her teeth into it. The old man sat stiffly upright, attacking his meal and eating it in precise steps – one, two, three, four – a military march across his plate. The young woman was bored, kept darting appealing glances towards her husband. The wedding band was bright on her finger and she twisted it up to her knuckle and down again. Her husband avoided her gaze.

When the pudding arrived they all took up their spoons and forks. The mother dipped her spoon into the cream and lapped it up with eyes half closed. The old man had refused cream and frowned at her. The young woman pushed aside the pastry and toyed with the filling. She watched her husband as he, like his father, concentrated on eating. She looked from one to the other: Is this what he will become?

And still the young man wouldn't look at her – as if he was wearing blinkers. Locked in this meal with his parents, he could focus only upon keeping going, getting it right, this meal that was so important. But as the pudding bowls were cleared away, his face sagged: God, and now there's still coffee to get through . . .

And neither he nor his lovely wife could see as I saw only

too clearly how afraid those parents were. How the old man felt death creeping up on him, an enemy he couldn't avoid. How the old woman, her body collapsed into shapeless dresses, shot acid glances at her slim daughter-in-law with her smooth skin and her firm high breasts.

So they sat, the four of them, like a team of unmatched horses forever out of step. Because young people never see their parents, they only feel them as towering monoliths, dark monuments in whose shadow they will always stand and to whom they will forever look, hoping for their approval, fearing their disapproval. Because Mummy and Daddy never become people with names, individuals who do not know, who also make mistakes as they balance on this thin shelf looking back at *their* parents . . .

When Annie came to help me in here, I made her turn my chair away so that I shouldn't see them when they came in. I closed my eyes.

'I've – I've got the bag, Lavinia.' Gregory stood uncertainly by the door.

I looked up. 'Well, come in, come in – don't hover over there like some sort of insect.'

He came towards me hesitantly. 'Do you want me to—'

'Just put it on the table and sit down, Gregory.'

It had become mildewed, I noticed first. A faint green haze dulling the bright weave. The clasp was rusty too. Maybe I won't be able to open it, I thought wildly, maybe the papers will have decayed . . .

I sighed. 'I suppose I should thank you—'

He waved his hand. 'It was still up there in the attic. We haven't yet made a start on the roof, though most of the new walls are marked out.' His voice changed. 'I do wish you'd come and see it, Lavinia. It's going to be so much better—'

'Enough of the propaganda, thank you, Gregory.'

We both looked at the bag.

'I gave it a bit of a dust,' he said after a moment. 'I hope that's all right?'

'If I'd asked you to burn it, would you have?' I said suddenly.

'Of course.'

'Without looking inside?'

'Lavinia, I wouldn't dream of—'

'You wouldn't even be tempted?' I watched him. 'Wouldn't even shake it to see what it was?'

He flushed. 'I've already done that. It sounds like papers – a lot of papers.'

'Well, at least you're honest.'

'I'm a monk – what do you expect?'

I raised my eyebrow.

He smiled, then asked after a moment, 'And how is our mystery guest? Still here, is she?'

'Yes.'

'Have you spoken to her?'

'We've had a few conversations. Why do you ask?'

'Oh—' He shrugged. 'I just wondered, that's all. I thought I saw her out on the fells the other day. I wondered if she needed any help. The fells can be quite bewildering if you don't know them.'

'No doubt she had a map,' I said coolly.

He nodded but went on, 'She just looked – well, rather forlorn – a bit lost all on her own like that. I'd half a mind to go after her and offer her support.'

'Succour, you mean?'

'Well—'

'Leave her alone, Gregory,' I said firmly. 'It's what she wants.'

'Yes – yes, of course.' He cleared his throat, then began again with a suspicious brightness. 'I think we'll be able to get the Dower House ready for you before the winter. Certainly before the hotel closes after Christmas.'

'I'd rather *not* think about that.'

'But—' He hesitated, frowning a little. 'If you could become *involved*, Lavinia,' he said earnestly. 'You'd enjoy the planning – you'd be interested in the rebuilding.'

'I'm too old to be interested in anything.'

'But that's not true,' he cried suddenly. 'Your life isn't over yet, Lavinia – you must know that. You're a strong person. It's not in your nature to give in to despair.'

'Gregory—' I was shocked. 'Gregory, that's quite enough.'

But he went on defiantly. 'I know you'd say I don't know you all that well, but I feel I do, Lavinia. And it seems to me that it's a crying shame – a waste, your wanting to shut yourself away from life like this. It's not like you—'

'I will thank you,' I broke in, my voice tightly controlled, 'not to have the presumption to tell me about the sort of person *you* think *I* am. I will thank you, Gregory, *not* to interfere.'

How dare you, I wanted to shout, how dare you try and raise the dead? I am not Lazarus, I will not be Lazarus, I will remain here in my sarcophagus, trussed in my winding cloths. How dare you try to summon up that other bright, brave Lavinia? I had buried her and now you drag her out to reproach me.

I must have clenched my eyes tight shut to push him out, because when I opened them again he was gone. Only Helen's bag sitting on the table in front of me, ready to spring open.

I didn't go to Helen's funeral in the end. I couldn't. At the last moment I told Teddy. We were standing in the hall at Belle House and he was putting on his thick coat. It was cold, autumn already crossing over to winter.

'I can't,' I said. 'I just – can't.'

He looked at me sadly. 'Oh, Vinny,' he said. Just that. But with all the delicate reproach he could bring to the words.

'I'll wait here,' I said. 'If anyone wants to come back.'

He shook his head. 'There's only us. You know that.'

But Bernard was there.

He came back to the house alone, while Teddy stayed talking to the monks. 'Lavinia, darling.' He enfolded me in his huge embrace. 'You look just the same – beautiful as ever.'

I laughed. 'You flatterer, Bernard, I'm white-haired, I'm wrinkled. I look in the glass and I don't recognize myself.'

I led him inside and he gazed about, awed. 'My God, darling, this place is straight out of the National Trust, with a good piece of *Homes and Gardens* thrown in. Now I know why you abandoned us. Who'd want the footlights and greasepaint when they can live in Arcadia?'

'You get staff in Arcadia,' I said drily. 'We can't afford them here – or decent heating. Come on, we'll go to my sitting room, it's warm in there.'

'But who's that?' He gestured to the portrait of the Dowager as we went past the dining room. 'She looks a right old battleaxe.'

'She was.'

He stroked his beard. 'Can't say I'd fancy having her glaring down at me while I ate. Why do you keep her here?'

'She's Teddy's mother, Bernard – well, was. Anyway, one gets used to it.'

He shuddered. 'I'd turn her face to the wall if I were you, ducky.'

The fire was burning brightly in my sitting room, glinting off the blue and white hearth tiles. It was a room I'd chosen for myself, to house my own furniture and mementoes.

'Sit down, Bernard. Drink?'

He shook his head, then, 'Oh, bugger the doctors – yes, I'll have one of your delicious Martinis.'

'The doctors?'

'I've had to come off the booze, darling,' he said, walking around the room, examining the little objects. 'Heavens, Lavinia, isn't this the Nefertiti I gave you?' He held out the alabaster figure that looked very small in his plump hand. 'Do you remember that season? When we had that glorious run all summer – couldn't put a foot wrong, full houses, worshipping notices. And your Cleopatra, darling – to this day I've never seen anyone match it.'

I handed him his drink and looked him straight in the eye. 'Bernard, what's this about doctors?'

'Oh—' He waved his hand. 'The flesh decays, Lavinia – some little problem that's just too boring to go into. You know,' he went on quickly, 'your Teddy is a very nice man.'

'I know.'

He sighed. 'You always had good taste in men, Lavinia. I always envied you that.'

I laughed. 'Memory gilds, Bernard. I remember some of your comments about my "consorts", as you so discreetly called them: "Not everyone's cup of tea, darling" – "A real original, darling" – "A pity he can't speak English, darling." Remember?'

'Well, your taste has improved obviously.'

I patted the sofa beside me. 'Come and sit down and tell me what's been happening.'

He sat heavily, then took a deep gulp of his drink. 'Ah, now that *is* good. You know, it's almost worth having things outlawed because of the pleasure one gets from breaking the rules – forbidden fruit, so much sweeter.'

'So what is this prohibition? And stop avoiding the issue, Bernard.'

'Ah, Lavinia, your Bracknell voice.'

'Bernard—'

He gave a resigned shrug. 'I had a little scare, that's all.'

'How little?'

'Well, enough to scare Kevin, anyway.'

'Kevin?'

'I know.' He looked sheepish. 'But what's in a name, eh? I did try calling him by his middle name, "Stephen", which really would be better, but he simply wouldn't hear of it – went off in quite a huff, the poor lamb.'

'Never mind the name, Bernard.'

'Well, I've got rather attached to him, you know,' he swept on. 'And it seems he's rather fond of me, so I have to be careful for his sake.' He grimaced. 'We're all getting older, darling – it's a bore, but there it is. Still, we'll put up a good fight before we shuffle off this mortal coil, eh?'

'Is he in the theatre, Kevin?' I asked.

'Oh, heavens, no. He's a British Telecom engineer. Came to mend my phones – you've no idea. Very stable man, though.'

I laughed. 'Oh, just your type, Bernard. You've always adored stability.'

'Well, as one gets older . . .'

'And the theatre?' I questioned. 'How's that little world these days? Come on, I want all the gossip.'

'It's not the same, Lavinia,' he said, taking another swallow of his drink. 'A lot of the style's gone out of it – the class. And the actors – well, maybe I'm just jaded, but they don't seem to have the talent that they used to. All they can do now is to take their clothes off and shout, not even project their voices properly. And so difficult to work with – tetchy, you know, and moody.' He shook his head. 'Of course, there *are* one or two good ones, there always is – the cream. But nothing like as many as there used to be. I'm actually thinking of retiring.'

'Bernard, you're not? What would you do?'

'Same as you – enjoy my life.'

'But you'd die without the theatre.'

'You haven't.'

Haven't I? Don't I miss the crowds, the camaraderie, the excitement? Aren't I just vegetating down here? That's another thing Helen took from me, I thought bitterly.

'Have you never thought of making a comeback?' he asked suddenly.

I shook my head. 'It's too late now, Bernard. And I couldn't have earlier, not after all that furore.'

'But that was years ago,' he protested. 'And nobody remembers all that, Lavinia, not these days.'

'Well—' I shrugged. 'I've lost my nerve, then.'

'Rubbish.'

'It's true.'

But Bernard had seen me act and I could feel him watching me. A shrewd man for all his bonhomie. He'd worked with too many actors.

'I'm not a member of your company now, Bernard,' I warned.

He sighed, stretching his legs. 'Well, I think it's a shame, you know. That damn play of Helen's – it was just a storm in a teacup.'

'Not for Teddy it wasn't.'

'But he harbours no grudge?'

'None.'

'That must be hard – for you.'

There was a pause. I turned my glass in my hands, took a sip and then said slowly, 'I never really thanked you for turning down *A State of Grace* when Helen presented it to you, did I? And yet you must have been tempted – must have known it would be a box-office success?'

'I knew what it would do to you, Lavinia,' he said. 'I wouldn't do that.'

'That was more than loyal.'

He sighed. 'Didn't stop it going on stage, though, did it? That little bugger of a director at the Playhouse picked it up quick enough. I told Helen when I'd read the play, I said: This is unfair, to anyone who knows her it's obviously Lavinia, and you're making her and her lover a laughing stock. Don't do this, I told her, ditch this play, never mind the commission, I'll wait for another year, let the muse really inspire you.' He shook his head sadly. 'But she wouldn't listen. I know I shouldn't speak ill of the dead, but she was always stubborn, Helen. She went running off to the Playhouse and of course that tarty little theatre had a slot they were desperate to fill.'

'But you could have got a lot of publicity,' I put in. 'And it would have been good for the company – you might have got higher grants, increased funding—'

'And I'd never have been able to look you in the face again. Come on, Lavinia, I'm no Brutus. But what I can't understand,' he added in a puzzled voice, 'what I still don't understand, is why? Why did Helen do it? Didn't she realize?'

'She *said* she didn't,' I replied heavily. 'She told me she thought that the play was just another satire like *All Greek*. She even thought I'd admire it.'

'Really?'

'That's what she said.'

He sighed again. 'And now she's dead – so young, such a waste. And the child too?'

I nodded.

'I'll say one thing,' he went on, 'it's the devil she ever met that Jack Arden. Slippery little man, that one.'

'Oh, but I always thought you rather . . . liked him?'

'Not my type. Pretty, yes, a real heart-stopper, but he knew it, which rather spoiled the effect. And I must admit to feeling some satisfaction that after I finally kicked him out of my company, his reputation as an impossible drama queen closed many doors before him. God, he was difficult to work with – that summer season with him in Greece . . .'

'Well, I can only hope it's finally behind us now – over,' I said resolutely.

'One can never be too sure of that.'

'How philosophical, Bernard,' I joked. 'Is that love – or a sign of the times?'

He smiled. 'I've had a brush with the Grim Reaper, Lavinia – it somewhat alters one's perspectives.'

'Was it very frightening?'

'Very. I'd rather not repeat the experience too soon.'

'Are you likely to?'

He shrugged. 'That's why I'm thinking of retiring. I've realized there's not so much time and I want to spend what time I have got with Kevin. I don't want to lose him like I've lost all the others, because I'm too busy with some silly little show for a back-end theatre that no one really cares about.'

'Oh, I think that's going too far—'

'I'll let you into a secret, Lavinia,' he said, leaning towards me. 'I've bought a little retreat in the Highlands. The house in London is on the market and as soon as it's sold—' He waved his hand. 'Off—'

'You're serious?'

'Never more so.'

'I shall miss you.'

'But you'll come and visit – both of you?'

'The Highlands?' I raised my eyebrow.

He laughed. 'You're still a fine actress, Lavinia, but come and visit *me* anyway, even though you don't like the place.' He stood up. 'I must go.'

'It's not that I don't like the Highlands,' I said, following him. 'It's just that—'

'You loathe them.'

'I had a terrible tour there – oh, years ago, when I started in the profession,' I said as we crossed the hall. 'The natives – so dour – "What time d'ye want breakfast, eight or eight-thirty?" And that would be on a Sunday. And the porridge—' I shuddered.

He laughed, reaching for his cape. 'We'll let you lie in, we'll feed you croissants specially flown over and you can pretend you're in France.' He swung the cape over his shoulders.

'The same one,' I mused, fingering the thick blue material. 'It must be immortal—'

'Unlike us.' He clipped it shut and leaned down to kiss me on both cheeks, his beard stroking my face. 'Don't let it be so long next time, Lavinia – and let's not make it only at funerals, eh?'

'You look after yourself, Bernard.'

'I'll let Kevin do that.'

'I want to see you again,' I called out after him to the dark.

The rain was driving thick and cold and out there in the Belle House burial ground Helen lay in the drenched earth and I never once visited her.

It is very late. I am alone in the room. I had asked Annie to bank up the fire because, I told her, I'd be awake for a while. She looked at me suspiciously. 'It's not good to go without sleep, Miss Mair,' she said.

'There'll be time enough for that later,' I replied.

She clicked her tongue. 'You do say some things. Well, there's your coffee there. I've put the cosy on the jug to keep it hot, all right?'

'Thank you, Annie.'

'And the brandy,' she added with a tinge of disapproval.

'I doubt I'll be needing that,' I said.

She smiled. 'Then don't stay up too late, Miss Mair – please?'

I look at the bag, put my hand on the clasp and push it gently. It slides open.

It had always been such an adjunct of Helen, this bag. She took it everywhere with her. 'It's big enough to take a change of clothes,' I said when I gave it to her. 'You won't want to lug a suitcase around when you're stagehanding with companies on tour in the provinces.' And she'd smiled almost for the first time since I'd found her alone in that dreadful state after her father died.

I reach my hand in and take out a thick file of loose papers. Clipped to the cover is a letter:

Dearest heart, I knew you would look at this one day when you were ready. I have put the sections in the order I think it best for you to read them, though this is not, I think, the order in which Helen wrote them. But they are better this way. I hope they will help you to understand, I hope they will help you to forgive, I hope you will read this with that openness of heart and the courage for which I have always so much admired you, my dearest Vinny – T.

And my hand is shaking so much that I cannot hold the flimsy page. Oh, but I thought that I had read everything he had written to me, that I had gathered up every scrap. I thought that there would never be anything else he could say and yet here is one last message, as if for a moment he crosses the abyss and kisses me.

Like a jack-in-the-box, the loss springs out – oh, my love, my love . . .

The door opens and the musician stands hesitating. 'Oh – I'm sorry, I didn't mean to disturb you.'

'Come in – I want to be disturbed.'

She closes the door and comes towards the fire. 'I couldn't sleep.'

'The curse of the performing profession,' I tell her. 'I could never sleep after a show – used to take me hours to come down.'

'But I'm not performing now.'

I shrug. 'Old habits die hard.'

We watch the fire. Layers of silvery-white ash flicker on the logs like the delicate feathers of a bird.

After a while she gestures to the papers – 'Are they yours?'

'My memoirs, you mean?' I laugh drily. 'No, Helen's.'

'Another play?'

'I don't know. I haven't read it.'

'Oh.'

'I was about to read it,' I say, adding slowly, 'It has been left for me to read.'

'Do you want me to leave you, then?'

She is standing by the fire, warming her hands, and just now she doesn't look at all like Helen. Maybe because I have lived with her for a few days, spoken to her, the resemblance has evaporated. But then she gives a small sigh, a shiver ripples over her shoulder like a waterfall, and suddenly my heart is hammering in my breast sharp and quick as a bell ringing.

'No – stay,' I reply unsteadily. 'I'd – like you to stay. I'd like company.'

She tucks herself into a chair close to the fire. 'I'll probably fall asleep,' she says with a smile.

'Well, at least that would be one of us.'

I take a sip of brandy and open the file. The pages are clipped together in four sections like a four-leaf clover.

I turn the first page . . .

ROOTS

He likes the vegetables to grow in rows, neat orderly rows like lines of uniformed schoolboys. As I watch, he pegs out the garden line, unrolling it very carefully along the ground, crouching to see that it is absolutely straight before slowly, deliberately, drawing out the drill with his hoe. I would like to stand beside him and help, maybe smoothing out the soil with my hands or keeping the tools out of his way, but he points to the little white fence (I was allowed to help him paint the fence) and he says, 'No, Helen, you stand over there. You can watch but you won't get dirty.' What he means is that I won't get in the way.

Mrs Baines leans over her fence, the flowered overall stretched tight over her broad shelf bosom, and says, 'It's a beautiful sight to see the Professor sowing his seeds, isn't it, Helen? Even my Arthur, God rest his soul, could have learned a thing or two from your father, that's for sure . . .'

I pretend I haven't heard her. She has a moustache and smells of polish and disinfectant. She doesn't come over to cook for us any more but twice a week she comes in to clean the house. I wish I was old enough to do the cleaning myself, because then it would just be Father and me and we wouldn't need anybody else.

I lie on my belly and watch as he bends over the drill and tucks the seeds into the earth. He shuffles backwards, feet on either side straddling the row. I concentrate very hard. Even if I can't help I can at least pray to the gods like the Greeks did to make the crops grow. Father doesn't know I do this, it's my secret.

When the row is finished he marks it at both ends with special twigs and then comes out of the plot to fill the watering can.

'Can I do it? Can I water them?' I run alongside him. 'Please, Dadda, can I?'

'It's very good of you to offer, Helen, but this is far too heavy for you.'

'I've got my little can – the one you gave me – I can use that.' I have followed him to the tap by the back door and am looking around impatiently. 'It's somewhere here – I'm sure it is. Do you know where? Have you seen it, Dadda?'

'You must learn to keep your things in their proper place, not scatter them about, Helen.' He turns off the tap smartly and begins walking back to the plot. 'If everything's in its place, then nothing gets lost . . .'

But I am running ahead of him, down past the compost bin to the shed to look in there, and then to the bottom of the garden, where at last I find it among the bushes in my special hiding place, where sometimes I peep through the peacock eyes of the fence to watch the trains go by.

'Look, Dadda—' I run out, waving the little can. 'Look – I've found it. Can I help you now?'

But he is shutting the gate. 'It's all finished now, Helen,' he says. 'Next time . . .'

He takes the tools back to the shed and I watch as he cleans the earth from them and wipes them over with a special rag dipped in oil. The rags are kept in a bag and the tools are propped on their racks, bright and clean. Then he wipes his own hands with another rag and, sitting up at the bench, takes out his log-book and smooths back the pages.

I press at his knee. 'Can I see? Can I write something?'

'There's plenty of scrap paper for you up at the house,' he says. 'You know this isn't for you to play with.'

'But can I *see*?'

After he died I found the log-book in the shed. There, recorded in his neat, small handwriting with the classical 'ε's and the curled 'α's were the varieties and the dates of sowing and harvesting of every crop he had ever grown. All carefully written down. And for what? As I leafed through the damp pages with their columns of vegetables that had long since been eaten, I could find no reason for his attempt to hold on to them. What was he trying to prove? Whom had he wanted to show? I tossed the log-book into the compost bin.

84

'Please, Dadda,' I say again now. 'I just want to *see*.'

He sighs. And turns to me with a look that runs like prickles over my skin. 'Run along now, Helen,' he says. 'Have you finished your homework? And all the verbs? If you're good we'll have a walk down to the pond before tea to watch the sun go down.'

I smile, draw back immediately, am pleased, am good.

But then, as one drop of lemon will sour a whole pint of milk, he adds, 'And you can tell me your verbs as we go . . .'

Oh, let's not do the verbs, I want to cry out. Please, let's not do the verbs.

We walk side by side. I try to make my stride fit his, running two paces sometimes to his one. But his stride is uneven, hard to match, I cannot quite find the rhythm to fall into. As we walk I must recite the verbs and he corrects me – '"I loose", Helen, present indicative active? And the imperfect active? And the pluperfect? Good.' His praise so delights me that I give a little skip and answer his next question too quickly, without thinking. 'No, Helen, that's not the present imperative active, that's the present optative active. Come now, *think*, you know this.' His voice dark like the sun gone in behind a cloud. And all the time I am trying to make my stride fit his. Because if I do that right, then the verbs will come right, it will all fit together like clockwork.

There is a wooden seat by the pond and on good days, really good days, it is empty. On bad days, Mrs Baines sits there like a toad with her knitting. 'Never you mind me, Professor,' she says with her oily smile and the hair quivering in the spot on her chin. 'I'll just sit here quietly and get on with my work. I won't disturb you and little Helen.'

But with her within earshot the verbs squash and slide in my mind, slipping away every time I reach for them. 'Now, Helen, passive and middle: aorist indicative? Aorist subjunctive? Aorist imperative? And the infinitives? And the participles? Come along, my dear, don't be stubborn.' He only calls me 'my dear' when he is displeased, as if the endearment can sugar his disappointment.

My answers to his questions become more and more out of tune, like a screeching violin. The verbs sound like someone straining soup between their teeth. Meanwhile, along the bench

Mrs Baines is clicking her tongue (not at her knitting), hissing the air over her thick false teeth. I used to think she followed us out there on purpose.

Now, I wonder how he was before, when he taught in the prep school. Was he patient with his pupils? Dogmatic? Those rows of stiff, bored boys. Did he enjoy forcing their minds into straight classical lines, into tables and pillars of verbs? Did any of them challenge him? Did they have nicknames for him? What did they say when they saw Mr Grey's long face approaching them in the corridors?

But we are still at the pond and the exercises have at last been bludgeoned to death by my stupidity. Even the ducks have walked away, shaking their tails in disgust. He sighs, takes out his pipe and turns it over in his hands. But he won't light it, though, not yet – he'll save it for the evening, when he sits in his chair after supper marking books. 'Everything in moderation,' he says. Still, he likes to hold it, smoothing his fingers over the stem and round the bowl.

When I went to the hospital to pick up his things, there was the pipe lying on the registrar's desk. 'I don't want that,' I said, pointing to it. But it would cause an uproar in their system were I not to sign for it and take it away in the stiff brown envelope they give you in those places. And so the pipe came back to the house. The pipe that had been part of his face, his hands, the pipe that had smoked messages as distinct as a Red Indian tom-tom, lay small and cold on the dining table, reproaching me with bitter tobacco voices: You left him all alone – you didn't care – you never loved him . . . As if the sourness of the years had been trapped in its coils, the tube blocked with his disappointment, the stem bitten round by the teeth of his disgust.

Now we walk slowly back to the house and in the silence I vow that next time I *will* get it right. Next time I will get the verbs *and* the walking right. Next time.

I am small. I peer around the high wings of his chair. He has a pile of exercise books on his lap and the light from the standard lamp falls gently over his shoulders. One hand is curved around his pipe, which smoulders gently, the other marks the books with his special red ink pen. His head rests very lightly against one wing of the chair.

'What's that, Dadda?' I ask, pointing to the letters.

He looks down at me, his green eyes very bright. 'That's an "alpha", Helen, and that's a "beta".' He smiles.

I smile back – broadly. I point again. 'And what's that one? What does *that* say?'

He is pleased with my interest and I win the prize I was hoping for. He lifts me to sit on his lap, holding me firmly with one hand and pointing to the letters with the other. I lean against him, feeling his voice tickling my back.

I am a quick learner. Every evening I clamber on to his lap and point at the strange letters and say their names. When I get them all right he pats my head and smiles at me. 'Clever girl, Helen. Good – very good . . .'

But I learn too well, because then he says that I must study properly. I must sit at the dining table (which is not used for eating any more, only for carving up homework) and write the letters myself.

'But can't I sit on your knee, Dadda?'

'No, Helen, not now,' and there is that little edge to his voice that I am learning to recognize.

And soon, as the letters twist into words and the words into sentences, I am faced with a tangle of symbols which I struggle to unravel. 'Now, Helen, *think*. You know what this is, my dear – we went over it again yesterday.'

At any moment – in the garden, over a meal – he will turn to me and demand, 'Form the third-person singular, perfect indicative passive – "it has been stolen". And the third-person plural, aorist indicative middle – "they summoned". Parse this.' Or later, tossing a quotation to me light as a shuttlecock and that little sigh when it falls dead at my feet, heavy as a shot bird.

It was like watching a swimmer far outstripping me. As fast as I might swim, I could never keep up. From time to time he'd look back over his shoulder – Come on, hurry up, I'm waiting – and then he'd shoot away again as soon as I came close.

I work so hard. But the tenses, the nouns and their declensions, the slippery endings and prefixes, the elisions and reduplications, all slither through my fingers like soap. At night I sleep with an open book beneath my pillow, I clean my teeth to the beat of the declensions – first, second, third. But my mind is like a broad meshed net and the fish just slide through.

'Did you ever go to Greece, Father?' I ask him one night – anything to take my mind off that mess of spaghetti on the page in front of me.

'I don't need to go,' he says. 'I have it all here—' tapping the Homer on his lap.

'But have you ever been?'

'Once,' he says. 'With your mother. When the university offered me the Chair, she and I went there to celebrate.' He hesitates, then adds suddenly, 'You were conceived there.'

I blush, look down, cannot imagine what has prompted him to reveal such an intimate fact. We never mention such things. These days he no longer even comes into my room to wake me in the mornings, just knocks discreetly outside my door. Though I remember that when I was very small he would sit on a chair by my bed and tell me the Greek legends, so that I'd fall asleep with the gods and heroes running through my dreams: 'When you're older, Helen, you'll read all this in the original . . .'

Now he bends over his Homer again, his finger tapping out the line, head nodding. I think of all the Greek that is in his head, coiled up in that small skull like a compressed parachute. I try to imagine some way of siphoning it off – if I leaned my head against his, would it all jump into my brain?

'Helen,' he says, without looking up. 'Are you working?'

I look down at my book again where the letters are dancing like fleas. It is cold outside and we have the electric fire on, but the room is not warm. I would like to sit on the floor close to the fire, leaning against his legs, but I'm too old for that now. From the mantelpiece Joy's photograph looks down on us laughing.

There are voices from downstairs. Loud voices – they have woken me up. They aren't shouting (Father never shouts), but the woman's voice is very clear and has reached all the way up here to hook me out of bed. I creep quietly to the half-landing, where I crouch, listening.

'. . . Well, then, I'll talk to her myself about Joy if *you* won't. Really, Harold, you're getting to be a dreadful old curmudgeon, locked away in that university of yours. The child's a girl – a little girl, Harold, and little girls need their mothers. At the very least she needs to know something about her if she isn't to grow up warped, for heaven's sake.'

I wince, but he answers her in the calm, measured tones of one who has silenced whole roomfuls of boys with just a look. 'There's no need for you to raise your voice, Lavinia. I can hear you perfectly well.'

'Oh, for God's sake—' She has made a bird of her voice and it swoops down on him. 'What do you expect? I come here and I find that there isn't even a photograph of her—'

'Lavinia, I really must ask you to—'

'Not one photograph—' She sweeps on fearlessly. 'There probably isn't one in the whole house, is there? Is there, Harold?'

'Lavinia, please—'

'How can you be so selfish? Yes, selfish, because that's what it is, to deprive the child of—'

'I really must object—'

'Oh, stop being so bloody stuffy.' She dives in like a plane about to fire. 'What's happened to you, Harold? Honestly, if Joy could see you now she'd have a fit.'

There is a sudden silence.

I have never seen Father really angry, never known him to lose his temper, but I am always afraid that if he does then it will be terrible. He would turn me to stone. Now in the silence I am afraid. Has she turned into stone, this brave unknown woman? Has she melted into a puddle at his feet?

Then there is a familiar sound – tap, tap, tap, as he knocks his pipe out. And her voice, very soft and low: 'Forgive me, Harold – I'm sorry. That was a really horrible thing to say.'

He doesn't reply immediately. There is the clink as he lays his pipe against the ashtray. When he finally speaks it is slowly, with great effort. 'There may be some truth in what you say, Lavinia. It could be said that I have been remiss with Helen.'

And it has suddenly struck me that they are talking about *me*. That this mysterious woman knows me though I have never heard of her. And though Mrs Baines says you are punished for listening at doors, I am riveted by this conversation, by myself being handed between them like a precious stone.

But there is movement, I hear his chair creak and I ready myself for a quick flight up the stairs.

'It's late,' he says. 'If you'll excuse me.'

She laughs. 'Actually, it's rather early for me. You don't mind if I stay up?'

'As you wish,' he replies. 'The spare room is ready for you. Just be sure to switch all the lights off – I've already checked the back door.'

He is by the door, I can almost see his hand on the handle, I am poised to flee.

'Well, Lavinia, I'll say good-night, then.'

'Good-night, Harold – I'll see you in the morning.'

'Yes.'

'With Helen?'

He stops. 'Of course with Helen,' he says, a little testily. 'Really, Lavinia, I'm not concealing the child.'

'Well, you've certainly kept her pretty much to yourself all these years,' she bursts out. 'Never a reply to a Christmas card or a birthday present.'

'I didn't want to confuse her.'

'Confuse her?' The bird is back in the room, beating on the walls, swooping from floor to ceiling. 'Confuse her – about what? That she has an aunt who cares about her? Her only living relative – her own mother's sister? Was that so difficult, Harold? Was that so confusing?'

'Lavinia, I – I thought it was for the best—' His voice is sounding less certain now. 'When Joy broke off contact with her family, I didn't think I should stir anything—'

'That was with our parents, Harold, not me,' she breaks in. 'And it was about your marriage – Mummy and Daddy were just being stuffy and hidebound and Joy was just being dramatic. The whole feud was ridiculous. If little Helen had come along earlier, before they'd died, Mummy and Daddy would have fallen over themselves to mend the quarrel and Joy knew it. As it was, because of her high-handedness Joy made a mess of the whole thing. But anyway, you know full well that Joy never lost touch with *me*. We wrote – even when I was touring, *I'd* write, even if Joy wasn't that good about replying. And I was here when little Helen was born. You can't have forgotten that?'

She stops and there is a long silence. It is so long that I am suddenly aware of my bare feet on the cold linoleum, the draught chilling my thin nightdress.

Then she starts again, but now her voice is so quiet I have to strain to catch it. Even so, each word is distinct as a single petal. 'It was cruel of you, Harold – never to let me know. Never to tell me how ill she was – never to get in touch. You know I would have come – I would have dropped *everything*. She was my sister – my only sister – and I loved her.'

'For God's sake, so did I – so did I,' he bursts out. His voice is raw. 'Don't you understand? It was all so sudden, so quick – there wasn't any time – and nothing I could do – nothing, nothing.' He is choking, spluttering. I cannot move up there on the landing, hearing Father cry. I am turned to stone.

But she has not been destroyed. I hear her talking to him, soothing him, making him sit down while she opens the cabinet and clinks bottles and glasses. 'Here, Harold – no brandy, but there's some sherry, which will do. That's right – go on, drink it. And some more.'

'Lavinia – I feel so ashamed.'

'Nonsense. A good cry never hurt anybody.'

The glasses clink again and he says something I can't catch and she laughs suddenly. 'Oh, Harold – now I can see just why Joy married you . . .'

They continue to talk, but their voices are low and I don't know if I even want to hear any more. Then the door opens very suddenly and I spring up and run to my room. I am afraid they might have glimpsed the flash of my nightdress and I lie in bed with the covers pulled over me and my heart thudding. But I hear his footsteps go straight past my door and into his own room, where he closes his door firmly.

I lie awake wishing that I hadn't eavesdropped and hoping that I won't go to hell like Mrs Baines says. After a long time I hear the sitting-room door close and light footsteps on the stairs. They stop outside my door. There is a faint jingling sound and I close my eyes tight shut and will myself to sleep.

She is tall. Taller even than I imagined from her voice. She stands in the middle of our sitting room, which looks drab compared with her kingfisher-blue skirt and emerald shirt. She has a gold-spangled scarf around her neck and is smoking a cigarette in a long holder.

When she sees me she smiles and holds out her hand. 'Helen,

darling – heavens, how you've grown.' She laughs. 'Now, that's a very silly thing to say, isn't it? All children think so. I did myself when people said it to me.' She takes another big puff of her cigarette, tossing the ash casually behind her towards the fireplace. 'But you see, you were only a very tiny baby when I last saw you.' She bends down to kiss me – there is a wave of fresh, spicy perfume.

Father nudges me forwards. 'Helen, say hallo properly to your Aunt Lavinia.'

'Oh, heavens,' she exclaims. 'You don't have to call me "Aunt" – it makes me feel positively geriatric.' She sits on the sofa and pats the seat beside her. 'Come here, Helen. We've so much to catch up on.'

'I'll make the tea.' Father hesitates in the doorway. 'And then you must have your breakfast, Helen. You don't want to be late for school.'

'Oh, bother school,' she says, but thankfully once he's left the room. 'You can miss the odd day, can't you? After all, it isn't every day you get to meet your only aunt, is it?' She is stubbing her cigarette out in Father's special Greek pottery bowl.

'I don't think Father would like it – if I missed school,' I say, trying not to look too aghast at the bowl.

But she doesn't seem to notice, blows sharply through her cigarette holder and tosses it down on the side-table. Her movements are quick and the bobbled fringe of her scarf trembles as she twists and turns. She wears a lot of bracelets that jangle as she moves.

'Oh, my darling,' she says lightly, 'you are grown up, aren't you? How old are you now? Ten? Eleven? Heavens, how did you *get* to be so grown up? I know I wasn't half so keen on school when I was your age. Your mother was, though,' she adds.

'Father says school's important,' I say.

She raises an eyebrow – it is a tiny but very expressive movement. 'Well, and what do you say? Do *you* like school, Helen?'

I shift a little uncomfortably. 'I – well, it's all right.'

She laughs again and smooths my hair with long fingers which are clustered with rings thick as buds. She moves her hands constantly as she talks, gesturing, making pictures, her bracelets running up and down her arms as she adjusts her scarf, or strokes my face, a finger drawing down my cheek or smoothing back my eyebrows. Her voice, too, runs up and down scales, now high, now low, a ball tossed in the air for me to catch. I have been reading Book Six of *The Odyssey* with Father and I think of Nausicaa playing catch with her maidens. I would like to tell her this but instead I listen, not so much to what she is saying – she is talking about my mother and what she was like and how sad it is for me to grow up without her – but to the light and shade in her voice. I am watching her face, which is bright when she speaks, her hair coiled in a tight bun on her neck like a great auburn conker that I would very much like to touch. She reminds me, I realize suddenly, of one of the goddesses in my old picture books – Artemis, maybe, or wise Athena.

Then Father calls us into the kitchen, where he has prepared breakfast. Lavinia doesn't eat anything, just sips the coffee he's made specially for her and hovers around the kitchen. She fingers the red gingham curtains over the window by the sink – 'Aren't these the ones Joy made when you first moved here, Harold? I thought so – I'm not much better at sewing myself, you should hear what my dresser says . . .' She looks out of the window – 'Is *that* your garden, Harold? But there aren't any flowers? I distinctly remember flowers last time I was here. And what's that interior fence for? A vegetable plot?' She looks at him in amazement. 'You grow your own vegetables? Oh, Harold, how dear of you . . .'

I can see that all this makes Father very nervous. He doesn't settle down to his toast and marmalade as usual, but stands beside her rather awkwardly, taking the occasional sip of tea and patting his pockets to feel his pipe.

When I have finished I go to the sitting room to pack my satchel. I am a bit worried in case she says something to Father about my skipping school, but she seems to have forgotten that. She follows me into the room.

'I want to give you something, darling Helen,' she says. 'It's something I want you to take great care of.' She opens her midnight-blue handbag, which is lined with soft pink silk the colour of Turkish Delight. 'Here.' She takes out a large photograph. 'This is for you.'

The woman in the photograph is smiling. Her hair is loose around her neck, shorter than Lavinia's. 'Is that you?' I ask.

'No, darling.' She looks at the photograph with me over my shoulder. 'That's your mother – that's Joy.' Her voice is layered in soft down. 'I want you to keep it somewhere you can see it – where you'll see it every day.' She draws a breath. 'Your mother was a very lovely woman, Helen – and a very happy one, too, that's what you must remember—' Her voice breaks a little. 'I'm sure she loved you very much . . .'

But I'm sure now – and I was almost sure then – that Joy didn't really love me at all. Not that she disliked me, but that I simply didn't warrant much attention. They should never have had children, my parents, should never have put a child between them. They should never have made a child watch that look which leapt between them, live and burning as fire. I had to witness that look and I knew there was none of the fire in it left over for me.

They put me to bed very early in the summer, while it is still light. I lie there listening to their voices rising up from the garden, happy and relaxed, laughing as they don't laugh together when I am with them. Then there is a formality, a constraint. I do not ever see them touch each other, caress, kiss.

And yet sometimes, maybe when we are eating at the dining table, when I am concentrating on keeping my elbows in or not spilling my water, sometimes I will glance up from my plate and see a look passing between them. It is as if a cord runs straight from her eyes to his, bypassing me completely. Not so much as if I am excluded but, more terrifyingly, as if I simply don't exist at all. There is the look, like a lighthouse beam, a spotlight bright on both their faces. I can sit there absolutely still and see it tangible and unreachable as the twist of colour in the heart of a marble. As if they are tossing a ball lightly, gaily, between them and I am piggy in the middle.

Time just stops.

And I am suddenly horribly afraid that we will be frozen for ever in this moment, like one of those Christmas tableaux, so I rattle my cutlery or drop my napkin and the look is broken as if a light has been switched off, and they turn to me with little frowns darting across their faces like swallows. And maybe she gets up then and, while clearing the table, brushes her hand over his head and he smiles and murmurs, 'Not in front of the child, Joy . . .'

The child. I am the child who stands outside their hallowed world. I lie in bed listening to their voices rising up from the garden, his pipe spicing the night air. I don't move from my bed, I am good, so good. I think that maybe I will win them over with my goodness. They sit out in the garden among the flowers I helped him plant. They talk, they laugh, maybe they hold hands. Sometimes they just sit in silence.

I lie awake listening.

So, the photograph stands on the mantelpiece in the frame Father has bought for it. He never refers to it – neither do I. I let my eyes blur when I look in that direction. As I get older the lovely bright smile, the sparkling eyes seem to be mocking me.

'Isn't she getting tall, Professor?' Mrs Baines leans over her fence, her double chins wobbling. 'You must be proud of her – she's going to be just like her mother, God rest her soul . . .'

But I am not like my mother, I have not inherited her beauty. I am plain. My face, like his, is long, my hair dry, an ugly old rust red. Yes, I am tall, but gawky, awkward, not, as the Greeks describe, loose-limbed. And I am not now unaware of the unconscious cruelty of my name.

'The child will be a comfort to you, Professor . . . Little Helen, so much like her poor mother.' Maybe they thought that if they said it often enough the mask of my features would be smoothed away and replaced by Joy's smile, her generous mouth, her large eyes. That I would behave like her, laugh like her. 'Such a solemn child, isn't she, Professor? Here pet, give us a smile. There, you look much prettier when you smile . . .'

It is the year of the fuchsias. We have planted many fuchsias in the garden, Dadda and I, to welcome Mother back. The fuchsias are pretty, like little ballerinas, and I have helped Dadda plant them with my bucket and spade. He has given me some marigolds to plant in a little patch of my own. We spend a lot of time in the garden. It is nice to have Dadda all to myself.

When Mother comes back, she looks strange, different. Dadda carries her very carefully to sit in a chair on the terrace and wraps her in lots of blankets. It's hard to recognize her, her face is yellow and she has a purple turban on her head. Her lips look very large and red.

'You've got to be very good now, Helen,' Dadda says, taking me to one side. 'Your mother's not been well and now she's got to rest.'

I look up at him, straight into his forest-green eyes. 'Will she get better?'

'Of course she will. Now, you stay with her in case she wants anything.' And he goes back down the garden.

I don't really want to stay with her, I want to go and help Dadda. I hope she stays asleep, but she wakes up and calls me.

As I get nearer I can smell her smell like sour fruit. She is saying something, mumbling so I can't quite hear, and I dread having to get close to that red mouth of hers to listen. I edge forwards and suddenly her hand streaks out and grips my shoulder – a thin, bony talon of a hand. She is smiling a terrible lopsided grin and squeezing my shoulder, with her nails digging in.

And then suddenly I realize what is so wrong about her. I can't see any of her hair. All that lovely rich red hair of hers is hidden up inside the ugly turban and it is this more than anything else which makes her look so strange. So I say with a laugh, as if it's a game, 'Why have you got that funny hat on, Mother?' And before she can answer, I reach up to touch it, but the turban slips and underneath her head is bare as an egg.

She gasps – I scream – the turban falls to the ground. Is her hair inside? Have I just taken off all her hair? She is croaking harsh as a jackdaw and now I can see her skull is criss-crossed with scars and scabs and tufts of shrivelled gingery hair.

I run crying all the way down the garden to the bottom where the fence is and the bushes can hide me. What have I done? What have I done? A train rattles past, so I do not realize that Dadda is there until he is standing right over me.

'I didn't do anything,' I cry. 'I didn't – I didn't do anything.'

'All right, Helen – all right. Stop it now.'

'But there's nothing there, Dadda – there's nothing there. She hasn't got any hair.'

'That's enough, Helen.'

'But her hair, Dadda. She's got no—'

'I said *stop* that, Helen.'

He stands, huge and terrible, blotting out the sun, and I am crying, sobbing, pressing my face against the rough fence. Then he bends down to me. 'Your mother's been very ill, Helen. You have to understand that . . .'

As he talks I look at the daisies studding the grass by his feet and I remember how, before she got ill, sometimes she would take me for a walk to feed the ducks and we'd sit on the grass by the pond and have a little picnic with biscuits and lemonade. And I'd make her a daisy chain to put on her head like a crown and she'd wear it all the way home, skipping with me along the pavement . . .

'You understand now, Helen?' He has finished speaking and stands up. I nod, looking down at my red sandals – red like the polish she sometimes wore on her toes to match her favourite dress, red like her hair. But I mustn't think about her hair.

'Good girl,' he says. And walks back up the lawn to the crumpled figure in the deckchair, who looks like an insect lying helplessly on its back.

I don't see her again. Or maybe I do and I don't remember. I have to stay with Mrs Baines and I am afraid that Dadda is angry and has sent me away. I look through the fence but he never comes out and the fuchsias are wilting in the hot sun. My little patch of marigolds is all shrivelled up.

'Has Dadda gone to teaching?' I ask Mrs Baines.

'That's right, pet.' She pulls me to her stuffy bosom and pats my head, but she doesn't look at me and I don't believe her.

And then one afternoon he is back and I am taken out to him in our garden. He is wearing a stiff shiny suit which is cold against my cheek as I run towards him and press my face against his legs. He pulls my fingers away one by one and makes me sit in a chair while he listens to Mrs Baines, who saws away, nodding and shaking her head for a very long time.

After she has left he goes upstairs and when he comes back down he is wearing his gardening clothes and I hop and skip around him. 'Shall we water the plants, Dadda? Can I help? Can I do something?'

He goes down to the shed and takes out the spade and I follow behind, still skipping, still chattering. He steps on to the lawn and with one sharp movement slices into it. 'I'm making a vegetable plot,' he says. 'You can watch.'

He rolls up the grass as if it is a carpet, working from one side of the garden to the other like a shuttle unpicking the flowers, the bushes, the shrubs, leaving behind just bare brown earth. 'We'll turn those into compost,' he says of the bushes all heaped in a corner. It seems to happen overnight, my pretty garden with the ballerinas and the soft sweet daisy grass just whisked away.

Then he divides the earth into four plots like a folded handkerchief. He digs out trenches and paths and encloses it all with a little wooden fence to mark out his territory. And he decorates this strange memorial to his wife with the fruits of the earth – carrots and onions and potatoes.

Daylight thin as skimmed milk. The fire is burned out. The musician has gone. I am alone and stiff and weary from staying awake. Outside, the birds are calling the dawn. When Annie comes in and finds me here she will be cross and concerned. But I cannot move, not just my hands but all my joints ache as though they are being crushed in a steel grip.

Seagulls cry. I remember them rising up behind Teddy as he ploughed a field with the new tractor that the Order had bought. 'They're right, these monks,' he called out to me as he came to the edge. 'They know a fair bit about farming – even teach this old dog a new trick or two. Wait for me, Vinny – I won't be long.' But I turned away dispirited, disgusted at his pliancy, his lack of pride. Left him to the gulls, walking quickly so that I should not hear them wheeling and cawing behind him, scavenging as he scavenged for the scraps of his estate.

And now? Now in their cries I hear only the sound of yearning, of a note never brought home to rest. Like a bird, Helen said, my voice beating against the walls. That child listening from the landing, admiring *me*. And watching from behind those reticent eyes, observing in the same way as I observe the guests now.

But, as Gregory said, I have not always been an observer. I have been part of the dance, whereas she, it seems, was always an outsider. Poor Helen – poor little girl. Oh, Teddy, I don't want to understand her . . .

'The young can be very callous,' I said to Annie as she cleaned the room this morning.

She looked up immediately. 'Has one of those young scamps said something to you, Miss Mair?'

'No, Annie, no – it's nothing like that.'   'You're sure?' She eyed me suspiciously. 'Because if any one of them's been giving you lip—'

'No – really, Annie.'

'You've only to tell me, Miss Mair, and I'll tan their behinds—'

'Annie,' I broke in firmly. 'I was thinking of myself. It would have been more accurate of me to say that when young – or even when old – one can be very callous.'

She leaned on her broom. 'You? Callous? You wouldn't hurt a fly, Miss Mair. Others been hard on you more like.'

'No, Annie, *I've* been hard. Selfish – and cruel – and—' I broke off. She was watching me with an expression of exasperating tenderness. 'Don't look at me like that,' I said sharply.

But she just brushed a strand of hair from her face. 'We all of us make mistakes, Miss Mair. It's only human.'

'But some mistakes are worse than others.'

She shrugged. 'Maybe – but then it's not as if you've killed anyone, is it?'

No, Annie, not with my bare hands. But I have committed sins – sins of omission, and who is to say that they are not the worst?

'Don't look so fretted, Miss Mair.' She came towards me and suddenly darted a kiss soft as a bird on my cheek. 'There – I'd trust you with a newborn babe. You're what my mam calls a *genuine* person.'

'Oh – Annie.' I looked away.

'I don't know much about most things, Miss Mair,' she said, picking up her dusters and tins of polish. 'Only cleaning and cooking and that, but my mam – well, she always says that if you've done something wrong and you're sorry, "The good Lord always forgives."'

'I wouldn't know about that.'

She glanced around, checking the room. 'Well, thankfully it's not our place to know things,' she said. 'We get in a right enough muddle as it is – leastways, that's how I see it. Just get on with our own work and not worry about the whys and wherefores, that's what I think.' She made for the door. 'Well, I'll bring in your coffee. Oh – ' she turned back for a moment – 'I saw Father Gregory talking to that girl the other day – what's she called?'

'Celia?'

She shook her head. 'That's not the name on the register. But you know the one I mean – the girl on her own.'

'I know.'

'Out on the fells,' she went on. 'I *was* pleased. She looks like she needs to make some friends, all on her own like that – and I think it's nice when people get to know each other here. Mind you,' she sighed, 'it's getting quiet here now, isn't it? Not many more guests booked. Of course, there'll be a flurry for Christmas and New Year, but that'll be it then until we open again at Easter. And you'll be going off before long, won't you, Miss Mair? Back to your nice little cottage. Father Gregory says they'll have it all snug and ready for you before the weather breaks. They're doing the roof now.' She smiled. 'You'll be pleased to get back into your own home, I reckon.'

'I don't know.'

'Of course, we'll be sorry to lose you – I'll miss you, but,' she added shyly, 'maybe I could come and see you – on my half-days? If you wanted me to?'

And how could I tell her, looking at her clear, clean face, that what I wanted above all, what I begged of that good Lord of hers, of Gregory's God, of Joy's pantheon of gods even, was that my life should be allowed to end here in this place of temporary refuge where I have been just another guest after whom Annie will simply air the room and change the sheets for someone else as usual.

'I've been walking—' The musician comes in, her face flushed and bright. 'God, it's windy out there – and the air, I'd forgotten how good it could taste . . .'

And in a flash I see Helen lying back in her chair out in the Annexe garden. She closes her eyes to the golden autumn sun

100

and runs her hands over her swollen belly like a potter raising a vase. 'God, I'm going to be so happy here, Lavinia. I'd forgotten how happy I could be . . .'

'Lavinia, can I talk to you?'

    'Not now, Gregory.'

    'But I want to apologize – I really *must* apologize. I should never have spoken to you in that way last time I was here – it was completely wrong of me.'

    'It's all right – it's forgotten.'

    'I feel so ashamed.'

    'Not now, Gregory – later – come back tomorrow. I'm reading now . . .'

COMPOST

I am waiting for the ambulance to come. I am sitting on the stairs in the hall. At my feet are little balls of dust which slur the diamond pattern of the linoleum. There are dried splashes where he has spilt his tea carrying it up. The stairs are dirty, the house is dirty. In the kitchen the plates and cups and bowls lined up neatly by the sink are all unwashed. I think he has mainly been eating cereal, there are dregs still caked in the bowls. Along the window-sill by the faded gingham curtains is a long line of sour milk bottles soldier-straight, waiting to be rinsed and put outside. In the sink itself is a heap of vegetables – early thin-skinned potatoes, new carrots, peas – but they are all soft and rubbery now, the earth hardened on to them like barnacles. The carrot leaves have yellowed and a swarm of tiny flies hovers over them.

I think he is asleep – I hope he is asleep. I will wait for the ambulance, sitting here on the stairs, and as soon as I hear them I will jump up and open the door so that they can come in and take him away, clean him up, make him look more like himself.

When I first saw him lying upstairs in his bed in the middle of a hot sunny day, I didn't recognize him. For a moment I actually thought he must be someone else, that somehow I had come back from university for the holidays to the wrong house. His face was smeared with bristles so that it was like glimpsing his features through a mist. I have *never* seen him unshaven. He breathed unevenly, the breath rasping in his chest, his lips very dry, cracked, his face collapsed inwards. He opened his eyes and for a moment while he focused I don't think he recognized me either.

It is very quiet in the hall. Distantly I can hear a train run. I remember how, when I was a child, I used to look through the fence and wave at the carriages, imagining the travellers setting off on their voyages like Odysseus.

And then suddenly I hear him. 'Helen? Helen?' His voice hoarse. And I think: I shouldn't have stayed here, if I'd been in the garden or outside the front door I wouldn't have heard him.

'Helen? Helen – is that you?'

As a child I was not allowed in Father's bedroom, the door was always kept shut. But in the early days, when Mrs Baines came in to do the cleaning, I would peep in at the two beds – one flat with a pink bedspread laid over it, the other neatly made, a rough blue blanket tucked tightly over the sheets. 'Run along, Helen,' he'd say if he caught me lingering outside. 'Have you finished your homework?'

And I have never seen him other than fully dressed. His shirt was never open-necked, his sleeves never rolled up. In the winter, when he came in from the garden, he shifted his feet quickly from his boots to his slippers, glancing at me warily. In the summer he wore socks even with his sandals. 'He's a proper gentleman, the Professor,' Mrs Baines would say admiringly as she leaned over her fence, watching him. 'Keeps his collar and tie on even when he's working his plot . . .'

So now to step into his room is a terrible breach and I stand in the doorway uncertainly. There are clothes scattered all over the floor, not just shirts and ties but underclothes I do not want to look at strewn blatantly on top of spread-eagled trousers. The room smells of a smell I do not want to identify, acrid, sour, the windows tight shut, the curtains drawn. On the table by his bed are open books and half-drunk cups of tea without saucers, and on a little plate is a curled cheese sandwich with one bite taken out and a fly crawling curiously over it.

'Helen?' He is struggling to raise himself from the grey pillows. 'Helen?'

I have to go to him. Have to put my arms around his thin body, feel his skin, be close to the stale smell of him. 'Lie back, Father—' I push him against the pillows. 'Lie back, it's all right, the ambulance will be here soon.'

'No ambulance—'

'You're ill, Father.'

'No ambulance – no hospital—' His voice is petulant.

'It's all right – it'll be all right.' I try to edge towards the door as his eyes close again.

'Don't go – don't leave me—' There is a catch in his voice like a squeaking gate.

'All right – all right.'

I hover in the room, looking around and trying not to. On the big dressing table by the window is a collection of silver-backed hair brushes. Later, when I go through everything, I will find her initials, JM, engraved on the tarnished silver. There are two cupboards, one of which gapes open so that I can see his suits and ties all hanging up, completely separate from the crumpled, shrunken figure on the bed. I have never seen his clothes as separate before, they have always been part of his body, his skin.

'Helen?' He calls again.

'I'm here – I'm still here, Father.'

He doesn't look at me but he nods. Then his hand lifts very slowly and points to the pile of books. 'Read to me,' he says.

'Read to you?'

'Homer—' And he quotes the first lines of the first book of *The Iliad*, his voice rough as sandpaper sawing over the words. 'Remember?' He squints at me, his forest-green eyes suddenly sharp. 'Now you. Recite.'

'I can't.'

A wisp of a sigh. 'Read it, then.' He takes a breath and adds almost as an aside, 'You always read so well, Helen. With so much feeling – just like your mother.'

I am stunned – and suddenly angry. All those years, all that struggling for so little reward, so little praise. His disappointment when I scraped through the exams, his disapproval when I told him I would study English at university, that anyway I wouldn't dream of going to *his* university here, that I wanted to get away, live my own life. 'Not everyone has to do Greek,' I said. 'And what use is it anyway – it's a dead language.' It was the worst insult I could throw at him but he just blinked. 'Whatever you say, Helen. You're old enough to make up your own mind now . . .' Washing his hands of me.

And now? It has come too late, I think, as I look down at the thin stranger in the bed. Oh, why couldn't you have said that to me years ago?

But I pick up the book and read to him anyway. Read of the feud between two Greek fighters whose bones have long ago crumbled to dust, if indeed they ever lived at all. And while I read I hear him mumbling the Greek with me, his lips slip-slapping over the sounds like a child shuffling in his father's slippers. And something makes me read quicker and quicker until he cannot catch up and then he stops mumbling and lies completely still.

When the ambulance arrives the medics are briskly cheerful. Have I packed a few things? Oh, no – I hadn't thought. Well, never mind, bring them when I come in, eh? Must be a bit of a shock finding him like this. Wasn't there any neighbour to keep an eye on him? No – on holiday. Mrs Baines for her fortnight at Clacton, I can see her floating on the water like a vast red balloon.

They put him in his dressing gown and wrap him in blankets, then strap him into a chair before gently carrying him down the stairs. He is mute, uncomplaining, keeps his eyes shut though he responds to what they ask him – move this way, lift his arms. His pyjama top falls open and I glimpse his dry grey skin, crinkled like a chicken neck. I look away. In his dressing-gown pocket is his pipe. It is the only thing he takes with him. Later I will be summoned to the hospital to pick it up.

It is not deliberate in the sense of being planned, it evolves naturally, gradually. There is a sense of rightness about it – a fitting equation.

It begins with the weeds daring to straggle over the neat paths. They play grandmother's footsteps, creeping across to the rich, soft soil of the vegetable beds when they think no one is looking. Then, more boldly, dandelions push aside the brassicas, they elbow away the swelling beetroots and turnips and burst into the light. And bindweed winds itself like a tight scarf around the necks of the onions, choking the life out of them. In the early morning when I go out, I find the silver trails of slugs meandering over the spinach, there are gaps in the rows of French beans, little stumps of plants with their leaves amputated. The brassicas he had not yet planted out are becoming cramped and leggy in the seedbed as they jostle for room. There are clusters of broad beans ripe and swollen, waiting to be picked. Sideshoots spring from the tomato plants, some of which are tied too tightly to their stakes – he must have staked them just before he fell ill, because I can see that already they need tying in again.

Mrs Baines has been trying to catch me for several days, and now as I turn away from the plot I see her back door open and she waddles down the path in her slippers, her hair still in its curlers, an old coat thrown hastily over her dressing gown.

'Ah – Helen, pet. I've been wanting a little word—'

'I'm rather busy at the moment, Mrs Baines,' I say, adding deliberately, 'There's a lot I have to see to for the funeral.'

'Of course, pet.' She pretends to wipe a tear from her eye. 'It's so sad – your poor, dear father. And all so sudden too—' She looks at me confidingly. 'I tell you, pet, it's kept me up night after night wishing – oh, if only I hadn't been away – if only I'd *known* the Professor was poorly. I blame myself, really I do. If I'd've been here, he would never have—'

She hesitates to say the word, so I say it for her: 'Died?' Now she is obviously wanting me to reassure her, tell her how grateful I am for the care she has given in the past, that of course it isn't her fault, etc., etc. But a budding revolt makes me say instead, 'Well, he certainly picked his moment.'

She tightens her lips disapprovingly. 'I don't know what you mean by that, Helen.'

No, I think, you wouldn't. 'I've got to get on with things now, Mrs Baines,' I say, and start to turn away.

'Oh, but Helen—' She smiles so that I can see her teeth. 'Helen, I'd like to help you.'

'It's all right, thank you, I can manage on my own.'

'Well, of course, pet, I'm sure – and I'm sure you're very busy, much too busy to—' She breaks off. 'Well, that's where I'd like to help.' She shifts her bulk, folds her arms under her bosom. 'I've had a little word with Derek – you know, my eldest – and you've only to say when and he'll be over.' She shakes her head. 'We all want to do our bit for the Professor – he was such a good man, so polite, a real gentleman, that's how I'll always remember him. Oh, but I'll miss him—' She dabs her eyes again. 'But we must be sure to give him a good send-off, don't you think? We must have everything just the way the Professor would like – yes, Helen?' Her eyes gleam, but I don't say anything, just wait. She edges closer to her fence and begins again, her voice lower, conspiratorial. 'So, I thought tomorrow evening – if that'll suit you? As I say, I've already spoken to my Derek and he'll take the night off from his darts team specially. You've no call to worry – I'll give him his tea here when he finishes work, all you have to do, Helen, is to let him in and he'll just get on with it. He's a good worker, clean – you won't even notice he's there. He won't make any mess or get in your way, and you'll be able to get on with all your arrangements for the funeral and the do afterwards—'

'I'm not having any "do",' I manage to break in.

'You're not?' She is taken aback. 'Are you sure about that, pet? Because I could always arrange something for you here. I could get my Dawn to help with the baking – oh, we could rustle up a spread between us, one that'd do the Professor proud—'

'I don't want anything,' I say again. 'Just the funeral – that's all.'

'Very good, then, Helen,' she says. I notice the 'pet' has gone.

'Well—' I turn away.

'But the garden,' she cries out suddenly. 'The Professor's lovely plot? You can't mean to – you're not just going to – you don't want people to see it all like this?'

And now I understand what she's been working up to. 'Mrs Baines—' I start to say, but she sweeps me aside.

'It won't take my Derek more than an evening – or even a couple, if we catch it quick now before it gets too bad. You just tell me when – the day after tomorrow? Or after the funeral, maybe that'd be better?' She is speaking quickly, as if she can herd me into agreement. 'You've only to say the word, Helen.'

'Mrs Baines, I don't want any help,' I say firmly.

She licks her mustachioed lips. 'Then – you'll be doing it yourself, will you, Helen?' she asks slowly.

'Maybe.'

'You don't want to let the plot go to ruin, do you?' Her voice is heavy with reproach. 'Not after all the work your poor father put into it.'

I shrug. 'It's not going to make any difference anyway. The university will be taking the house back.'

'All the more reason to keep it nice,' she puts in. 'You'll want to leave your father proud, won't you?' She peers over my shoulder. 'And you've a lovely crop of beans ready for the picking there, Helen. You're not going to let *them* go to waste, are you?'

I've had enough. I turn away and start walking before she can stop me. 'I've got to go now, Mrs Baines,' I say over my shoulder.

'You think about it, Helen,' she calls out after me. 'We'd soon have it all spick and span for you. Think of the Professor – think what *he'd* say—'

I slam the back door.

There are clusters of blackfly on the tips of the broad beans. If I look closely, I can see whole colonies of them feasting on the tender shoots, milking the plants' sap. He used to say, 'Get the spray from the shed, Helen, quick now. I've got to catch them early . . .' I'd watch from the fence as he sprayed every leaf and stem and flower with absolute thoroughness.

Now I stand in the middle of the plot and study the blackfly. Some of them are strung all down the stems like seams of coal. If I ran my hands along I could squash them, but I don't, I just watch as, silently, they maul the nascent beans. The plants are very tall, the beans hanging like thick fingers, nails dirty with blackfly. Some of them, I notice, are still flowering – obviously he hadn't finished taking the tops off. I suppose they will continue to grow upwards until the frost comes to kill them off. I wonder how high they'll get – Jack and the beanstalk? One row has deep purple flowers – a new variety he must have been trying out. White or purple, it doesn't seem to make any difference to the blackfly, though. They enjoy them just the same.

The service is surprisingly well attended. Colleagues from the university, students he has coached, dons and lecturers. As stipulated in his will, it is led by the university chaplain, with whom, it appears, Father has played chess one afternoon a week for several years. I hadn't known that. Neither had I known of the new edition of *The Oresteia* he had been working on that a trio of old bearded professors tell me about. They shuffle towards me in their dark shabby suits and speak one after another like the chorus in Greek theatre: '. . . such an eminent academic . . . will be sadly missed . . . his eye for detail . . . and his meticulous

study – *Doric, Ionic and Aeolic Dialects in Homer . . .'* They recite
the title of his book all together in one voice. Then sigh, take a
breath and begin again, passing the conversation between them
like a rugby ball down the line: '. . . a masterpiece . . . definitive
. . . must be preserved . . . must be preserved . . .'

It is a while before I realize that they are asking for his
papers. 'Take them,' I say. 'I don't want them. Come to the
house and take what you want – otherwise I shall only throw
them away.'

Mrs Baines, decked out in black like a funeral barge, nods to
me from a distance. We don't exchange words. She has brought
all her family – 'to make a good show' – and they stand stiffly
in their dark suits and dresses – 'a credit to her'. No doubt she
disapproves very strongly of my red and white summer dress –
'and she wasn't even wearing stockings . . .' She has sent a large
wreath of laurels and carnations which no doubt she thought
looked distinguished.

When the service is over, I have to stand in the crematorium
gardens while people approach to shake my hand. They come up
one by one and look shy and uncomfortable and embarrassed,
as if I were the Queen. I realize suddenly that they are all men.
Old, middle-aged, dry, stooping men. Men with lank hair, men
with no hair, men with false teeth that click over their gums as
they speak, tall men, short men, men whose hands clasp mine
tightly, men whose hands waver, men whose touch is soft and
clammy.

I wish I was wearing gloves.

And all the time the tomatoes are ripening and falling, swollen, from their heavy trusses. The summer warmth draws
all the plants upwards to reach for the sun. There are great
bursts of dandelions among the potatoes, buttercups creep
through the unthinned parsnips, chickweed squeezes between
the radishes. The lettuces have shot great rockets up to the
sky, the early peas rattle unpicked in their pods, their foliage
drooping, discouraged. The runner beans are still flowering,
pretty scarlet splashes that wind over the ground, searching
for something to climb up – they have snaked through the
legume bed and are reaching for the brassicas. I notice that
some of the flowers have set and slugs are eating the small

bright beans as they develop. Does it hurt, I wonder? Is it like being eaten alive?

I go down to the supermarket and buy my vegetables ready-sliced and frozen. The carrots and potatoes are cut into little cubes and the peas are shelled. I put my leftovers into the dustbin for the rubbish men to take away – I have thrown out the compost bucket that used to live beside the back door.

It is good growing weather, hot in the day, a little light rain in the evening. There is an abundance of snails which can hardly keep up with the profusion in the plot. If I stand at the top of the plot I can still just about distinguish the rows and the four separate beds, though the grass has blurred the edges of the paths and the vegetables themselves trail away into a thicket of green.

In the seedbed the brassicas are really fighting for space now. The potatoes are flowering – a sign that it is almost time to lift them. Unsupported, the maincrop peas are falling over like drunks – some have crawled over to the early peas to lean on their sticks. It is amazing how fierce, how desperate, this fight for survival can be. I stand by the back door watching it.

I can throw my coat over the banisters now when I come in. I can sleep with my door open. I can leave lights burning all night. I can put my plate and bowl into the 'wrong' cupboard.

He liked order, particularly in the kitchen. 'Everything has its place, Helen,' he'd say, putting the crockery back after a meal. As if the cup and the plate and the bowl were all parts of a Greek verb to be fitted together and then unscrewed. He even cooked like that, with a recipe book that had steps – one, two, three – logical, methodical, a system for every-thing.

The university is being self-consciously generous. I can remain in the house until they find a new professor for the Chair. But I will have to sort out his things, bag them up and get rid of them. The professors have been. They stood very awkwardly in the hall, too embarrassed to venture into the sitting room and help themselves to his papers, which I handed out through the door: '. . . so generous . . . so kind . . . such a contribution . . .' One of them stepped forward boldly. 'But your own studies, Miss Grey? Your father had hoped – he always thought you were so *able.'* I laughed. Oh, yes, I could just imagine him telling them that I was 'able'.

His room is tidy now, the bed covered up, the cups and plates cleared away. There is a thick layer of dust on the glass surface of the dressing table – so thick I can write my name on it. I go to the chest of drawers. Inside are his shirts, his socks, his underclothes – these I put in the black bin bags distastefully. Some of the shirts have a shower of holes down the front from where occasionally his pipe would explode like a volcano. Some of the socks are worn through, but they are still rolled up in a ball and put away in the drawer. Everything neat, everything in its place.

I open the doors of the first cupboard. There are the suits he wore – thick brown tweed for winter, thinner brown flannel for summer, the cloth shiny with age. His shoes are lined up, his dull ties hang from the rack.

But there are a few surprises.

At the back of the cupboard I find the bright orange scarf I gave him one Christmas. 'Very nice, Helen . . .' It is still in its wrapping paper, the folds ironed flat and new while his old beige scarf hangs threadbare from its peg in the hall.

And in the second cupboard I find Joy's clothes. All of them. Her dresses and skirts and shirts. I even recognize one or two. There is a red cotton dress with a tight waist and full skirt and two big daisy pockets embroidered on the front. I put my hand in and pull out a handkerchief with her initials embroidered on the corner.

At the back of the cupboard I find all their letters.

I recognize his handwriting immediately but hers, Joy's, I have never seen before. It lopes boldly over the thin wartime paper, defying the shortage and describing the rationing, the Blitz, how she was 'doing her bit' driving a bus and dodging the bombs. She says how her parents had wanted her to come back and stay in their safe country house with them and her little sister, who, she says, has also written to her, saying that when she grows up she wants to be an actress. 'Poor Mummy and Daddy,' she wrote, 'I suppose they can only hope that at least Lavinia's young enough to grow out of it . . .' She wrote that if her parents knew she was still in touch with him '. . . they'd have an absolute fit. Can you believe it? We're in the middle of a war, there are bombs falling everywhere, people are *dying* – and all they care about is a moribund class system. Never mind your joining up and being an officer now with the hush-hush people. As Lavinia might say, "God, what fools these mortals be . . ."'

He wrote back more cautiously. Maybe they shouldn't correspond. He really didn't want her to go against her parents' wishes. And was she really sure she didn't want to continue with her degree course? After all, she had only another year of it to go.

She replied that she was perfectly happy driving her bus. She told him not to be silly about her parents: '. . . they don't know the first thing about you, Harry, and it's none of their business whom I write to . . .' She told him she looked forward to his letters: '. . . almost more than eating my whole week's butter ration in one go on hot toast. You can't deny me this. Sometimes it's really bloody here – cold and dark and everyone's tired and short-tempered. We've all had about as much as we can take . . .'

I read them all, sitting on the floor of his room, leaning against the bed. Read every page of every letter, the envelopes spilling out all around me. And as I read I feel them standing on either side of me, their gaze running over my head as if I have simply been a stone cast between their lives which they flowed over.

In the early letters they swapped epigrams in Greek but the censor soon stopped that. He still urged her to continue her studies: '. . . but your degree is so important, Joy. You are such an exceptional scholar. I have never coached anyone with so fine a grasp of the subtleties of the Greek language . . .' She wrote back that she couldn't very well lock herself away in ivory towers studying the Peloponnesian War when she had the real thing going on all around her. He quoted from *The Iliad*, she from *The Odyssey*. She spoke of the gods and their quarrels, he of the heroes and their trials. In this early stage their letters sparkled and danced like water running downhill, both showing off to each other.

But as the war continued and he was posted further away, they seemed to become more intimate. 'My dearest Harry' – 'My darling Joy'. And I wonder, had they become lovers then? Maybe when the bombs obliterated his parents' little terraced house in north London, maybe then, when he was granted leave to come back and bury them both and sort out what was left of their possessions. Because the tone of their letters changed after that, becoming tinged with loss, as if each of them had only just woken up to what might happen to the other. Even Joy sounded afraid: '. . . and I don't want to lose you, Harry. So many people have lost their loved ones. Please, *please*, be careful. Your work cannot be as safe as you say – *wherever* you are. Please, promise me you won't do anything gallant. Let others be the brave ones and fight this bloody war . . .'

I read them all. I read them right to the end, when he tells her he will be demobbed, that he has resigned his commission and will look for a post or a lectureship that will enable him to continue with his research: '. . . and I've thought that what I'd really like to work on is a study of Homeric dialects. A huge project, I know, and I would welcome your support. But how about your own research into the Eleusinian Mysteries? I do hope you will consider taking that up again . . .'

Oh, yes – my father, my mother. She standing by the barrier at the station to welcome him. Did they run into each other's arms? Did they embrace? Was there a shining light about them that shut out all the noise and confusion of the platform?

At the bottom of the box I find their marriage certificate: 'Harold George Grey to Joy Eleanor Mair. September 1945.' It is from a register office. No doubt if they could have had an ancient Greek ceremony with Hera and Hestia and the other goddesses of the hearth attending them, they would have done so. But they settle for a register office.

There is only one more letter and I don't know why it's been kept. Sentiment maybe? 'Dear Joy, I've tried talking to Mummy and Daddy but they just won't listen and they say that if I bring the subject up any more they'll stop my elocution lessons with Miss Thorley and I couldn't bear that. Because they see the post first in the mornings and they know your writing, I really don't think it's safe for you to write to me here, but I'll set up some system with a friend at school. And when I leave here in a year or two and go to drama school, I'm sure we'll be able to meet properly then. In the meantime, please don't forget – your loving sister, Lavinia.'

I sit back on my heels and look at the mess of paper around

me. Then I gather it all into my arms, every sheet and envelope, and take them downstairs. In the sitting room I move the electric fire away from the hearth and open the flue. Then, using the matches that are still on the side-table by his chair, I start a little fire in the empty grate and toss the letters in one by one, as if I am feeding fish to a captive seal.

At first when I see his handwriting illumine and flare, I instinctively reach out to save it, because the destruction of his words, his thoughts, has always been sacrilegious. But then I sit back on my heels again and watch the flames gobble him up. The fire burns quick and bright.

When it is over there is a thick layer of sullen ash in the grate which flutters in the draught. I look at it for a long time. I expected to feel relieved, satisfied even, but instead there is a sour taste in my mouth and I can feel him looking over my shoulder, shaking his head.

I have no parents now, I tell myself. I am free. I can do what I like and never again will I have to fail his expectations. But maybe I am giddy from breathing in smoke from the fire, for, though I do not hear his voice, I can see him standing there quite clearly, turning away from me with that little sigh which never really cloaked his disappointment.

It is getting colder. The days are shortening. The potato haulms are dying down and beneath them, I know, will be a treasure trove of potatoes. Those carrots that have forced their way through the matted undergrowth are broad-shouldered, burly, clustered together because they haven't been thinned. The parsnips touch edge to edge, they wave their leaves to try and catch my attention. Beneath the surface the wire-worms and small slugs will be devouring all this unexpected food, making little holes in the roots and tubers like Emmenthal cheese.

Most of the legumes have withered now and the first frosts will soon finish off the rest. The stems cling to their supports like ragged sailors to rigging. In the seedbed the stunted brassicas are hearting up, making miniature cabbages and cauliflowers, there is even a stalk studded with tiny Brussels sprouts. The leeks are bunched together, wavering reeds in the wind. The aphids have all but disappeared, killed off by the cold, their

115

work is left to the beetles, the slugs, even the birds, who are foraging now for winter food. They will find food enough here, I think. There is a row of swedes that he had sown just before he fell ill. Determined, the seedlings bristled up, conquering even the chickweed that tried to smother them. Now the roots are fat, purple-topped. I imagine the birds feasting on them in the winter.

Leaves swirl down, blending the beds even more into the surrounding paths. He used to gather them up and keep them in a large pen by the compost heap to make leafmould. Now they form a sodden mat on the beds, bitter as old tobacco.

The tomatoes have shrivelled from cold. Soon the frosts will blacken what is left of their leaves and they will droop from their stakes like executed prisoners.

I watch all this. I watch. And tell him when he questions me without words, as he has started to do: It is a process, the inverse of your building verbs and neatening cupboards and cooking by numbers and cleaning the house room by room all in order. This is *my* process, I say. But he doesn't answer.

In the drizzle of the autumn rain he stands by the compost heap, looking at his vegetable plot. He is wearing his green serge gardening jacket that I took down from the back door only yesterday to add to the piles of bags in the hall. The rain forms a mist around him, I see beads of it settling on his shoulders, his sleeves. The smoke from his pipe plumes gently over his head. He doesn't move, just stands there, looking.

I say to him: You've got what you wanted, haven't you? You're back with your wife. You did it on purpose, didn't you? You got away as soon as your 'duty' to me was done . . .

He doesn't answer, just looks through me at the ruin of his plot, at the leaves and the stems and the sodden rotting vegetation.

You can't stop me now, I say to him. I can do what I like now. And I move towards him, but he melts away, becomes part of the rain, the mist, the cold autumn wind.

I can see him from the kitchen window, I can see him from the upstairs rooms. When it is raining and dim, when it is dusk and the light is uncertain, I see him standing by the compost heap, slowly blinking his forest-green eyes, his hand curved round his pipe, whose embers glare at me furiously.

116

Maybe he sees a different plot. Maybe he sees his own plot with the straight lines and the clean beds and the crops all growing in precise rotation. Maybe he doesn't see me at all, maybe he ignores me because I am not there, as I have never been there, as I have always been some cipher, a leftover, an irritating little irregular verb that cannot easily be tucked into a sentence but makes its own rules, demands its own construction.

But I am afraid that he knows very well what I've done. I'm afraid that when I leave this house, even when I go to some other place, he will come with me. Always there at the end of a garden, at the back of a queue, in a bus, a shop, a library, café or lecture hall, watching me.

It rains all day now, rain drumming on the windows. I have drawn the faded kitchen curtains so that I should not see him.

The rain becomes heavier, louder, it knocks at the windows, at the doors. There is a swirl of wind and more loud knocking and then I hear someone calling my name.

I open the front door and Lavinia stands there, holding her scarf over her head. 'Helen, darling – I came as soon as I could. I'm so sorry . . .'

And I look at her and think, Lavinia, yes, Lavinia, maybe she will drive him away.

∞

I tell myself that I am too old to change now. Too old to alter my opinions, my judgements about people and life – and Helen. I say I am terse and crabby and that I think I have won the right to behave irritably, to expect everyone to accommodate me.

But I find that this is becoming more and more like a part I am acting. A part I slip into easily enough but one that isn't fitting as close as it used to.

I am shedding a skin. Each day and with every section of Helen's papers I can feel it loosening, becoming hard, a casing I will slither out of. And now I feel Helen watching me, not critically, as she felt her father watching her, but simply as one would observe any interesting process – as she observed the dereliction of his vegetable plot, as I observe my ageing – with clarity, as a witness, a recorder of events.

Still I am wary, though. This new skin is tender and raw and I dare not expose it. The slightest breath of wind would injure it.

'Do you talk to your God, Gregory?'

'I try to – in prayer.'

'And are your prayers answered?'

He smiled. 'You should know better than to ask that, Lavinia. Who among us can say that their prayers are answered?'

'So you don't have a hot-line to God, then?'

He laughed. 'I wish I did.'

'Then what's the good of it – if even *your* prayers aren't answered?'

'God's ways are mysterious, Lavinia. It's not for me to try and impose my will on him.'

'That's a textbook answer if ever I heard one,' I said sharply. 'Pour me some coffee—' I pushed my cup towards him and began again. 'You don't strike me as the kind of man who'd do something for nothing – you're not that stupid.'

'You can't make bargains with God. It just doesn't work like that.'

'Doesn't it?' I looked at him. 'Then why are you making this bargain? Why dress yourself up in skirts and forswear family life? What's in it for you, Gregory?'

'It is,' he answered slowly, 'a form of service.'

'Really?' I raised my eyebrow. 'But I thought your God was all for procreation. Isn't that what he's so busy promoting – "Go forth and multiply"?'

'It may be . . . that for some of us . . . it is better that we don't have a family life,' he said haltingly. 'We would make . . . bad husbands, ruthless fathers.'

'So you offer up the whole flawed package to your God?' I snorted. 'He must be patient indeed to put up with such substandard goods.'

'Lavinia—' He looked at me. 'Why the inquisition?'

I waved the question aside and took a sip of coffee. 'So, for your reward you get to sit – after a lifetime's denial – at God's right hand, is that it?'

'I don't count on it.'

'You don't?' I curved my voice. 'But surely *you* don't have doubts? Surely *you* never think that all your efforts may be wasted – that your religion is a pipe-dream – a story?'

He looked down. 'I'm only human, Lavinia.'

'And?'

'And what?'

'And what do you do then?' I asked fiercely. 'When you're in despair – when your God leaves you? When you're on your cross?' I held his eye. 'What do you do then, Gregory?'

'I pray,' he answered.

'Even though you can't?'

'Even then.'

'Even though you don't believe in what you're praying to?'

'Even when all the demons are riding my back – I stay on my knees. It's all I *can* do.'

'I see.' I softened my voice. 'I suppose this should be acknowledged as an admirable strength?'

'Or a form of pig-headedness,' he said with a smile.

'But it gives you comfort?'

He shrugged. 'Not always – not so I can count on it.' He gave a sigh. 'Though the more I think about it, the less I see anything in life as being certain.'

'That's the sort of geriatric wisdom *I* should be credited with, not you.'

'Maybe I'm learning from you?'

'I wouldn't bother.'

We sat in silence for a while. Outside the rain was driving across the lake in bands like sleek grey otters. On the fells I could glimpse the white forms of sheep sheltering beneath the bright orange bracken.

'Teddy used to tell jokes to sheep,' I said suddenly. 'He said it was a good way to learn about the indifference of life. He'd stand in the middle of a field and when they'd all calmed down and stopped running away, he'd tell them jokes. And he'd always pause, too, before the punchline and they'd just look at him—' I broke off. 'It is one of those things I remember.'

'Yes,' he said reverently.

'Don't, Gregory.'

'Don't what?'

'You know—' I looked at him sharply. 'Those spun-sugar angels of yours – just don't.'

There was a pause.

'So,' I began again, 'I hear you've been talking to the musician.'

'How did you know that?' He was surprised.

'Annie saw you out on the fells. I hope you didn't plague her—'

'Lavinia!'

'—or intrude on her privacy.'

'We spoke about music,' he said defensively.

'Music? A subject you know so much about—'

He flushed slightly. 'I offered her the use of the piano.'

'Which piano?'

'At Belle House.'

'I don't remember a piano there,' I said, perplexed. 'Teddy and I certainly didn't possess one.'

'It was bought for Father Paul,' he explained. 'He's teaching a few of the novices. We find it helps to have music as part of our retreat meditations.'

'Where is it – which room?'

'The back room downstairs – the one with the tiled fireplace.'

My sitting room. And what of the rest of the house, I wondered? Is it all completely changed? Have you stripped the cushions from the window-seats in the morning room? Are there refectory tables lined up in the dining room? And have you removed the high double beds with their bolsters and their brass fittings to replace them with hard bunks and rough grey institutional blankets?

'. . . of course, I told her that none of us would bother her,' he was saying. 'But that if she needed an instrument to practise on, then she was welcome to use ours – we keep it in good order.'

'And what did she say?'

'She said she'd think about it.'

'She didn't mind?'

He gave a little shrug. 'She was a bit skittish at first – when I told her I knew who she was—'

'I'll bet.'

'—but she didn't seem offended. Lavinia, you don't have to be quite so protective of her,' he rallied. 'She struck me as being perfectly capable of looking after herself.'

I was stung, looked quickly out of the window. 'Well, that's all very good then, isn't it?'

He didn't answer but after a moment began carefully, 'I – I wanted to ask you, Lavinia—'

'Yes?' I kept my face turned away.

He took a breath. 'The Dower House. It'll be ready soon – we've almost finished the roof.'

I stared stonily out of the window.

'It really looks quite different,' he went on. 'Larger – brighter with the new windows. And when it's all redecorated – would you like to see the colours we've chosen? I think you'll like them – but of course if you don't—' He was fumbling in his pockets. 'I've got the swatches here.'

I raised my hand. 'Gregory – I'd rather not.'

He looked at me steadily for a few moments, then said quietly, 'It's not the same, Lavinia. Trust me, there's nothing to be afraid of.'

'Who said I was afraid?' I snapped.

'Well, going back to places can be—'

'It's not about fear.'

He seemed about to reply, but then stood up. 'I have to go,' he said. 'I won't be able to see you again till next week – we're rather busy at the moment with the new retreats we're holding.'

'Whenever—' I waved my hand carelessly. 'Any time, it doesn't matter.'

He went to the door, but then, turning back, said suddenly, 'I do pray for you, Lavinia.'

'Really?' I made my voice inflect. 'Not for my conversion, I hope. That *would* be a waste.'

'For your well-being,' he said gently. 'Your peace of mind.'

I didn't reply.

But it is not that I am afraid – or at least, I don't think so. Although Teddy once said that there were really only two forces at work in the world: love and fear. Everything came down to one or the other. So maybe I am afraid. Of the Dower House? Even though I am assured that it is changed and new and painted in God knows what foul, tepid colours. No. Of the land then – the fields and hedges and trees? The land where they lie expecting me.

I have escaped – like the musician has escaped. We are both escaped prisoners met out on the fells. Why should I go back? Why should she? Because, Teddy would say, it is easier to sing with the music than to keep trying to push the tune out of your mind.

I reach down for the carpetbag . . .

LEGUMES

He never moves in his sleep. As if he arranges himself like a model – head turned slightly away, one arm flung up on the pillow – and then holds that position all through the night.

I sleep in a tangle of bedclothes and pillows and sweat, pushing the sheet away, then pulling it back to cover myself. I look at him lying there so beautiful, so far away. I let my fingers hover above his nostrils so that his breath will gild my nails.

In the morning he will wake very early and, stealthily, careful not to wake me, he will slip out of bed and stand by the open balcony doors looking at the dawn. I will lie completely still, keeping my breathing even, my eyes half shut so that I can just peep through the lashes. I have not slept. I have waited for this moment, this glimpse of his privacy. Later I will sleep, wasting the hours while I wait for him to return from rehearsals.

Quite naked, his golden body outlined by the sun – the god Apollo smiling on him – he will stretch like a cat in the cool pink early morning. Then he will come back into the room and quietly open the cupboard doors to position the mirrors so that standing between them he can see his whole body, back and front, bending and stretching as he performs his exercises.

From the bed I watch him. I hardly dare breathe. I don't stir. I am never completely sure that he doesn't know I'm watching, that, as always, having an audience doesn't inspire him to even greater effort. But oh, he is beautiful. His muscles so lithe, so taut, his sinews slipping and pulling, their tight outlines clear as if drawn in pencil. He flexes and bends, his toes spread out, gripping the polished stone floor. I would like to be the ground under his feet to absorb his sweat. I would like to be one – just one – of his toes, curling when he commands me, part of his body.

I watch. I watch.

When he has finished he has a sheen of sweat like fine down over his body. In the quiet of the room I can hear him panting slightly. He closes the cupboard doors, goes into the bathroom and I hear him practising his vocal exercises as he showers, running his carefully cultivated voice up and down the scales, in and out of breathing patterns. On a good morning he will recite a few lines, maybe even a whole speech, first one way, then another, now slow, now fast, with the inflection here or there, darning himself around the words tirelessly like an expert needlewoman.

His emerging from the bathroom is my cue to wake up. I move and make small sounds – I think I do the whole thing rather well – and when I finally open my eyes he is sitting on the bed, holding a towel round his waist with one hand while with the other he flicks drops of water over me from his wet blond hair. I must pretend to be irritated, must pretend I do not find it funny, pretend that my heart does not leap when I see him – Jack, bending over me, Jack, wanting me.

And then he says something silly and crass, something so trite that I really shouldn't be taken in by it, but even though part of me recognizes that, the other part of me, the greater part, is looking up at his blue, blue eyes, eyes that have all this Aegean Sea in them – this sea that surrounds our island and is not wine dark but clear and blue and sparkling – and this part of me, this *all* of me, is thinking: Oh God, gods, let him be mine, let Jack be mine – I know it won't last but let him be mine . . .

It is hot – even now in early summer. Hotter than anything I have ever known. I feel the heat slithering over my back and slipping slick fingers inside my shirt. I have already taken off my tights and my jacket and have rolled up my sleeves. Even with sunglasses, the light is bright, but I do not want to wear them anyway because they shut me off, making me into just another blank-faced tourist, when instead I want to be part of this island, part of its life, part of the local people who sit in the shade beneath the awnings sipping thick coffee and clicking beads as they watch the holidaymakers go by.

The luggage is at my feet – two separate suitcases and Lavinia's carpetbag with my writing things. I had hoped when we stood in the chaos of the arrivals bay at the airport that the carpetbag might have got lost, but it came through eventually, riding the carousel serenely like an ugly duckling. You should have taken that as hand luggage, he said irritably. I told you, Helen, it could easily have fitted into the cabin and now because of it we might miss the ferry. When he is annoyed he nips with tiny teeth like an angry kitten, but the sting isn't painful, it serves only to remind me that he is there, beside me.

The quay is very busy. I sit at this table in the shade of the taverna, grateful that we have at last arrived. Alternately I sip cold drinks and hot sweet coffee, and I watch it all. The small boats herded together in the harbour, the suntanned people leaping from deck to deck, flashing their white teeth as they call out to friends, helping the tourists into the boats with strong dark arms. They speak very quickly, twisting words and sentences together and spinning them over the water like bright discuses. I can even catch a word here and there – sea, market-place, right, left – the same words, ancient words. When Father came to Greece, was it like Chaucer walking down Oxford Street, I wonder? How much did he understand? The old lists of verbs and declensions are stirred in my mind.

Jack has gone to find a room. I have in my mind exactly the room I want. It is in one of those whitewashed houses at the top of the town overlooking the sea. There will be an outside staircase cluttered with pots of geraniums and at the very top will be our room. Not too large, plain white walls, simple furniture and a soft clean double bed. There will be a balcony with more plants and a cane chair where I will sit and watch the people as they walk up the steep narrow streets, the women all in black calling out to each other as they carry their baskets of fish and fruit and olives, and the tourists setting off with their creams and rucksacks, their pallid skins marking them off as outsiders. But I won't be an outsider. I will belong here – I will have a place. I will become known to the islanders, who will greet me as I come down for my breakfast in the morning or my lunch in the afternoon. And when Jack returns from rehearsals, we will both be hailed with smiles and waves as we walk through the little town hand in hand, he striding so fine, so beautiful by my side. By the time his play opens, we will be well known. The patron will welcome us into his taverna and set down drinks and little dishes of olives and pistachios for us to nibble while he stands back smiling, proud to have us sitting at his table. In the evenings while Jack is performing I will work on the new play I am writing for him, and now the pages will flow smoothly, piling up, my hand moving swiftly, confidently across the paper. And when it is finished – and it will be written in such a burst of inspiration that it will be finished very quickly – then Jack will read it and look at me with admiration, with respect, almost with a tinge of apprehension that he should be the lover of such a talented woman. Maybe he will even—

Quick, Helen – quick, I've got a taxi—

I open my eyes. He is grabbing the suitcases. Come on – have you paid for your drinks? He throws down a few notes. Now, come on, quick – I had a hell of a job getting a car as it is, I don't want the bloody driver hijacked by somebody else. Come on – I'll explain later when we're on our way.

The taxi is very old, very rusty. As it moves away I can see the road through holes in the floor by my feet. I turn towards him, questioning, but he just smiles that smile of his that somersaults my stomach. Trust me, he says, you'll see.

Already we have left the little town. We are driving up towards the top of the island. Over my shoulder I can still see the sea, but it is like a distant painting now, almost part of the sky, no longer liquid and moving. The driver mutters something I don't catch but Jack leans over the seat and they exchange a few words. Jack turns back to me. Close your eyes, he says. Go on – it's a surprise – close your eyes. I obey, then feel him binding his kerchief around my eyes. It is warm and damp and smells of him – sharp and musky, like smoky lemons. I am trying to protest but he takes my hand: Trust me, he says. To the ends of the earth, I think, but I don't say anything and try to look a little peeved so that he shouldn't be too certain of me.

The car turns sharply left, slowly bumps over a very uneven track for a few hundred yards and then stops. The engine is switched off and there is a deep silence which engulfs us. Don't peep, Jack says. And then he and the driver have got out and taken the luggage.

I sit in the car feeling the heat beating down through the roof. I could move a little to where Jack's side of the car is in shade, I could lift the blindfold and peep out, but I do neither. I sit listening to the wind, the rasping insects, the silence.

I'll help you, he says, opening the door suddenly and taking my arm. Here, lean on me, it's all right, I won't let you hurt yourself. I can hear the laughter at the back of his voice, he is happy, he is pleased, so why should I worry – isn't this all I've ever wanted? I feel the touch of his fingers and I tremble slightly. It's all right, he says quickly, I've got you.

He guides me over the rough ground and behind me I hear the taxi start up and drive away. I can feel the sun very hot on the back of my neck and am about to start questioning him again when he squeezes my arm. Three steps up, he says. That's right – good, good. Then we walk into sudden shade so unexpectedly cool that I shiver and he laughs. The ground is very smooth now under my feet and just as I have realized that we are indoors and if there are other people about then I must look ridiculous, he whips off the blindfold with a gleeful cry: There!

We are standing in the centre of a large hall. There are glass panels high up in the roof through which I can see the sky. The walls around us are frescoed with old paintings – or maybe not so old, I can't tell, though I take a few steps towards them. Beneath my feet is a smooth marble-flagged floor. There is a huge ornate staircase curving upwards like a giant wave.

We seem to be quite alone here.

Well? He is grinning. Well, what do you think? I knew you'd be impressed – it's stunning, isn't it? I'll tell you how it happened. And as he speaks – a typical Jack story about chancing to meet a man who, hearing that he was one of the actors come to perform in the festival, etc., etc. – he is capering, no, *prancing* around the hall on the balls of his feet like a court jester. He beams: And he's letting us have the villa for – he waves a dismissive hand – a piffling rent because he's mad keen on the theatre . . .

And suddenly I realize that this is no day trip he's brought me on. This villa, this mausoleum, this empty Cyclops cave has swallowed up my friendly intimate harbour room.

We've got the whole place to ourselves, he goes on, the gardens, everything. He sweeps his arm: Look at it, peace and quiet and no interruptions, no distractions . . . No little chats with people in the tavernas, I think. No sitting in the square watching the world go by. You'll be able to get on with my play, he says, coming towards me, his arms outstretched, his steps springing as if he walks on marshmallows. You'll have all the quiet you need to work in. Well, what do you say, Helen? Well?

And what choice do I have, really? On one side is our little room in the town with the geraniums and the balcony, but it is no longer ours, it is only mine, and if I look, I see that it is cramped and noisy and maybe it has beetles, cockroaches – oh, I don't know, some ghastly infestation. But here? Here is Jack, with his arms wide just waiting to welcome me. Here is the palace he has found where I will be locked away as his princess. Here is our private kingdom, never mind the stone the Cyclops has rolled up against the doorway, never mind the fact that if I speak aloud my voice echoes across this cave and whips back at me.

No, Jack is standing there with that smile on his face that could so easily tighten his lips into a petulant sulk. He is walking towards me, but he could just as easily be walking away. He catches my look. I knew you'd love it, he says. And I am rewarded, folded into his arms like cream into a cake, his hands sliding under my shirt, his fingers whispering over my breasts and teasing my nipples into taut aching points all alive to the touch of him.

We clamber over each other fast and furious as legumes growing in summer heat. Fingers like tendrils wind in each other's hair, lips fasten like suckers on each other's skin. Is this my sweat? His sweat? My spit? His spit? When he pushes into me I feel my back arch and I press him against the bed so that I am pushing into him, I am penetrating him, it is *his* body *I* am riding. His hair is damp, no longer golden but dark as my own. The curls in his armpits are matted and sharp as I bite – there – where the skin is tender, where the taste of him divides my mouth like pepper, like ginger, like cloves. He is holding my hair with one hand, pulling my head away. Look at me, his eyes command, look at me. And I look and look at the twist of his lips as he comes, at the curl of his mouth, at the cry that creases his eyes and scrolls his face, crumpling his beauty. Oh, I look at you, my lover, my love, I look at you. I look and I know that with every jolt of my body, every grip of my nails, every turn of my hips, you are for this moment utterly, completely and wholly in thrall to me, thinking only of me, conscious only of me. That I hold you as a man holds his dog at the end of a chain. That I could crush you in my hand as I would an empty can after I have drained the contents down to the last sweet drop.

We have climbed to the top of the island. It has been a hard, long, hot climb, irritating, with the paths petering out and rocks slithering under my feet and thorny bushes grazing my ankles. Jack leapt ahead, light as a deer, springing from rock to rock. From time to time he looked back and called out to me, but he never waited.

Now we rest under an olive tree. Far below, the sea is spread out like a blanket. Just across is another island which I can see quite clearly. If I stretched out my hand I could touch it. Like a god, I could lift that little spot right out of the sea. From up here the water between the islands looks as still as earth.

Today is our last full day together. Tomorrow Jack will start rehearsals and I will be alone. Tomorrow he will take the motorbike he has hired for himself and drive down through the town and out to the old amphitheatre where the rest of the company will be waiting. Tomorrow, he says with a rapacious smile, you'll be able to start my play, won't you, Helen?

I am lying beside him in the shade. We are close enough to touch but we are not touching. As with the islands, there is all this sea between us.

It is quiet. So quiet that I hear the silence pressing down around me like cotton wool. There is only the rasping of the cicadas, the wind which never stops, the dry rustle of the olive leaves. No voices, no cars, no hubbub of human activity. In the town there must be people chattering and the restless to and fro of customers at the tavernas. There must be boats starting up as they leave the little harbour, there must be laughter, shouts, the cries of children, the singing of radios, the mutterings of women as they toil up the hills with their buckets of water, the clicking of the old men's beads as they sit in the shade, measuring the pretty women in their bright sarongs and bikinis.

Here there is only the drying, withering silence, the wind that flings dust at the open windows, the sun that beats down out of a pitilessly clear sky.

129

I watched Jack leave on his motorbike, his hair feathered by the wind, his white shirt pressed against his chest. Can't I be that shirt? Can't I come with you? No, I stood by the door with my smile and my wave, watching till he was out of sight and listening until even the sound of the motorbike was swallowed up in the silence. Upstairs he had left his damp towel on the floor. I picked it up and wrapped myself in it, but it was cold and clammy and smelt only of the sea. But on his pillow I found two fine golden strands of hair and down in the sheets there were stiff splashes of semen. I lay trying to remember the pressure of his arms around me, his face in the moonlight as he slept.

But now I have washed and dressed, I have eaten my breakfast standing in the kitchen dipping the dry bread into the thin honey, fighting the wasps off. I have looked out at the arid garden Jack likes to boast about. I have even stripped our bed, washed the sheets and towels and hung them all out to bleach in the sun. If there were ingredients I would cook, if it wasn't so hot I would walk, if we weren't so far from the sea I would swim, or sit in one of the tavernas drinking lots of little coffees and listening to that half-familiar language all around me.

But maybe Jack is right, I think, as I go towards the State Room where I have dumped the carpetbag. Maybe I need to be cut off from distractions.

I'll make sure you can really work, he said, when he heard how I had cobbled together *All Greek to Me*, writing backstage on the props tables during acts, jotting down notes between tours, stuffing the notebooks into Lavinia's carpetbag and forgetting them for weeks, months even, until, offered more work as a stagehand, I'd pull them out again. That's not how a genius should work, he said, putting his arm around me. I won't have you be distracted, not when you're working on *my* play . . .

Sometimes – and it is rare, only for a second – I will glimpse an accent flattening those lovely vowels of his that have been cultured as a pearl is cultured. But somehow I can never quite lever the question in. Where are you from, Jack? Where were you born? He weaves a tight cloth. Once, I commented that surely his parents must be proud of him – what did they say? I can't remember how he evaded that one, I was so concentrated on my serve that I failed to volley back his quick reply. But I did glimpse a postcard one day, addressed to him in a different surname, and reluctantly he admitted that he had taken 'Arden' as a stage name. It's a theatre name, he said, and it gets me to the top of the cast list even if I'm playing a spear carrier with only one line to deliver. Jack Arden – yes, it looks good on programmes. But is he even 'Jack'? Maybe he is 'Jason', or 'Jay', or 'David', or 'Miles', or 'Patrick', or – God only knows and I don't ask. Don't look a gift horse in the mouth, as Mrs Baines would say.

We called it the State Room because it has a dining table – the only decent table in this sparsely furnished villa. The table is very long, mahogany, surrounded by chairs pushed up against the polished surface. This will be perfect for you, Helen, he said. Look at all this space – no more cramped desks for you. I bet you've never had anything like this before, eh? No, I had notebooks with torn pages that I crammed into the top of the carpetbag when I went shopping for props, I had café tables that wobbled as I snatched a piece of dialogue, I had the back of a bus ticket as I stood in the rush hour overhearing the other passengers, I had old felt-covered props tables against which I could only write in soft pencil. No, Jack, darling Jack, I have never had anything quite as luxurious as this.

The blinds are drawn tight against the windows to keep out the sun, but thin stripes of light finger the slats and creep over the table. At least it is cool, I think, as I approach the carpetbag, lying so casually where I left it in the middle of the table – at least it is dim. I could almost imagine that this is the quiet back room of some taverna in the early morning before the tourists wake up and the town comes to life . . .

The room is large, runs the length of the villa. There is a huge ornamental mirror hanging on the wall and a pair of stiff armchairs still covered in dust sheets. The table was covered in a sheet too, but Jack whipped it off as if presenting a gift: You'll be able to work here, won't you, Helen? Plenty of room . . .

Yes, I think, as I unpack the carpetbag, there is plenty of room. I can spread all my notes out so that I can see each separate sheet of paper, each snatch of conversation. I will only have to stretch out my hand and what I want will be there. And so, as I set the notes out, as I make all those piles and layers and cross-references and connections, I suddenly have a sense of excitement. Maybe I *can* do this play, maybe I *do* know what it is about, maybe it *is* a good idea after all. And I notice that I am beginning to fall in love, not just with the thought of finishing the play and handing it over to Jack, not just with that sweet delicious fantasy of him reading it and looking at me with astonishment, but also with the play itself, that I might enjoy writing it, that it might be a pleasure.

So, I look through the notes and move the pieces of paper from one pile to another, I take out my pad and make fresh notes, new connections, I think of other plots I could introduce, other characters. I even write brief descriptions of them: Yes, she will carry an umbrella, a man's umbrella all the year round – yes, he has a green striped tie – he wears shorts and a T-shirt – her hair must be one of those bouffant hairstyles because he will say – he will say—

And suddenly I stop. He will say? No, all right, then she will say – she will say? But I cannot hear what she says, I cannot hear what any of them say, and descriptions and costume notes and clever little plot lines are not enough. Sooner or later these people must open their mouths and speak.

There is a beam of light crossing the table. How long have I been in this room – a long time? Long enough. Maybe I've done all I can today. Maybe Jack will be back soon. Maybe . . .

I look at the notes. They form a little island in the dark sea of the table and already they have curled slightly in the warmth.

And now I cannot even lift the pen, cannot even put the cap on it. Maybe, if I say the right incantations, if I whisper the right words, if I pay the right price, maybe a clever little Rumpelstiltskin will write the play for me. I will come in here one day and find it all done, tied up with a red ribbon and sitting on top of the carpetbag.

I get up from the chair and leave it a little back so that Rumpelstiltskin won't have to move it out to sit down – I almost put a cushion on the seat for him. Then I close the door very carefully behind me and tiptoe away. For the rest of my time at the villa I will blur my eyes when I go past that door, as I used to with Joy's photograph. Sometimes I will think I can hear paper rustling. Lying beside Jack in the night, I will catch the faint squeak as of a felt pen moving across a page and then I will smile and curl up close to him: Your play is being written, my love . . .

*　　*　　*

So, how's my play coming on, Helen? All right, all right – he holds up his hand, I know you don't like to be hustled. But it's coming on well, is it? Go on, you've got to tell me something to keep me going, you've no idea how hard Bernard is making us work out there. All right – but I don't see why you should be so damned secretive about it. Can't I see just a little? But it is going to be another good one, isn't it? Like *All Greek*? And you'll win another award, eh? And we'll become famous – *the* theatre couple. Oh, we're going to make it, you and I, Helen, our names in lights, we'll be celebrated, fêted . . .

Beware the sin of hubris, Jack, I think, as he speaks. Hush, the gods will hear you – don't tempt them. But he who has been so favoured by the gods will not be visited by their wrath – I will. And maybe they turn their wrath on me because I thwart their plans for making their darling golden boy shine as brightly as they do.

So I place my fingers gently over his mouth to silence him and he licks my palm, his tongue rough as a cat. I guide him away from the closed door – Bluebeard's dangerous room, to which I will not allow him access.

But it won't last, I think, as I lead him up the stairs and into the shower, where I peel his shirt off and sponge him down under the cool water until he is clean and fresh and his erection presses heavy and wet against my belly. It won't last, it won't last, I think, as I go down on my knees and take him in my mouth. He leans back against the tiles, his eyes shut, giving himself up to me. I draw him in deep, feeling the soft skin roll over my lips, smearing the salt driblet at the tip across my eyes as if it were holy oil. And I suck him until he forgets, until I forget, until he is only a pair of hands holding my head and drawing it slowly, determinedly, back and forth over him.

Sometimes, sitting in a bar or a restaurant, on a train or a bus, or even walking down the street, I will say something to him and he won't hear me, won't even turn his head to reply. He will be engrossed in watching someone – a woman dawdling, a man fumbling for change, a tramp digging through dustbins. And later, when I watch him on stage, I will suddenly recognize the slope of his shoulders or the querulous inflection in his voice. There is the old man, or the young girl, the hesitant foreigner, or the black man's defiant swagger.

And as we sit at a table eating, as he gestures to the barman for more drinks, as he laughs just that little too loudly, throwing his head back and slicking his hair with his fingers, I will wonder: Who are you being now, Jack? The waiter? The fruit vendor? Who are you being now, chameleon extraordinaire, as you lay your arm so casually over my shoulders and draw the threads of my hair between your fingers? And who now, as you slip the sleeves of my shirt back, as you hold my head between your palms and solemnly, as if in a ritual, kiss my eyelids, the right, the left and then the right again? Who now, Jack?

I never dreamed that such a beautiful man would be interested in me.

I was sitting in the stalls with Bernard, watching the first full rehearsal of *All Greek*, feeling very nervous at seeing my words that had been so flat and contained on paper suddenly billow up and float across the stage. I want to collect up all those words and stuff them back in the carpetbag. It's terrifying – the play seems to have no contact with me, it is out of my hands now and I can hardly recognize it. Of course, I know it *is* my play, even the changes that Bernard hammered out have been approved by me. Night after night, the two of us sitting opposite each other at his partner's desk, his dark cloak slung over the back of his captain's chair: Let's have another look at that speech in the first act, Helen, darling. Onwards and upwards – we want to get it right, don't we, ducky . . .

But is it 'right' now? I worry as I watch. If it is, then why do I feel so afraid? Can't I stuff the parachute back into the bag?

Between scene changes Bernard turns to me: It's good, Helen, it's going to be all right. It is one of those rare moments when he is not aiming for an effect but speaking truthfully, from the heart. He goes on. And every playwright feels as you do at this point. But how does he know how I feel? He smiles, rubs his beard, leans closer to my ear and whispers in his impeccable English: You're shitting yourself, darling – it's written all over your face . . .

In the break I wait in my seat while the others go out for a breath of air and a quick drink. I close my eyes and let the stillness of the theatre quieten me. It is so different sitting on this side of the stage from being part of the team at the back. Here the actors regard me almost with suspicion, even actors I have worked for as a stagehand only nod to me now as if I have crossed over to another camp.

I will gather myself together before they run through the next act and I have to sit expressionless again, watching my words being tossed between them, embellished with unexpected gestures and pauses. Oh God, I don't know if I like this . . .

And then there is the sound of theatre seats being tipped up. Footsteps approaching. I open my eyes. He stands in the row before mine, his head slightly cocked, a sheaf of gold hair falling over one eye. He is wearing a leather jacket slung casually over his shoulder and as I recognize him I think distantly: That suits the character he's playing, maybe I will suggest such a touch to Bernard when we go over the costumes. And I am telling myself this to take my mind off the fact that he is handsome, that he is looking at me, and I have never felt comfortable with good-looking men. He is scrutinizing me with unmistakable appraisal in his eyes and I am quailing.

It's going to be a great success, he says looking down at me in my seat with his cat's smile. He holds out his hand, the fingers are lightly tanned and the fine hairs dusted gold. May I shake your hand? he asks. Maybe some of your luck will rub off on me. We both laugh. His touch is firm, dry, and he continues to hold my hand quite casually as he goes on: Come out to dinner with me, will you? I'd like to take you somewhere special – to celebrate. It's such a great play, really.

With a little pressure he releases my hand. Then – and I don't know how he did this – he manages to blush, a real blush working over his face and up to his forehead, turning him pink as salmon. He looks away as if embarrassed – oh, my Jack, as if you ever were. You'll probably hate me saying this, he says with masterful uncertainty, in fact you've probably had dozens of people saying this to you but— And he breaks off just there, playing the pause. You see, he begins again, but still hesitant, I've got this idea for a play. And then it all tumbles out as if quite spontaneously. It's just an idea, you know, it's been knocking around in my head, and I wondered – I just wondered if I could possibly – he is slowing now – if I could, well, talk it

135

over with you. I just wondered— And then he takes a step back so that he is pressed against the seat behind him, thereby playing his best card – did he already know how effective that threat of withdrawal could be? But before I can even pretend to consider my eager agreement, he bursts out: I do *so* admire you . . . God knows by what black arts he manages to get so much meaning into those words. God knows how he succeeds in conveying exactly what he would like to do with me, the promise, the crisp sheets, the little bites ringing my neck as he feasts off my blood. God knows – but he is an actor and actors can perform these feats on- or off-stage as long as there is an audience.

But I do not know all this then. All I know as I try to match him with a pitifully uncasual shrug of my own, as I try not to let him see the empty pages of my diary, is that the warmth of him is spreading over my shoulders as if he is the sun melting my spine, sucking the marrow from my bones.

I did not anticipate the success.

The papers are full of it – reviewers, critics, other playwrights, directors, they all want to meet me, to interview me, to shake my hand and make suggestions for new projects. A producer says he'd like to discuss making a film, maybe *All Greek*, maybe something new, he'll get in touch. A West End theatre will arrange a transfer when the run in Bernard's theatre comes to an end.

Bernard says I will have to get an agent, that I must be careful not to take on too much. What did I tell you, ducky? he exclaims, proudly steering me through the throng at the awards party. I knew it would be a success – you just listen to wise old Bernard, he'll make sure you're all right . . .

And there stands Lavinia in midnight-blue satin with a red scarf flaming over her shoulders. She still manages to look more of a star than I am, I think ungraciously, even as she opens her arms and kisses me on both cheeks: Darling Helen, I'm so proud of you . . . I am wearing a plain black dress and wish I had accepted her offer to help choose a 'costume' for me. I look dowdy – I feel dowdy.

People are expecting me to say clever things, to be witty as the play is witty, to make them laugh, to be incisive and sharp and quick. But my brain has slowed to a standstill, I can barely answer questions coherently, I cannot keep up with the brilliant conversation sparkling all around me. All these people with their high laughter and their faultless make-up, dextrously balancing plates of canapés and glasses of wine.

The compère says I am a modern Aristophanes, which raises a good laugh. But when I go up to collect the award, I stumble through my acceptance speech and later I am aware of Lavinia's tinge of disapproval: Such a pity you didn't mention Bernard, Helen dear. He did give you so much help, after all – and he is commissioning the next one . . .

The next one? Jesus.

But then Jack is at my elbow, holding my arm very firmly. I won't let you go, his hand says, stroking the inside of my wrist. It's all right, I'm here . . .

And suddenly the party is fun – the lights and the voices and the conversations. Suddenly now I have found a voice and I am saying all those clever things they wanted me to say. They stand around me in a little circle, waiting for my next remark. But maybe Jack is the ventriloquist and I am his dummy, maybe it is he who floats the words through my head and I who speak them, because he has only to hold my hand as he is doing now to unlock my mind and turn it towards him like a flower spreading the heart of its beauty into the light.

Lavinia meets me outside the West End theatre to which *All Greek* has transferred. But you will be careful, won't you, Helen? she says. Jack Arden, I mean – he has quite a reputation, you know.

I shake my head, try to raise my eyebrow in imitation of her. No, I don't know what she means.

She sighs. I notice while she is gathering herself to speak again that there are streaks of silver in her bronze hair and a network of lines creeping over her face which do not dissolve but rather are deepened when, as now, she is worrying. You are growing old, Lavinia, I think coolly. And I admit there is some satisfaction there. She who has been so beautiful is now crumbling, while I, who have never had any beauty to speak of, am at least still young, still able to attract a man. You've had your day, I think, as I watch her take up her lower lip between her teeth unconsciously. My star is rising while yours . . .

You see, Helen, she goes on, I've heard – well, darling, it's just that he's not the *kindest* of men – understand?

But as Jack comes out and greets us both, I see how she watches him, how her eyes slick over his thick gold hair, and I realize suddenly: She wants him, that's why. She wants to warn me off and have him for herself.

So I deliberately put my arm through his and stand with my hip pressing intimately against him, smiling while he tells Lavinia how he and I will be in Greece soon with Bernard's company for the festival there – weren't we lucky? And he's so sorry to hear of that play she'd been in being broken off like that – he shakes his head gravely. Such bad news – and he'd heard that the production had been so *innovative*. Well, critics. And he throws up his slender hands in exasperation, leaving me without any contact with him. What do they know? he says. His hands are floating out of my reach like butterflies, but just as I am about to catch one— Well, lovely to meet you, Lavinia. Maybe we can all have a meal together when Helen and I get back. Good luck, something's bound to turn up, it always does . . . He waves, smiles, and thrusts his hands deep in the pockets of his leather jacket, out of bounds to me. We turn away and I don't even bother to try for his hand again, but content myself with walking as close to his side as I dare so that at least the people passing will know he belongs to me.

These nights he has been coming back to the villa very late. Rehearsals, he says – we rehearse in the evenings, when it's cooler. There's no point in coming back all the way here, he adds. Besides, I don't want to disturb you in the middle of the day when you're hard at work, do I? He ruffles my hair and I turn the conversation aside deftly, as one would turn a blade.

Later, when I ask him, he replies casually: Oh, mostly we go to the beach, rehearse a bit, go over the lines. I look at him incredulously. Well, yes, he admits, we swim too, and the girls sunbathe. He laughs: Some of them are getting quite dark now, it'll be good for the play though, all those swarthy Trojan women. And Bernard goes off for a siesta, he adds with a wink: I think he's having a little cheek to cheek with one of the fishing boys, they're always hanging round him . . .

And you? I want to ask. Are you having any cheek to cheeks,

any little whispers with one of the swarthy women? Have you tumbled the wardrobe yet? Preened the chorus? Brushed the thighs of the lead?

Now when he comes back late at night he is too tired to make love, too tired, he says, even to allow me to caress him. Jack, who could make love three, four times in a night. Jack, with his boundless energy, now complains of the heat, the insects. Jack, who when 'resting' has worked in a slaughterhouse carrying bloody carcasses. Jack, who has been willing to take any tiny crumb of a part just to be on stage, now grumbles that Bernard is cutting his lines, that Bernard has it in for him, that Bernard keeps criticizing him unnecessarily in front of the others. I won't stand for it, he scowls darkly, I won't let him make a fool of me, he'll see . . . Oh, and Bernard was asking after you, he adds later, when we are lying in bed. He wants to know why you haven't come down to see him yet. I told him you were very busy, working on your play . . .

So one day, without telling Jack, without even mentioning it, I wait till his bike has disappeared, then get up and wash and dress carefully and put on suncream and a hat and set off on the long walk down to town.

At least I am doing something, I think. At least it is better than being locked in the villa or going out for those dull lonely walks. There was one day when I climbed up to the top of the island again and looked out at the tiny puffs of white boats sailing across the vast blue table of the sea. I imagined the people trailing their hands in the cool water, laughing, talking. Maybe they were looking back and watching this little island melt away, the harbour and houses and beaches becoming indistinct. I remembered the legends – Scylla and Charybdis, the Sirens and their island of skulls. I thought of Poseidon and imagined him rearing up out of the sea, gigantic, broad-shouldered, covered in barnacles, weeds streaming from his sea-green beard. I thought: Maybe if I pray hard enough, he will pluck out this island and toss it away from him, and myself and the empty room where my little Rumpelstiltskin should be working will be shaken into the sea like matchsticks . . .

But today, as I walk the long miles into town, I am thinking of how I will surprise them all. I have my plan ready. First I will go to the taverna by the harbour and sit in the shade and drink cool drinks to prepare myself. Then I will walk out to the amphitheatre and sit very quietly at the top of the steep sloping seats and watch them rehearse. When they have finished I will come down the steps and take my place by Jack's side among them. They will all be so pleased to see me.

The walk takes longer than I expect and when I get to the harbour it is almost lunchtime. I sit at the taverna. It is rather bewildering to be among so many people again, to see the bustling and hear the shouts and chattering when I have been alone for so long. And then, just as I begin to think of setting out for the amphitheatre, I see Jack come around the corner. I am about to hail him, am already half out of my seat, when he stops, turns and calls out to someone just behind him. She comes at a run, long white-gold hair streaming behind her, long gold legs in white shorts – Atalanta sprinting for the hunt. She stops by his side and they stand there together: the Heavenly Twins. Then she laughs – white teeth gleaming, her breasts in their tight little bodice stretched taut and high and inviting, and he draws her towards him and kisses her long and hard and full on her ripe strawberry lips. I can feel his hands stroking the nape of her neck beneath her thick hair, I can feel his mouth hot as pepper, his sharp teasing tongue. I can smell the rush of sweat on his body, the length of his erection pressed against her – against me . . .

That night he does not come back. I sit out on the terrace under the stars. I have prepared olives, bread, wine – but he does not come back. The mosquitoes whine, but if they bite me I don't notice. When the candles splutter and burn down, I don't renew them but sit under the arch of the night where the eyes of the gods mock me from the stars. From their vantage point they can all see me and they whisper to each other – Hera and Aphrodite, goddesses of marriage and love. They look down on me without pity, while Zeus holds the heavens steady and keeps the night calm for all those who are out in the velvet dark making love.

I have stopped crying. I have stopped pleading. What do they care, those gods? What have I ever done for them? I have made them no sacrifices, poured them no libations. Instead I have taken their language and customs and rituals and held them up for ridicule. No, Zeus has raised his golden scales and my side has dropped to the ground. I cannot look for help there.

But someone has been on my side. Not one of the great Olympians, but perhaps a minor deity of this island who slipped through the villa and shimmied into our bed one night, rousing him from sleep and making him turn to me. And maybe that kind deity borrowed the girdle of Aphrodite, draping it around me so that I was made beautiful, irresistible. Maybe she stirred my womb with her fingers as one stirs the soil before sowing seeds so that the earth is made ready and fertile.

The bloody bike broke down, he says, leaning against the door of our room. It took me all night to find a mechanic to set it right and by the time he'd finished I hardly thought it was worth coming back and waking you.

Not one of your better stories, Jack. But I don't say anything, just nod, trying not to look at him as I take my clothes out of the cupboard and lay them on the bed.

I'm really sorry, Helen, he tries again. I know you must have been worried. Come here. He tries to embrace me, but I dodge past into the bathroom. I push aside the suncreams and take my toothbrush – not much here, really, he can keep the soap and the toothpaste. I come back out.

What are you doing? he asks.

I have gathered all my clothes together and now I look at them again. No, too much to carry. So I separate them into two piles, one much larger than the other. These are the clothes I will discard. The two tight dresses that he bought for me. The shorts. The bikini. The jeans. The short skirts that I always felt too exposed in. All the shirts I stole from him and never washed because they had his smell in them. The half-cup bras. The black lace knickers.

I know from experience that I can get a change of clothes and underwear in the carpetbag and I scoop these up from the bed and take them downstairs.

He follows behind me. What are you doing, Helen? Helen, speak to me – tell me.

I pause outside the State Room and he catches up with me, tries to take my arm, but I am holding the clothes tightly. Helen – please? He is looking genuinely worried and for the first time I take in his face: he is unshaven, his eyes bloodshot, there is a dirty rim around the collar of his white shirt. And suddenly it strikes me – what is he doing back here on a rehearsal morning three days before the opening night?

The play, he says, I'm packing it in. I can't stand any more of Bernard sniping at me. He can use one of his fancy fishermen to play the part – he's cut it to shreds anyway, so there won't be much to learn. Anyway – he takes a step closer – I've got better plays to come from you, haven't I?

My play? Well, if he wants to see my play, then here it is. And I gesture for him to open the door.

Of course, he doesn't realize at first. He sees the notes and the open pens and the lines of writing on the pages. He is excited and leafs through it all eagerly as I roll my clothes into a bundle and pack them in the carpetbag. Then I see the realization slowly break on him. He doesn't act this, it is genuine Jack astonishment, the wave drawing back gradually, cresting, peaking until—

Is this it, then? He glares at me, holding a sheaf of notes out in his hand. Is this it? He is not shouting yet – he can't believe that I haven't got a manuscript hidden away in the carpetbag that I'm clutching so protectively. Helen? he asks.

I look down at the mess of papers, dusty now and faded from the sun. The uncapped pen is dry, lying just where I left it on the blank pad. So, Rumpelstiltskin didn't do his work then. But that also means I am not in debt to him, I have no bill to pay, I am free.

This is all you've done? He waves a fistful of paper in my face. This?

You can crumple it up, Jack, I think calmly. Go on, it's the kind of dramatic gesture you'd like to make. Light a fire with it, make paper darts – use it to pen love letters to your newly discovered goddess.

I've given up my part in the play for this? he shouts at last.

But you'll charm your way back into it, Jack the lion-tamer, I know. Once you've washed out the dandruff I can see flaking on to your shoulders and smoothed down the peeling skin on your nose. When you've changed your shirt and deodorized your armpits, you'll go striding back into that amphitheatre and Aphrodite who loves beauty will set a charm about you to bewitch them all.

Haven't you thought of me, Helen? he rails. Haven't you – at all?

I study him once more before I leave. Actually, he is not a tall man, slightly built, and his voice, now that I hear it unguarded, has more than a trace of an accent scraping his vowels.

It wouldn't last – I knew it wouldn't last. All he ever wanted was to hitch on to my coat-tails and have me carry him to the stars. Maybe I am numb and the pain will come later, but I don't think so. I have finished worshipping at his shrine, I have burned my fingers and paid my dues. But I have also snatched a prize from him, something he will never know about, something he will never miss because it will never have been his. Now I actually pity him for the days he has left to himself.

I ride at the prow of the ferry boat. I am laughing. The wind and sea spray my face and my hair streams over my shoulders. I feel the engines drumming under my feet and through my whole body as the boat cuts through the water. My hands are folded over my belly, where my prize rests safe and warm. But because I look ahead so arrogantly, I fail to notice the Furies clinging to the stern behind me.

I lay the page down, my hand trembling. God, but Helen's passion there on that island is almost frightening – and it is all the more fierce for being stoppered. She never actually speaks. And the speech of others, unpunctuated as it is, seems not quite real, as if none of us ever penetrated that shell of hers.

Do I begin to admire her, then?

But there was always something dangerous about her, some unpredictability that kept me off balance even during those long hydrangea conversations that we shared in the Annexe garden. I can see her now, leaning back in her deckchair, her eyes half closed to the golden autumn sun, her hands clasped over the round ripe fruit of her belly. And I see myself sitting beside her, telling her everything, and in my own state of innocent contentment unable even to conceive of being betrayed . . .

'But what would you have done, Helen,' I asked, 'if I *hadn't* run into you last week in the theatre foyer?'

'If you hadn't rescued me and brought me here, you mean?'

She looked at me wryly – always something a little mocking in her eyes.

'Well, darling,' I said lightly, 'you were in a bit of a state, weren't you?'

'As I was when you scooped me up from Father's house after he died. Heavens, Lavinia – ' she laughed – 'I don't know what I'd do without you. You're like a fairy godmother, always appearing when I'm crying among the pots and pans, and whisking me away to the ball. First, finding me all that backstage work and now this little house – I really don't know how to thank you.'

Is it me, I wondered? Am I just being oversensitive? A little touchy perhaps at the sight of her fruitful belly so proudly displayed? But no, I told myself, it's only banter, only Helen's way.

'You don't have to thank me,' I replied. 'As I've already explained, the Annexe needs someone to live in it now that my – friend – won't be using it any more.' I was still carefully reticent.

'And you're sure your "friend" doesn't want any rent?' she asked. 'And doesn't mind my redecorating?'

Isn't there a glitter of – what – suspicion, mischief, in her eyes? Some emphasis in her voice? Again, I pushed the doubts aside and answered her evenly, 'I've told you, Helen, there's no need for any rent – you're *family*. And as for the redecorating – well, you know I still don't think you should be doing it all yourself.'

'In my condition?' Her mouth puckered.

'You know what I mean,' I said, a little primly. 'It can't be good for the baby.'

'I know what's good for her,' she answered, stroking her belly tenderly.

I looked away.

She stretched languorously. 'Anyway, even if I hadn't run into you, I'd've found somewhere to live eventually. I could hardly have brought up my baby in a bedsit, could I?'

'Well, it was a close thing,' I said reprovingly. 'Why didn't you get in touch with me as soon as you got back from Greece?'

'We've been through all that. I didn't want anyone to know—'

'But surely I'm not *anyone*, Helen?'

She didn't answer. A train went past and she smiled. 'You

know, I do like being near trains again,' she said. 'I suppose they're familiar – like Father's house, remember?'

I nodded, then asked, 'And after your father died – if I hadn't "rescued" you then, would you have gone back to university?'

She laughed. 'God – no. I'd flunked most of the first year anyway, they were already thinking of kicking me out – I just saved them the bother. I'm no clever academic, Lavinia.'

'Oh, but you can't say that,' I protested. 'What about *All Greek*? Everyone agrees you've written a highly intelligent play—'

'Fluke.'

'Oh, come now – Bernard told me how hard you worked on it.'

She shrugged.

'How's the new play coming along, by the way?' I asked. 'I saw Bernard the other day and he was saying he hoped to catch a glimpse of it before the deadline so he knew what to prepare for.'

Her face hardened immediately. 'Sent you to check up on me, did he?'

'Helen – no.'

'Well, I don't like to be pushed.'

'But he's only *asking* – and he did commission it.'

'In my own time.' She bit a corner of her nail. 'I'll do it in my own time – the deadline's not till the end of next month. Anyway,' she added, 'I don't want Bernard to see me – like this.'

'But – darling,' I laughed. 'Surely you don't think that Bernard will *mind*?'

'I just don't want him to know,' she said stubbornly. 'I don't want *anyone* to know.'

'Not even Jack?' I suggested gently.

She flared: 'Especially not Jack – I've told you that already, Lavinia.'

'But Helen, darling, shouldn't you think again? After all, he *is* the father and—'

'She's *my* baby,' she interrupted fiercely. 'No one else's. And if Jack does find out – ' she looked at me menacingly – 'then I'll know who's told him.'

'All right, all right,' I backed down hastily. 'There's no need to get worked up . . .'

I visited her every day after the rehearsals for my forthcoming American tour. Sometimes she was out in the garden pulling up weeds, clipping back the straggling bushes that Teddy used to sigh about. Other times she was paint-splattered as she finished another coat of stinging yellow or vibrant blue. Some days she was pleased to see me, other days she was nonchalant, but always there was a frenetic energy – she must get more plants, more furniture, more rugs. She must decide on a colour for her bedroom, *their* bedroom – 'She'll sleep with me, of course. I couldn't make the little lamb sleep all on her own . . .'

I brought her presents: a decorated porcelain bowl filled with spicy pot-pourri, a small table for the hall, pictures, books. And a large china pot of blue hydrangeas that stood between us in the garden as we talked.

I was relaxed, expansive – unguarded. Teddy and I would marry next spring, when I came back from my tour. Nothing can disturb me, I thought, as I watched Helen picking the hydrangea petals and tearing them carelessly.

Some evenings we shared a bottle of wine in the garden as we watched the sun go down. We laughed over theatre stories, the mishaps, the characters – Bernard and his merry men . . . So when one night she asked casually, 'Tell me about this little house, Lavinia. Who is your mysterious "friend"? Do tell me – please,' I couldn't refuse. And I told her the whole story just as she asked. I told her about Teddy and our long, secret affair. I told her about Eve and how her recent death had left us free to marry. I told her about the Dowager and the estate and the Church and how we'd had to be so discreet. I told her how we used to meet here. I told her how Teddy had laughed when I'd confessed to him my impulsive offer of the Annexe to her. I told her about Belle House, where we'd be living after we were married. I told her how happy I felt with him, how lucky I was to have found him. I told her everything. And I enjoyed telling her – it was a relief to be so free and open when I had been forced to be secretive for so long. And it is appropriate, I thought, now that Helen is living here, for her to understand what this house has meant to me.

She listened carefully, attentively, soaking up my words as the walls soaked up her bright paints. She smiled, nodding sympathetically as she poured more wine into my glass. But behind her smooth face her brain must have been clicking like an abacus counting up the beads of my story, moving the words into speeches, scenes, acts. *A State of Grace* – I must have all but written it down for her.

But sometimes, maybe when I went upstairs to the bathroom – a virulent green – or when I paused on the landing as a train rumbled past and the shutters trembled, sometimes I would suddenly remember the house as it had been before, when it was only mine and Teddy's, how dim it was then, how quiet. And part of me would feel uneasy at having brought Helen here, casting out the cobwebs and the worn comfortable drabness.

So to cover my misgivings, I brought her more presents: napkins, tablecloths, cutlery. 'But you must pay me a penny for each of the knives,' I told her with a smile.

'Superstitious, Lavinia?' she chaffed.

I laughed. 'You may think it's only superstition, but you've still got to pay up.'

But she never did.

We sat in the garden, the windows wide open behind us, the smell of fresh paint drying. She tossed the hair back from her face. It was darkening again, growing out the perm and the highlights she'd had put in before going to Greece and which I'd thought had made her look brassy. Now her hair hung straight and heavy as a curtain, so unlike Joy's naturally buoyant waves.

I sighed, remembering Joy, remembering the past. 'It's such a pity,' I said, 'that neither of your parents lived to see *All Greek*. Your father—'

'He'd have hated it,' she broke in. 'You know that, Lavinia.'

True, I thought. But said loyally, 'You don't know – but even so, he'd have been proud of your success.'

'Prouder if I'd got a first in classics,' she retorted.

'But the film,' I persisted. 'You can't say he wouldn't have been pleased about that?'

'Actually, the film might not come off,' she said carelessly. 'I don't really mind. They've sent me wheelbarrows of money for it and what with that and the royalties for the play, I shouldn't have to worry about – oh—' She broke off suddenly, clutching her belly.

'Helen? Helen, what is it?' I was half out of my chair.

147

'It's all right.' She smiled beatifically. 'It's just that every time she moves inside me I feel so – so—' There was a look of utter absorption on her face.

'You don't know that it *is* a girl, Helen,' I said, trying to keep the sourness out of my voice.

But she just smiled and looked at me pityingly. 'Oh, I *know*, Lavinia – I *know*. You wouldn't understand – you couldn't, could you?'

I succeeded in keeping my face completely impassive while I felt the sympathy that I had built up for her so carefully, tumble in one breath like a house of cards. No, Helen, I thought, I wouldn't know. You see, I had my foetus scraped out of my womb like so much offal all those years ago when, by chance, Joy found that she was carrying you. I watched her become rosy and round while I was thin and pale and barren. And when you were born, Helen, when Joy brought you home from the hospital in your thick cotton blanket – you so small, so perfect, with your clutch of dark red hair and your wavering hands – then I felt the womb I no longer had contract inside me and a voice cried, But that's my baby, that baby should have been mine.

No, Helen, I wouldn't understand.

But you have not turned out to be my baby, I thought, as I watched her heave herself out of her chair and go into the house. You have turned out a stranger. And, if I am honest, I have never felt comfortable with you. I was jealous, yes, of Joy for having you, but now that I have you to myself I cannot continue to pretend that I care for you as I would a daughter of my own.

So it is better, then, that I keep my distance from you in future, I decided, as I stood up to leave. We will not really become close. I have done what I can for you now – there is nothing you can do for me.

Sins of omission . . .

I suppose the Annexe must be just as Helen left it. Teddy didn't have it cleared out – he didn't have time to, between her death and his there was barely a month.

So it must be just marking time down there in that tucked-away corner of London – waiting.

I wonder how it looks. Quiet now? The gaudy walls faded

maybe? Thick dust on the tables – cobwebs in the corners – mice scrabbling in the kitchen? And all their things – the child's pictures on the walls, her toys and books. Helen's clothes in the cupboard or lying untidily on the floor.

But maybe the quiet waves of silence and the wash of the trains passing have cleansed that house. Maybe it is empty as a nutshell. Maybe a wind has streamed through, sweeping away the detritus like a river carrying off fallen trees after a storm . . .

I should get rid of the place, sell it, give it away. It is just another loose end.

The lake is covered with a thin mist in the mornings now. It is like that veil of spun glass that used to wrap the Christmas tree when I was a small child. I remember clearly as yesterday, Joy and I waking very early on Christmas morning, tiptoeing past our parents' bedroom and down the stairs to where the tree towered in the drawing room. I remember how we stood there, awed, Joy's hand tightly clasping mine as we watched the tinsel and lametta and silver baubles winking at us.

And I remember, too, an Easter with Teddy at the start of our affair, when we dared to slip off for a few days to a country inn. They baked us fresh hot cross buns and I can taste them now, the warm spice, the thick butter, the sharp sweetness of the honey.

'We'll get fat and ugly,' I said to him.

'I won't get fat, I'll get plump – and you could never be ugly, Vinny,' he replied.

'Well, plump then – we shall both get plump.'

'Yes.' He smiled. 'I shall become plump and dull, and you won't want anything more to do with me . . .'

Oh, I lived so keenly then, rushing up to meet life with the very edges of my body. Now my food tastes of sawdust and I dread Christmas. So, maybe Gregory is right and I have become cowardly, timorous, proud of my suffering. Maybe it is time to put that Lavinia away – God knows, I am sick of her.

The musician paces the room, glances out of the window at the rain, turns back, kneels by the fire, poking it, throws on more logs and gets up again, goes back to the window.

149

'You're restless,' I say.

'Oh—' She turns away. 'I'm all right.' Her hair falls into her face and she flicks it out of her eyes impatiently.

'Your hair's grown.'

'Yes.' She tosses it back again. 'I don't have to keep it short any more. I used to before because I couldn't bear it getting in my face when I played, but now—'

I catch her eye. 'You'll have to go back. You know that, don't you?'

'No – no – not yet – I can't.' She goes to the fire, picks up a stick and breaks it into small pieces, which she throws into the flames.

'It's not so difficult,' I continue. 'People will help you.'

She doesn't answer.

'You'll be happier. I know – trust me. It won't be – *can't* be as bad as you fear—'

'How do you know?' She turns on me suddenly, her face – Helen's face – spitting. 'You don't know what it's like – no one knows. It's like stepping off a cliff – stepping into *nothing*. How can *you* understand that?'

And for a moment I see Helen standing by the window in the guest-house before the child was found. She is tearing at her face with her bitten nails, her hair lank and matted, still dripping with the rain, which beats down mercilessly outside. 'You don't know what it's like, Lavinia,' she cries, her words hard as bullets. 'You've never risked having a child – how could *you* know anything?'

No, I think now, as the musician comes towards me contritely. No, Helen, you were right. I never took that risk. I squandered my chance years ago on a casual affair and a bodged abortion. You were right, Helen, I have buried my head in the sand and thought I was wise. I have scraped a hole in a rock and called it living.

And I don't know if I am thinking of the musician or myself, but I turn to her now and say fiercely, 'Don't be a coward – don't give in. If I have to push you over the edge myself, I will. Leap, damn you – leap.'

I have been having dreams. This is unusual. I wake in the very early morning and have to push aside the tangled images which hang over me thick as jungle creepers. I am driving a car – not my old sports car or Teddy's Rover but something huge – a lorry or a coach. I am driving, but the car doesn't move – or I cannot engage the gears – or I put my foot on the brakes but they don't work. There is a moment of panic even when I wake – I feel my heart thudding – and then there is the sound of the birds outside, the rustle of wind, the calling of sheep as they pass by on the fells.

These dreams are not like the ones I had after Teddy died. But I never considered those to be dreams. They were encounters. He'd be in my bed – I could feel him in my arms, feel the weight of him, the roughness of his face pressed against mine, smell his sweat slightly acrid like a horse, run my hands over his chest, down his legs to his feet with their large middle toes. This isn't a dream, is it? I said to him. No, Vinny, he smiled, this isn't a dream . . . Waking from one of those encounters was like having my heart torn out of my living body and I reached for the brandy.

No doubt that shrink of Helen's – Dr Elspeth – would have something to say about all these dreams. No doubt if Helen had dreams, Dr Elspeth analysed them too. Tidying up all the loose ends, putting Helen's mind in order, allowing her to find the voice with which she set down these disturbing accounts of herself.

Dr Elspeth wrote to us after Helen died, apologizing for being unable to attend the funeral – God, I was grateful for that. She expressed her condolences, her 'deep sympathies', and finished:

Helen was well on the road to recovery in herself. She had gained significant insights from the writing she did here. Had she lived, I'm sure that Helen would have been able to continue with her life in a new and meaningful way . . .

And that's the rub. Had she lived, would I be talking to her now? There would have been just Helen and myself – an uneasy equilibrium. Would she have visited me? And would I, hungry for contact, afraid of being old, of dying and being forgotten, would I have clung to her as the old cling to their young relatives, grasping at their youth, their promise of immortality?

151

Because there will be no one left after I have gone. No mark of my family, my genes will be extinct. Myself, Teddy, Helen – we have left behind no remnants. As if one of those vengeful ancient gods pulled up our lineage root and branch.

I had never before considered this to be important, but now I find that it is an eerie feeling to leave nothing behind. I had thought it would be a relief to go out with a clean pair of heels, but now I find that it is lonely. I would like there to be someone of my blood, some member of my tribe, to carry on – even if only in a minute way, a flash of red hair, a flair with words, a certain stubbornness – the line of my family.

I have seen photographs of the First World War battlefields. For miles a whole landscape will hold nothing but debris, shell holes, tangles of barbed wire. And then suddenly in the middle of it will stand a tree. Its leaves stripped, its branches broken, but still there, maybe the only survivor of a whole forest.

I am that tree.

The last of Helen's sections is in my hand . . .

FURIES

They have chased me here to the gingerbread house. I didn't want to come back – I never wanted to come back. If I peep through the cracks in the shutters, I can see them huddled up against the foot of the magnolia tree where I had buried the spare set of keys. Their wings are folded over each other and they look as if they're sleeping.

I sit here on the floor under the table where they cannot see me. Sit and wait.

It is very quiet. Now that my breathing has slowed, I can hear the silence. No trains – they don't run through the night. There is a little light filtering through the shutters which makes shadows of the carved hearts and flowers like negative photographs. She would have outlined them with one tiny sugarsnap bean of a finger, tracing their patterns on the floor. And then she would have looked up at me and smiled.

I remember now. Before we left, I swung the shutters to and disconnected the phone and turned off the gas and electricity so that now there is not even the hum of the fridge. Automatically when I came in I tried the light and when it didn't come on I thought they had done something – cut the cable, or spread their bat wings over the house, cloaking it in darkness. But it wasn't them. I remember how I'd consciously switched off the two handles so that the house went completely quiet. It reminded me of when I first came here with Lavinia. 'Go on, Helen,' she said, pushing open the front door. 'Go on – go inside . . .'

I don't know what time it is now. My watch is still on the bedside table at the hotel I stayed in yesterday. I suppose if I don't get back there someone will find it and take it in part-payment for the room.

I must sit very still and give them no reason to become

153

suspicious. If they hear me moving, they might come up and tap against the shutters.

It is suddenly hot in London now. Furies weather. Where they come from it is always hot and they spread their wings and soar on little eddies of hot wind. Here it is like an oven door open. I have walked through the streets with them close behind buzzing: Walk quickly, or we'll get you . . . Children play that game – I'm coming to get you – screaming with excitement as they chase each other in the playground. She used to outrun all the others, her hair flaming out behind her.

One evening when they were chasing me, a child on her bicycle sped past, hissing at me from the corner of her mouth: 'You're a witch – you're a witch.' Maybe she saw them billowed out behind me, maybe she felt their rancid breath.

Another night – or maybe it was the same one, I get confused about time – they played a game with me. Chased me across all the bridges in central London from the north side to the south side and back again, criss-crossing the river in huge stitches. I thought: Maybe they want me to throw myself over. God, if *that* was all they wanted. So I stopped in the middle of a bridge and hooked my leg over the railing, leaning forwards. But they were swirling all around me then, like dirty water, and they pulled me back and set me to walk faster and faster. They will not let me throw myself in front of cars, or buses, or trains.

But tonight they chased me straight here. Not along the riverside, their favourite route – they like the tired wash of oily waves against the banks. Nor through crowds, where they make me invisible so that a horde of drunken jeering youths will simply part before me, the Furies masking their eyes with webbed fingers.

No. They chased me here – to the gingerbread house.

This afternoon I sat by the window in the hotel room and watched the day slowly thicken into night. Saw the people drain out of buildings and seep into pubs as the twilight descended like a soft blanket, the streets emptying of cars, a little breath of cool wind. And I thought: Maybe I'll sleep tonight, maybe I'll get through a whole night. My head wasn't aching and I felt lighter. Maybe after a sleep, a proper sleep, I'll be able to think about it all. And then I heard them sniffing down the corridor, heard the rattle of their claws in the chambermaid's trolley, their wheezing breath in the whine of the lift, and tapping, tapping until they were outside my door . . . I didn't pause, didn't hesitate, stood up, left the window. Furies inside a room are a million times worse than Furies outside.

I don't plead with them now. I don't beg, or pray, or hope. I let them chase me. I try maybe to outwit them, but even that means nothing. I will not try to escape. There they are, clustered at the base of the magnolia tree like large black umbrellas.

I had not intended to come back here.

When I dug up the keys, I expected them to come at me at any moment. I scrabbled at the ground with my bare hands: 'Shall we play buried treasure, Mummy? You bury it and I'll dig it up . . .'

Of course they could come in here. They could slide beneath the door, or through the keyhole, or between the slats of the shutters. And maybe while they besiege me they are gathering their strength to do just that.

Come the autumn they will hide in every pile of dry leaves. They will skitter across the pavements, their bird bones clicking like dry twigs. In winter they will leave tracks in the snow, omens, messages for me to read – where they have been, where they are waiting for me.

Through the kitchen window I can see the moon. It hangs low in the sky, heavy as if filled with liquid – a woman in her ninth month. I said to her once: There's a woman in the moon. Look, see her face, see how she smiles? But my little moonbeam didn't say anything, just nodded.

I've found some candles. They didn't seem to notice when I got up, or maybe they just allowed it. I have melted the candles on to the floor and taken some paper to write on. I am still sitting here beneath the table, out of their direct line of sight, but I have pulled the cushions down from the sofa: 'Shall we make a nest? Let's play nests . . .' giggling with her friend, Melissa.

I could take one candle and float through the rooms like a ghost. Softly, softly, do not wake her, she is sleeping. And my little house curved round her like a shell.

Sometimes in the night, long after she had demanded her own room, I'd wait till she was asleep, then tiptoe in and crouch on the floor by her bed just to watch her. She slept with her face half hidden and her stubborn little back turned towards me. Her hair flared over the pillow, bright even in the dim light, and her breathing was so soft I could only just hear it, little wisps of sound leaking from her mouth. Precious outbreaths that I'd want to draw deep into my own lungs.

When she was newborn I'd lie awake for hours listening to her shallow panting breaths, terrified that after each one she might simply not bother to take another. The thread of her life seemed so fragile, so lightly held. It was like watching an unprotected candleflame.

Her birth was dreadful. The pains starting late at night, and being all alone here, the house no longer friendly, the wind rattling the shutters, and the scent of Lavinia's pot-pourri making me feel sick as I lurched down the stairs to the telephone. By the time they got me to the hospital I was screaming. But it wasn't meant to be like this, it was meant to be warm, joyous, loving. And I wasn't meant to feel so alone. People rushing past, gowns billowing behind them, faces masked, beady eyes bending over me, arms holding me down and someone screaming, screaming as I struggled to get free from the hive of insects swarming over me.

They say it is the first few moments of a child's life that are the most important. Mother and child must form a bond, imprint themselves, recognize each other. She looked at me with large dark eyes as if at a stranger. Who are you? she said. As if she'd forgotten all the conversations we'd had.

And then she cried. Cried and cried, mosquito wails that protested at what I had done, forcing her to be born, tearing her out of that safe warm place where she'd turned and danced joyous as a dolphin. I held her and rocked her and begged her forgiveness: Oh, my darling, I'm so sorry, I'm so sorry . . .

Time is flowing very strangely. It seems to have slowed now and I am tired. Maybe it has stopped altogether, left behind in my watch on the hotel table. Maybe I have been here for many nights. Maybe I have always been here.

They stand there, Father and her. They stand with linked arms, laughing. There is a joke they share, something I'm not party to. It's obvious, they say. Can't you guess?

She had many secrets. A secretive child. If I went into her

156

room without warning, she'd curve her hand around her toy or book *instinctively*.

Beneath her bed is an old chocolate box I thought I'd thrown away long ago. She must have squirrelled it out of the bin and hidden it. I found it just now. I sat on the floor of her room, pulled off the gaudy pink lid with its glassy-eyed kittens, and a cascade of shrivelled conkers spilled into my lap. And suddenly I could see her dancing ahead of me in the street: 'Look what I've found – look, Mummy . . .' She must have filled her pockets with them and hidden her lustrous treasures here under the bed, where she thought I would never find them.

The moon is shining bright out there in the garden, where shreds of her voice flutter like ribbons. She crows to herself as she picks up a pebble or a shard of old crockery. What have you got there, darling? 'It's a secret,' she purses her lips. 'A secret, Mummy . . .' Little hands pushing me away.

She has a terrible intelligence, my daughter. Terrible as the thousand-headed Hydra, or the monsters in the Underworld that Father used to describe. And yet those creatures that the heroes did battle with are nothing compared to the intelligence of my daughter. She has lion eyes which can look through me, defy me, turn me to stone. When I cleaned her room – Really, Marigold, it's time you learned to do this for yourself. Come on, pick up those toys. Don't argue, Marigold – she would suddenly turn on me with a bitter defiant look that twisted my heart like a Chinese burn. So that the worst part of being a mother was discovering that the child I had given birth to was completely separate from me, a stranger, someone I might possibly never know.

It is at least peaceful in here. Quiet. No sound from the Furies outside. I could almost be tempted to try and escape, but they would see me then. Instead I will sit here in the flickering candlelight, as if in a cathedral.

She wanted to go to church. 'I want to go like Melissa – she goes with her mummy – *and daddy*.' This was being added recently. She'd started to ask precociously pointed questions. 'She's so sharp she'll cut herself' – I could just hear Mrs Baines saying it.

I said: No, Marigold, don't be silly, we don't go to church.

'But you make me say my prayers before going to bed.'

True. Every night I made her kneel by her bed and whisper some verses I'd stolen from a prayerbook, while I stood behind, watching her. Those prayers were an insurance, a small offering to placate the gods who circled above my darling, always threatening to take her away.

'I want to go to church like Melissa.'

So we went one Sunday. It can't do her any harm, I thought, it can only protect her.

There were candles everywhere burning in rows on iron racks in front of painted statues. I could hear Father giving his lecture about sacrifices and offerings and burning the fat for the gods.

We sat at the back because I didn't want to get too close and she looked around her with wide eyes taking it all in, the incense and the gold robes, the little chiming bells and the white-ruffed altar boys. And all of a sudden it frightened me to see her so absorbed, I didn't want her to look up at the garish cross like that.

We have to go now, I whispered, and reached for her hand.

'But, Mummy—'

Now, Marigold. Don't argue.

I saw her look, saw her temper boil up, but I held her hand and pulled her behind me out of the pew.

'But *why*?' she kept saying when we were outside and walking away. 'I *want* to go to church – Melissa goes to church – all mummies and daddies go to church . . .'

I held on to her hand all the way in the bus and down the road until we were back in the house. After a while she stopped protesting and just glared at me mutinously. I have won this battle, I told myself, I will not let them take her. She is mine.

What will happen to me? Will I have to remain here? We have reached an impasse – I am in here, they are out there. Who will move first?

Sometimes they make me stand in the middle of the pavement – Do I go left? Do I go right? – their wings beating so hard around my face that I can see nothing distinctly and I have to wait there like a doll until they weary of the sport and push me onwards.

But I am tired. Tired of the running. Tired of the memories bursting like fireworks – Marigold giggles behind the paper parasol, she dances in the candleflames, her shadow slides along the walls. Maybe the Furies' pursuit would be more bearable than this – my mind writhing like a cut worm, lashing like a loose cable in a storm – Marigold – Marigold . . .

'What a beautiful little girl,' they all said. People stopped me in the street, in the park: 'Isn't she lovely. You must be very proud of her . . .'

Hair like a bright flag waving as she ran ahead, always ahead: 'Mummy, can we go and feed the ducks now? Can we go to the swings? Bet you can't catch me? Go on, push me higher, *higher* – I want to see right over the whole world.'

'She's going to be a beauty,' they said. 'And so bright too, so intelligent . . .'

When she brought her work home from school it was decorated with red and gold stars, bright as her hair that skipped down the street: Don't go so fast, Marigold, not out of my sight . . .

She wriggled out of my arms as soon as she could walk. As soon as she could stagger on her little fat legs, she was away waddling down the path: No, Marigold, you can't go there . . . She'd glance back at me, crowing.

She didn't look anything like me. And I told myself that she didn't look anything like *him* either. But when she regarded me with those lion eyes, when she pouted that peach mouth . . .

She claimed her own room as soon as she could talk. 'Melissa has her own room – she doesn't sleep with *her* mummy. I want my own room – I want to sleep in *my own* bed.'

But, darling, you'll be afraid on your own, won't you?

'I'm not afraid – I'm never afraid of anything.'

Don't be silly, Marigold, don't boast. (The gods might hear and punish you.)

But she didn't creep into my bed in a storm, I crept to hers – just to see she's all right, I told myself. And there she was, sitting up bright-eyed, excited.

'Close the door properly,' she ordered, after I'd kiss her good-night.

Marigold, I say a little sternly, you know the rules. The door stays open just in case.

(In case of what? In case she wakes and, oh, blessings, calls for me in the night? In case I want to push it open silently and watch her as she sleeps?)

No, but she sleeps tightly, her back hunched under the blankets, her face hidden under her arm. She sleeps so quietly I can barely catch her sweet breath.

Whatever I have done, however I have wronged them, whatever punishment they wish to impose on me, I will accept it. I will do whatever they demand. Here – see my suppliance, I rub dirt on my face, I burn hot wax on my palms. Let *me* eat the sin, let *me* suffer and burn for all eternity. But spare her. Save her. At the moment of sacrifice let her be snatched away like Iphigenia, daughter of Agamemnon. But before you hide her with your cloak of invisibility permit me one tiny glimpse so that I know that she is well. If Demeter can have her Persephone returned to her for even half the year, then let me have sight of my darling. O gods, hear my prayer . . .

Little scenes from her life:

I said to her: If you ever get lost, if by some accident you ever find yourself separated from me when we're out, you know what to do, don't you?

She was chewing a strand of her hair, looking bored, kicking the chair leg.

Marigold, listen to me—

'Can we go out to the park?'

Later, this is important.

'I want to go *now*—'

Marigold—

She sighed, straightened a little. 'And then can we go?'

I pulled the wet strand of hair from her mouth and ran my finger down her cheek. Listen, I said. If ever you get separated from me, this is what you must do – it's very simple. Are you listening?

She nods.

I hold her gaze. You must sit down, I say.

There is a moment's silence. Then: 'Sit down?' She looks at me incredulously. 'Just sit down?' her voice rising in disbelief. (I have a sudden uncomfortable glimpse of her as a rebellious teenager: 'You can't *make* me take my make-up off . . .')

Wherever you are, I say, you must just sit down.

'In the middle of the street? What if I'm in the middle of the road, I can't sit down there, can I?' She looks pleased with herself.

I keep my voice very even. You get to the pavement, Marigold, and then you just sit down.

'But I'd feel stupid.'

I think for a moment. There'd been a case in the papers – there was always a case in the papers, but I wasn't going to let it happen to my child.

If you simply close your eyes then it won't be so embarrassing.

She thinks about this. At least I've managed to catch her attention. 'Just sit down?' she says eventually.

That's right.

'And close my eyes?'

Yes.

'And when I open them?'

Then I'll be there.

'But what if you aren't?'

Then I'll be on my way.

'But I can't just sit down in the middle of the street and close my eyes,' she scoffs. 'It's silly.'

You can, I tell her. And you will. You sit there. You don't go with anyone, you don't speak to anyone, you don't let anyone take you anywhere. You just sit there.

'I don't know . . .' She says this like a businessman turning over a proposition. 'I'm not sure.'

Listen, Marigold, I say. It's highly unlikely that this will ever happen, but if it does I just want to make sure you'll be all right. I hesitate, then say carefully: There are people – people who aren't – very nice to children.

'Why?'

Why what?

'Why don't they want to be nice?'

I don't know, I sigh. It's just that some people are – funny about children. But she is looking bored again. So, I say briskly: What do you do if you get lost?

161

'I sit down.' But she doesn't sound as if she means it.

Marigold, this isn't a joke, I say roughly. This is serious.

She blinks, takes a breath. 'I sit down – and close my eyes – and wait for you.' She finishes and looks up at me. 'Now can we go to the park?'

You sit down, you close your eyes, you don't move and you don't go with anyone – understand?

She nods.

And should someone ask you – should a woman ask you – you say you're waiting for your mummy and you don't budge. You stay there until I come and find you. Yes?

You see, I want to say, there are demons and hungry ghosts out there who want to steal you away. But I don't say this. I stroke her head that used to nestle in the palm of my hand, that once rested against my heart and was washed by my blood, that now contains a whole world I cannot enter.

When she was very small she had tantrums. She threw herself on the floor if she didn't get her way and lay there stiff as a board, her tight fists beating the ground. I'd pick her up and lay her gently across my knees and hold her, just hold her until her rage subsided and she softened into tears, like a shirt that has been starched and then is rained on.

There was a spring day when we went on a picnic to the park. We sat by the pond and she ran to and from the edge, tossing bits of her sandwich into the water, laughing as the ducks bobbed to retrieve them. Suddenly the sky darkened and heavy streams of rain sheeted down, soaking us both. She ran up to me, her arms outstretched, her head bent back, the rain peeling her face. I was on my feet, already gathering up the sodden food and stuffing it into bags, but she just grabbed hold of my hands and pulled me away: 'Let's dance, Mummy – come on, let's dance—' And we tangoed and waltzed and galloped across the grass, my little wet seal slipping in my arms.

I bought her a parasol with fish and flowers painted on fragile paper, the wooden ribs bright blue. She was very proud of it and twirled it round her head as she strutted down the street: 'Look at me – look at me, Mummy . . .'

In the garden she laid it opened out on the ground and played behind it so that I couldn't see her. I could hear her giggling with her friend, the flowers and fishes trembling in the breeze.

But it got left out in the rain and was spoilt. The rain weakened the thin paper, which tore when she opened it too impatiently. I said I'd get her another for Christmas or her birthday – but I kept forgetting.

On Guy Fawkes Night we had a bonfire in the garden. I bought fireworks and she squealed and gasped as they shot into the sky, her face brighter than all the rockets and Catherine wheels put together. We ate hot potatoes roasted in the ashes, and toasted marshmallows and sausages. When the fire burned down, she cuddled up to me and we sat warm together looking up at the stars. Her hair smelt of smoke and autumn leaves and I could feel the little pulse in her neck beating strongly against my fingers.

Sometimes there is a sound in the house – a door creaks, feet patter on the stairs – and then I know that she is here. I hear her playing upstairs, her feet light as leaves. But if I go to look, she will disappear back into the stillness of her room like dolls in a doll's house returning to their positions with that fixed wooden smile on their faces as if they've never been alive at all.

Lavinia was right about one thing, I decided after her visit, we did need a holiday. Marigold was looking pale, tired. 'Outgrown her strength,' Mrs Baines would say.

I passed my test and bought a small car. We could take a driving holiday this summer, I said. What do you think, Marigold?

She was rocking in her chair at the table, tipping it back so that it balanced only on two legs.

Don't. I pulled her forwards sharply. Well, what do you say – a holiday, eh?

'OK.'

We could get a cottage – somewhere nice, just the two of us?

'OK.'

You don't sound very enthusiastic.

She shrugged, then looked at me carefully. 'We could go to Aunt Lavinia's house—'

She's your *great*-aunt, I said.

'Well, to her anyway – we could go there, couldn't we?'

I don't think so.

'Why not?'

We'll find somewhere else. Somewhere new.

'Great-aunt Lavinia's house is new,' she persisted. 'We've never been there. And she said we could go – she said we could go whenever we liked. She said they had animals there – horses and cows and sheep and everything – and she said—'

We're not going there, I said firmly. Now, where else—

'Well, it's not fair—' she broke in. 'That's where *I* want to go.'

Marigold—

'You said *I* could choose.'

Marigold, we won't go anywhere if you don't behave.

'Well, I don't care—' She reared up from the table. 'We never do what *I* want to do – it's not fair . . .'

The caravan was alone in a field. It was already dark and Marigold was asleep. I carried her in and laid her gently on one of the beds, but she woke up.

Lie here, sweetheart, I said. I'll get the things in from the car.

'But it's dark,' she whimpered. 'And I'm cold. Don't leave me . . .'

It was cold, but the air was crisp and smelt like clean sheets, so broad and open I could take great gulps of it. The night was full of strange rustlings and hootings. Marigold cuddled up close to me and I curved my body around hers to give her my warmth. I felt her breath butterfly my hands, her eyelashes rippling as she dreamed.

In the morning it was still cold and our field was covered in a thick mist. We drove down to the small town and I bought her bright yellow waterproofs and a bag of fudge. We had lunch in a steamed-up café and I let her have as many chips as she wanted: We're on holiday, I said. So she licked her fingers and ate two portions.

When we came out it had warmed a little. We drove into the

narrow back lanes that twisted and curved around the hills. The landscape was bare and beautiful and we just looked at it all, not saying much. After a while the sky cleared and the sun came out and I stopped at a little lay-by at the foot of some hills. Let's get out and stretch our legs, I said. We can walk to the top and look at the view.

It was one of those deceptive ranges – just when you think you've reached the summit you find there's more hill behind. I was worried that she'd get tired, but she ran ahead of me, her long legs springing over the bracken.

Aren't you tired, darling? I asked her.

'No, I'm fine. I could go on for miles and miles—'

I smiled. It's all those chips you ate.

'Here, Mummy – ' she held out the bag – 'have some fudge – it's got lots of energy.'

We stopped for a breather. I was suddenly aware of the quiet. There was only the sound of the wind and the distant call of sheep. The sun had gone behind a cloud and when I looked back I couldn't see where the car was.

We've come a long way, I said. Don't you think we ought to go back now?

'Oh – but we've *got* to see the view.'

I don't know if my old legs will make it, darling.

'Have another piece of fudge—' Then, lowering her voice secretively, she added, 'It's magic fudge.'

Oh, my angel, I laughed. Here, give me a kiss.

She pressed herself against me for a moment – and then she was gone.

Like foul breath, like the Furies' breath, the mist came down very suddenly. They must have been up there on those hills tracking us, but I never heard them. Once, I looked over my shoulder – maybe I heard something, a twig crack, or a ewe bleat, but there was nothing, only the mist seeping stealthily over the hills, grandmother's footsteps creeping up behind me.

Zeus with all his thunderbolts could not have invented that mist. So which one of them was it? Which of those gods opened their hand and let the mist fall out fine as a veil? Maybe Jack pleaded his rights, and the gods – always on the side of the father – granted his prayer and flung out a net of mist to entrap me.

Marigold? Marigold? Darling – darling, come here—

Not even the sound of sheep cropping the grass. Not even the sound of the wind.

Marigold? MARIGOLD?

My shouts hit a wall and bounce back at me.

MARIGOLD – COME HERE.

I am stumbling over rocks and bracken. Uphill? Downhill? Was the drop to my right or to my left? Just below my feet or way off in the distance? I stop, panting for breath. Listen. Wasn't that something? A call? A shout?

MARIGOLD – WHERE ARE YOU?

A ewe sheltering beneath a rock suddenly rushes to its feet and scurries away.

Dark now – Oh God – getting dark now. How long have I been here? How long since she – since we—? But, of course, she will know that *downhill* is where the car is. Even now she could be there waiting for me – God, why hadn't I thought of that before, instead of wasting all this time? Quick – downhill, quick. God, this bloody place is vast— Quick – *quick*. But it'll be all right, it'll be all right, she'll be by the car, it'll be all right . . .

'There, love, there now, we've got you. Give her your coat, Ben, quick, she's half frozen. That's right, love – drink this, that's it. More tea, Ben – and plenty of sugar. Yes, love, we've called out the Rescue and they'll be here in a moment. No – you stay here, that's right, the Rescue's coming. Drink this – that's right . . .'

'Yellow waterproofs, you say? Nice and distinctive – we'll have her down in a jiffy, don't you worry. And she's got some sweets with her? Good, that'll keep her strength up. No, you stay here – no, you've got to stay here. Dave, stop her, for God's sake. That's right – we can't go looking for two of you now, can we? You stop here. We've got radios, we'll let you know as soon as we – Jesus, Dave, hold her. Get the doctor to give her something – quick . . .'

'Just hold steady – that's right – you'll just feel a little sting – that's it. Just to calm you down a bit. There now – it's all right – it's all going to be all right . . .'

Stop. Stop the day. Stop time. I don't want time to move forwards. Nothing must change. We must stay at the same time and not see the distance increase as of a ship pulling away from shore.

Isn't there a law somewhere? Didn't Einstein or one of those people invent a law? A law that could make you stop the world, halt it and then slowly, very slowly, like pushing furniture on heavy castors, couldn't you push the world back? If we all pushed, if we all joined together, if I explained to everyone in the world, surely then they'd help? Surely they'd understand? That we could push the world back to how it was – push it back just for one day, no, not even as far as that, just for a few hours, just to that moment when I had her hand – when I felt her small sticky fingers, her grubby palm, the narrow band of her wrist – when I had her hand – when I had her hand in mine.

Lavinia at the guest-house. She leans forward and the pity in her voice rushes down on me. 'Oh, Helen – my dear—'

Don't, I say. Please – don't.

I travel on the train. Sometimes I am alone in the carriage, sometimes there are other people. It is a small old-fashioned carriage. There are blinds to cover the windows but I don't draw them. I am searching – one eye on the communication cord. I am ready to pull the cord and leap out of the train as soon as I see her.

But she's canny, artful. As I travel towards London she could just as well be travelling back up to the hills. Maybe we have already passed each other – maybe she is in one of those trains speeding north. Maybe I should get off this train and catch another.

But she has a sense of play, I have to give her that. And she's clever too. Sometimes she lets me catch a glimpse of her – a flash of her hair which I saw on the top deck of a bus as I stood on the pavement. The bus was building up speed to beat the lights but I could see her hair very distinctly, that unique shade of copper and auburn and gold. Except that she had grown, she was taller, older, a woman already. I ran alongside the bus and shouted. I would have flung myself in its path if only I could have got in front. I called up to her, waving my arms, beating the side of the bus, but she never turned, never looked down at me, and then the bus slipped through the lights on amber and was gone.

Cunning child. I hear her laugh in a cinema, her laugh that distinguishes her, that I would recognize among a million other laughs. We are all sitting in the dark and suddenly I hear her laugh behind me – or is it in front, or at the side? I can't tell, and when I run around looking, calling for her, they all stop laughing. Laugh – laugh, I tell them: Go on, keep laughing . . . But they put hands like iron on my shoulders and take me out.

Of course I see her yellow raincoat everywhere. In the street, in the shops. I see it on grown women, on men, on old ladies. I see it in showercaps hanging in the chemist. Once, I saw it as a bright tablecloth in a basement. That's her coat, I shouted – that's her coat. Where did you find it? Where did you get it from? I gripped the bars and wouldn't let go until they threatened to call the police.

I see her running in parks, I see her smelling the flowers – swinging high in the playgrounds – flinging sheets of bread to the ducks.

In the spring, when the daffodils are in bloom, I will see her everywhere.

Soon it will be time for me to leave. Daylight is coming – the Furies dissolve. They cannot chase me back here again. Maybe I will catch another train and look for her one more time on the hills. Or maybe I will contact Lavinia and tell her to cleanse this sweet, low-eaved house of the witch who lives here. Because this is a poison house with its gingerbread walls and icing-sugar roof, and I am the witch that enticed the children with biscuits and cake and then locked the door so that they couldn't escape.

It has been a long night – there are still pockets of shadow in the corners. I blow out the candles. There is a distant rumbling and then the house trembles as the first of the trains goes past.

It has been one of those startling blue late-autumn days.

Even so, when Annie approached the window determinedly this morning, I pleaded, 'Don't open it, Annie – please.'

'Miss Mair – but it's lovely outside, like July,' she coaxed.

'Maybe later, in the afternoon – or tomorrow.'

'But tomorrow you'll be going out for real,' she said cheerfully. 'Remember? Father Gregory's coming to pick you up in his car in the morning.'

'No, I don't remember.'

'Come now – you can't pull the wool over my eyes. You told me yourself, you did – last week. You can't go changing your mind now.'

'I may yet if I want to,' I said petulantly.

But she just smiled. 'I think it's *so* exciting. For two pins I'd come with you myself just to see your face. Father Gregory says you won't recognize your little cottage.'

'Really?' But Annie doesn't notice subtle shades of inflection – as she says herself, she's a simple girl.

Now my hands are aching. Where are your Furies now, Helen – you with your cauterized, unmarked voice? Let me tell you. They have settled around my chair to pinch my knuckles and twist my fingers – they saw at my bones.

The wind is picking up, it wrinkles the lake. Clouds mass, sheep cluster beneath the rocks. The gulls fly in twisting bands out towards the sea.

Maybe it will storm tomorrow.

Those last scenes are welling up. I can no longer hold them back . . .

Finally I had managed to get through. His phone had been out of order and even now the line was very bad.

'Teddy? Teddy?'

'Vinny – is that you? I can hardly hear—'

'Oh, Teddy—'

'Vinny, are you all right?'

'Oh, Teddy—' I pressed the receiver close to my ear as if that might bring him nearer. 'Teddy – they've found the child—'

'Found? Is she—'

'No – no – she's *dead*.'

'Oh, God. How?'

'Exposure. They found her the day before yesterday – there's been freak cold weather here. She was hidden under a rock – just *sitting* there. Oh, Teddy—'

'How's Helen?'

'I don't know. She's—'

'What? Vinny, you'll have to speak up, I can hardly hear you.'

'She's gone,' I shouted. 'Helen's gone.'

'Gone? Gone where?' His voice became faint again.

'I don't know – I don't know.' I leaned my head against the wall in the dingy corridor. I could hear a television booming in the 'Lounge'. A plastic ivy by the phone brushed my face.

'Vinny,' he called. 'Where? Where's Helen gone?'

'I don't know.' I began to cry. All that time I hadn't cried. From the moment at Belle House when I had received Helen's raving, incoherent phone call, I had been dry-eyed, practical, setting off to 'rescue' her again. But now, after the nights spent with her raging, the days trailing behind her as she shouted herself hoarse on the cold bleak hills, now I was crying. 'Since they found the child – ' I stammered – 'Helen's just – disappeared.' I could hear only the faintest wisp of his voice. Oh, Teddy, I wanted to say, it's all my fault, because I've never really liked her – because I'm still angry at what she did to you. Oh, Teddy, I've laid a curse on her . . .

He was speaking, but I couldn't hear what he was saying. Later, I would realize that we could have put the phone down, tried again for a better line, but at the time I couldn't break that connection however tenuous it was – couldn't bear the thought that I might not be able to reach him again.

'Oh, Teddy – I don't know what to do.'

'You're sure Helen's not up there?'

'I don't know – she could be anywhere. I've had the police looking – someone thinks they might have seen her at the train station.'

The door to the 'Bar' opened and the landlady emerged, peered at me inquisitively. Later, I would think: But why didn't I take Helen to a different place, a hotel instead of that ghastly guest-house, somewhere she might have been more rational? But at the time – at the time I could make none of the right decisions.

'Where do you think she's gone?' Teddy asked in a lull on the line.

'I don't know.'

'The Annexe?'

'I've tried ringing but I think the phone's off the hook – and I can't leave here to look for her, there are things I have to do. Oh, Teddy – ' I burst out – 'I had to identify her.'

In the hiss of his indrawn breath I heard the pneumatic doors closing on the lift as it took me down to the cold basement. Trolleys lurked in the corners, bright polished steel rims and edges. A strange smell I didn't want to identify. The chessboard pattern of the floor – oxblood-red squares and veined cream tiles. Inside the room were high metal tables – with runnels. I could already see her body under the sheet – so small, like a broken-off square of chocolate, her feet didn't even come half-way down the table. A curl of her hair dangled over the side. I could have identified her just from that.

I was crying again and he was saying over and over, 'Oh, that poor woman – that poor woman.' And it stung to know that he wasn't thinking of me. Selfish Lavinia.

'I'll go and find her,' he said.

'But you've never met her – you don't even know what she looks like.'

'That doesn't matter.'

'But God alone knows where she is – she could be any-where.'

'I'll start at the Annexe – I'll leave now.'

'Teddy, you can't—'

The sea of crackles parted for a moment and his voice came through suddenly loud and firm. 'Vinny, I have to do something for her—'

And then the waves joined up again and swept him away.

'Are you ready, Lavinia?' Gregory stands beside me. 'I've got the car waiting.'

'Well, I didn't imagine you came here by flying carpet,' I snap.

He smiles. 'Is there anything you want to take with you? A book, perhaps? Or something for the journey?'

'For heaven's sake, Gregory, we're only going ten miles down the road, not half-way across the world. *And* this is only a short *visit*, remember?'

But it seems everyone is humouring me today, my tetchiness runs off him like water.

171

'Nothing you need then.' He reaches out his hand. 'Come on.'

Teddy sank into the chair in my sitting room. 'God, that's better.' He stretched out his feet to the fire.

I hovered anxiously. 'Are you all right? You don't look very—'

'Nothing a stiff whisky won't fix,' he said with a smile.

'Of course – I'll get it – you just stay there.'

'I wasn't thinking of moving.' He gave a weak laugh.

I poured a large measure into his tumbler and a brandy for myself. I thought I could feel him watching me, but when I took him the drink his eyes were closed and my heart twisted at how tired he looked, how pale and exhausted.

'Here—'

He took a sip and nodded. 'Ah, that's better.'

I sat on the arm of the sofa to be close to his chair. 'I could make cocktails if you want?' I offered.

'No—' He waved a hand. 'This is fine. But you know – ' he smiled ruefully – 'it's at moments like this that I really *ache* for a cigarette.'

'Then sod the bloody doctors—' I slammed my glass down. 'You shall have one – I've got some upstairs.'

'Vinny—' He looked at me in surprise. 'So you didn't throw them all away?'

'I haven't touched them – I just kept them for emergencies.'

He reached out and took my hand. 'Oh, Vinny, you've done such a lot for me.'

'What? Giving up cigarettes because you had to?'

'Not just that—'

I looked away uncomfortably. 'I'd hardly agree. In fact – I think I've been quite unbearably selfish.'

'Vinny – no—'

'Not marrying you—'

'There's still time for that,' he chuckled.

I made to stand up. 'I'll go and get the cigarettes.'

'No – don't bother. The ache's gone – that ache anyway.'

'Was it very bad?' I asked after a moment.

He closed his eyes again. I could see the veins on his eyelids quivering.

'It was, wasn't it? Tell me, Teddy.'

He took a deep breath. 'Helen was all right at first – really quite calm. She opened the door to me at the Annexe – didn't even seem too surprised at meeting me for the first time like that. She said she was glad it was me who came to find her, because I'd always seemed to think kindly of her. I told her I'd come to take her somewhere quiet where she could rest a bit.' He rubbed his forehead tiredly. 'I wasn't sure whether to tell her about Hill House—'

'You'd already thought of taking her there?' I broke in.

He nodded. 'On the way down to London, I remembered it from when I was there after the war. If I *could* find Helen, it seemed the ideal place for her – quiet, you know, secluded. I stopped at one of those motorway places and managed to get hold of the number and I spoke to a Dr Elspeth.'

'But you *did* tell Helen where you were taking her?'

'Yes.'

'And she was all right – I mean, about going there?'

'Oh, yes—' He took another swallow of his drink. 'As I say, she was quite calm, you know – quite normal, really. I thought she seemed an interesting person,' he added, glancing at me.

I ignored the look. 'And the child?' I asked. 'Did Helen say anything about her?'

He shook his head. 'And I didn't want to bring that up either – I didn't know how she'd react. I just asked if she wanted to bring anything with her and she said she wanted to find a bag she had—'

'A bag? You mean a suitcase – or a rucksack, or something?'

'No. It was a carpetbag – she found it in one of the cupboards. Actually, she said you'd given it to her.'

'Her writing bag—' I took a gulp of my drink, the brandy burned.

He nodded. 'Yes, she said she'd been writing.'

'She said that?' I looked at him incredulously. 'Writing? You're sure?'

'I asked her – in the car while we were driving – what she'd been doing and she said walking around London and writing. She said she'd stayed at an hotel but she couldn't remember which one.'

'Writing— I'd never have expected that.'

He gave a shrug.

'So, it was all right, then, the journey?'

He sighed. 'All right at first. We drove part of the way, then I stopped for a rest and something to eat. By the time we got back on the road it was getting dark—' He stopped.

'And?'

He seemed to brace himself. 'Then – she wasn't so good. She stopped talking, wouldn't respond to anything I said, kept looking behind her all the time as if she was – I don't know – searching for something—'

'For the child? God, how macabre—'

'No, not for the – I do wish you wouldn't refer to her like that.' He was suddenly sharp. 'She had a name, you know.'

'She didn't like her name,' I said defensively. 'She told me.'

'Vinny, I'm sorry – I didn't mean – I'm just tired.'

'It's all right. Go on – in the car when it was getting dark—'

He rubbed his eyes. 'She got very – well, you know, looking behind her, fidgeting, shifting around in her seat. I tried to have the radio on but that wasn't a good idea – she got very agitated about it.'

'Oh, Teddy—'

'I was just terrified that she'd unlock the door and leap out.'

'So – what did you do?'

'What could I do?' His voice rose. 'I just put my foot down and broke all the speed limits – I drove as if the hounds from hell were after me.'

'Oh, Teddy—' I tried to take his hand. 'I'm so sorry – dragging you into all this.'

'It's not me you should feel sorry for.' He drained his glass and set it down. 'Anyway – we got there. You know,' he said after a pause, 'Hill House has changed quite a bit since my days.'

'I should think so – it's almost fifty years, isn't it? What did you imagine – that the place would still be full of war cases?'

'Well – it was strange.'

I gave a wry smile. 'Skeletons in the cupboards, darling?'

He chuckled. 'Ghosts under the lino, more like – but they don't have lino now, it's all carpeted. Still looks the same from the outside, though – the long glass esplanade where we used

174

to sit when it was too cold to go outside. Mind you, it's full of plants now. Funny really, going back,' he mused. 'At the time I was so *ashamed* of having to be there – and the Dowager wasn't exactly complimentary about it – funny farm, and all that.'

'It might have done her some good to spend time there herself after your brother's death,' I broke in. 'Anyway, by the sound of it you were a nervous wreck after the war – that Japanese camp, your friends—'

'I know – I know.'

'But you got to the place in the end,' I said after a moment. 'With Helen?'

He nodded. 'And I was damned relieved, I can tell you.'

'And the doctor?'

He brightened. 'Elspeth – Dr Elspeth, it's all very informal there now. Well, she seemed to take it all in her stride – got Helen inside and everything. She didn't want me to tell her too much about Helen, said she'd rather hear it all from her herself. I think she'll be well looked after – Dr Elspeth seemed a knowledgeable woman. We're lucky they had space for her. Tragic, tragic – the whole business.'

'Well, I think you've done very well,' I said reassuringly. 'I'm sure Helen will be very grateful.'

He nodded absently, still staring into the fire. 'There is one thing,' he said slowly.

'Yes?'

He looked at me and suddenly I knew what was coming. 'We'll have to decide – Helen will have to decide – what to do with the child?'

It is bright – brighter than I remembered. Although I have been seeing daylight sitting by the window for all these months, it is not the same as standing outside in it. And the air – the air is thick with scents. I can smell grass, sheep, the fells – even the water of the lake.

'Down the steps – that's right—' Gregory has my arm firmly in his, Annie hovers at my other side. I can feel her excitement beaming through her yellow dress. She exchanges looks with Gregory over my head as if I were a child. 'Mind the gravel now, Miss Mair,' she says. 'It's not very even—'

'I can manage – I'm not lame, you know,' I say tetchily.

'That's right – lovely,' she squeezes my arm. 'Oh, it's so nice to see you out of doors – I can't tell you—'

I am folded into the car, the door closed carefully. Gregory comes round and takes his place beside me. 'All right?' he asks.

'Just get on with it, Gregory. Stop making such a fuss.'

He leans towards me and for one awful moment I think he might be trying to offer some sort of embrace and I shrink away. 'Just put your seatbelt on, Lavinia,' he says.

But at last I have found something I can fight back on. 'No,' I say firmly. 'I draw the line.'

'But, Lavinia, if we have an accident—'

'Then I'll be grateful to your God for evermore – you can sing hymns over my grave. Now just drive, Gregory.'

I stare straight ahead. The horizon is a burning autumn blue. From the corner of my eye I can see Annie waving but I don't respond. Gregory starts the engine.

'Here?' I looked up at Teddy, shading my eyes from the sun with my hand. I had been planting the early autumn bulbs in the borders at Belle House. 'Helen said she wanted the child buried *here*?'

He nodded.

'But why – why here? Helen's never even been here.'

He shrugged. 'Because of you, I should think, Vinny. After all, you're her nearest relative.'

'But I still don't see why?'

'Never mind why,' he said tersely. 'It doesn't matter *why*. To tell you the truth I was honoured.'

'And you agreed?'

'Of course I agreed – as I say, I feel honoured—'

'And the Order? What do you think they'll say?'

He drew himself up. 'The Belle House burial ground is a private family plot. In this case it's *my* say-so that counts, not theirs.'

So, I thought, you'll stand up to them for *her* sake but you won't for your own.

I turned back to the border. 'Looks like it's all decided then,' I said coolly.

I thought he walked away. I stayed bent over the soil, digging out holes for the bulbs, working hard and fast in the tight soil though my hands were aching with the effort and I knew I'd have pain with them in the night. But when I looked up he had only moved to the stone bench by the drawing-room window and was watching me.

'Leave that, Vinny,' he said gently. 'Come and sit down for a moment.'

'I've got to finish or we won't have any spring flowers,' I said stubbornly. 'The Order may not care about such things but I do.'

'Vinny—'

'Someone has to do it,' I went on. 'If they don't think it's worth paying for a proper gardener – if they don't care that the gardens are going to ruin—'

'Vinny—' I could hear the smile in his voice. 'You're having a little rant.'

'Maybe.'

'Come here—' He stretched out his hand.

I got stiffly to my feet and went to sit beside him. Gently, he pulled off my gardening gloves and stroked my painful fingers and for a time we just sat there quietly in the sun.

Then he began in a low voice: 'Vinny, I really do think you should—'

'Teddy, don't—' I broke in. 'I know what you're going to say. Please – don't go on. I've had enough – really.'

'But you *will* go and see Helen?'

'Of course – later – not now.'

'And—' He hesitated. 'It's all right – to have the child here?'

To have her haunting the estate? To have Helen visiting – God knows, maybe even moving in here? I shuddered, but said tightly, 'It's your decision, Teddy. It's not up to me.'

'But if you mind—'

I gave one of my best laughs. 'Teddy, darling – why should I mind? I was just surprised, that's all.'

He squeezed my hand. 'Then I'll arrange it.'

'Will – will Helen come?' I asked after a moment. 'For the funeral?'

He sighed. 'I'm not sure. She didn't say and I didn't want to press her. It was enough that she'd made that decision – a big step forwards, Dr Elspeth told me. And she's been writing more,' he added. 'Dr Elspeth says that's very therapeutic for her.'

'Does she say – what she's writing about?' I asked carefully.

But he shook his head. 'I don't ask. Part of the treatment – confidential, I should think. At least it's helping.' He stood up. 'I'm relieved we've sorted out about the child. Bless you, Vinny.'

'Me?' I looked up at him. 'What for?'

'Oh – just for being you.' He bent and kissed me, then turned towards the house, saying over his shoulder, 'I'll just give Hill House a ring to say I'll be up tomorrow. Helen *will* be pleased . . .'

And what could I say? Nothing. The sourness in my stomach, the ache in my bones. Nothing. The sniping when I saw him setting off in the Rover wearing his best suit and his spotted bow tie, carrying the pick of the flowers *I* had struggled to grow. Looks dapper for her, I thought. Doesn't bother to dress himself up for me any more . . . Ugly, childish, whining voices. Spends all day with her – doesn't care about me . . .

Helen didn't attend the funeral. Neither did I. For once I thanked the pain that bit my nerves and crucified my joints. Teddy stood alone by the grave that I could never bring myself even to visit. I imagined him stiff, attentive, doing his duty. When it was over, he went straight up to visit Helen and didn't come back till very late.

'But what do you talk about?' I asked him.

'Oh—' He shrugged. 'Sometimes we don't talk much at all – we just sit together.'

So, now she steals his silences.

'Does she mention the child?'

He shook his head sadly. 'No – not at all. I wanted to describe where she lies – I've thought of a beautiful memorial statue I'd like to erect for her there – but Helen won't let me tell her anything. Later maybe she'll be able to face it all . . .'

Every few days he'd be up there with Helen. He no longer seemed to care about the estate, didn't try to discuss things with the Order, but just let them make their own decisions to root out hedges and raise the rents. Even his dogs got less attention, they shuffled around me all day while he was away, moping until they heard the Rover turning into the drive, when they'd be off, bounding towards him.

'Bless you, Vinny,' he kept saying. 'You're so understanding . . .'

Lavinia, teeming with bitterness, smiled back.

We drive quite slowly until I tell Gregory to speed it up. 'We're not going to a funeral,' I say. 'Put your foot down.'

The window is open and I can feel the breeze on my face. It is startling to see so much variety – fields, houses, roads, cars. We drive through villages – shops, busy people – God, I'd forgotten what it was like, all this life outside. And then I pull myself up sharply. No, I will not let myself become ensnared, no, I do not want my horizons widened. No. No. No. Like a drum beating time in my head until I am weary of the argument and just gaze out of the window anyway.

Teddy stood implacable at the far end of the dining room. It was late autumn and very cold but I hadn't lit a fire, hadn't thought it worthwhile – too much bother now to fetch the wood and clear the ashes. An electric fire would be simpler.

But looking at him now, I wished I had taken the trouble. A fire would have warmed the large gaunt room where we still ate our meals, might even have warmed him as he stood there beneath the portrait of the Dowager, looking, for that moment, very like her.

He had returned late, bone-tired, his eyes bloodshot, even his hands wavering as he picked at the food on his plate before pushing it away and getting up. 'I've made all the arrangements,' he said, his voice very flat. 'They'll be bringing Helen's body down here tomorrow. We'll have the funeral the day after. Nothing elaborate – I've spoken to the Order, they'll send one of the monks to officiate.'

'But I don't know if Helen even believed—'

'It doesn't matter,' he cut in. 'None of it matters – not any more.'

'Oh, Teddy,' I cried, 'don't say that—'

But he just looked at me wearily. 'I tell you, Vinny, this has just about broken me.'

'Darling – no—'

'I never expected that she would die – just out of the blue like this.' There were tears in his eyes. 'And she'd been doing so well – everyone thought so – Dr Elspeth *said*—' He was like a bewildered child. 'Why didn't she *tell* anyone if she wasn't feeling well? They might have been able to do something before it was too late, but now—'

'You could say,' I suggested carefully, 'that it's for the best.'

The look he gave me was scalding. 'No, Vinny, I couldn't say that. None of this was for the best – *none* of it. It's all been a – a bloody *waste*. Jesus – Jesus Christ!'

I had never heard him swear, never heard him take his Lord's name in vain before. I stayed very still and the voice in me whispered: So, now she's stolen his God from him, stolen his faith, there's not much else she can rob him of any more . . . It seems impossible to stamp out those voices. Like a hidden leak, you stop up one outlet and they simply spring from another, seeping through hairline cracks in your reasoning and bursting out to race in an unstoppable tidal wave to the forefront of your mind.

He went to the door. 'I'm going to get a drink.'

'Oh, Teddy—' I half rose. 'Do you think you should? You know the doctor said—'

'Fuck the doctor.'

He slammed the door behind him.

I am beginning to recognize landmarks – that field at the top of the hill where he practised his ploughing – the village we've just passed through. And this wall running alongside the road, I remember him telling me how once, for a dare when they were children, he and his brother had walked along the top of the flints all the way down to the village, and their father had beaten them when he'd found out . . . Soon now, on my left, we will pass the big hay meadow – and on my right will be that wonderful line of beeches – yes, here they are, burning with autumn . . .

Gregory is driving more slowly. He drives well, economically, his hands moving deftly from steering wheel to gearstick. He hasn't tried to make conversation and I'm glad of that.

Now he is indicating, pulling over, and we turn through the gates. We have arrived.

'I thought we could go straight to Belle House first,' he says as he drives swiftly past the hedges that surround the Dower House. 'I thought you might want some tea.'

I look at him.

'Well – some refreshment anyway – before you go to have a look at the Dower House properly.'

'I'd like a drink,' I say. 'You'll be able to offer me a drink, won't you?'

'I'll see what I can do.'

'What a diplomatic answer, Gregory. I take it that's a "no"?'

'Well, Lavinia, you see, we don't actually—'

'I should have brought my own supply,' I break in, with as much acid as I can muster.

He doesn't reply, or if he does I don't hear him. Because suddenly there in front of me is Belle House – the perfectly symmetrical proportions, the warm honey-coloured stone, the Virginia creeper that was Teddy's weakness – 'I know I should cut it back, Vinny,' he said every year, 'I know it'll pull the house down if I'm not ruthless with it – but for that one week in autumn when it just *flares* . . .' Oh, my Teddy, I think as I look at it, did you see it flare before you died? It is flaring now though the monks, efficient as ever, have cut it back hard.

Gregory comes to a halt by the main entrance and switches off the engine. He gets out and helps me from my seat. I am a little stiff, a little shaky, but I push his hand away and go over to the stone bench beneath the drawing-room window.

'I'll stay here,' I say firmly. 'You can bring me my *drink* out here.'

'You don't want to come inside?'

'No.'

He nods and turns away.

'And don't send any of your representatives to check up on me either,' I call out after him. 'I can still bite, you know.'

The stone bench has warmed in the sun. I have drunk the coffee, though I crumbled up the biscuits and tossed them on to the grass which now covers the borders. From time to time one or two of the monks go in or out of the house, but they pass me without comment or even so much as a look. Gregory has them well schooled.

And as the clouds pass gently in the sky I turn over those pebbles that have rattled in my mind: Teddy, Helen, the child. I can feel Teddy here – feel him in the stones of the house behind me, in the ground beneath my feet. I almost expect him to stroll around the corner, the dogs loping by his feet. He smiles: Vinny, I knew you'd come . . . And I reply: I didn't want to come, I wasn't going to come. He looks at me: But you have come, you've come back, Vinny – I've missed you . . .

I need a stick, I think, as I pull myself to my feet. If I am going to be walking around, it will be easier with a stick. But for the time being I must content myself with going slowly, gingerly, round the corner of the house to the back, where I disappear from view.

It seems a long way and when I reach the small gate I lean against it for some minutes to rest. It is very quiet. Many years ago one of the Dowager's ancestors planted cedars of Lebanon around the little plot and now they have grown huge, spreading out massive branches like arms to shield the dead.

No one comes here. The surrounding hedges are left wild – even the monks seem to respect that. Now they are dotted with the last of the wild flowers – poppies, rosehips, a few gangly foxgloves.

I push open the creaking gate and walk down the path, looking from side to side. They are all here: the Dowager in her vault with her husband and her adored Christian. And rows and rows of her ancestors' graves – some of the headstones so old that the inscriptions have worn away and there are only shallow dents where letters were carved. Grass grows over them – it has not been cut but left to seed itself. There are brambles twined around some of the stones and a few ripe heavy blackberries.

I should have brought flowers, I think – to give myself something to think, because my heart is thudding too fast and I am feeling more than ever that I would like an arm, a stick, a person here to lean on. Everyone brings flowers . . .

And then quite suddenly I come upon it.

They have laid him in a corner by an elder tree whose leaves are a brilliant yellow. They have given him a simple slate headstone with just his name and dates carved on it. The stone is rough-hewed, unsmoothed, the edges jagged. That's not like you, I grieve – you should have had the honey stone, something I could touch, not something so forbidding.

There is a bench opposite and I sit down heavily. Someone, though, has been bringing him flowers.

In a vase is a bunch of gold chrysanthemums that stand out against the grey stone like sudden sunlight in a storm. It should have been me, I reproach myself, I should have been here watching over you.

The creak of the gate wakes me. For a moment I can't remember where I am. It is cooler now, the sun sinking behind a hill and the plot covered in shadow. Gregory, I think as I hear the footsteps. Well, I could do with a strong arm to lean on for the way back.

But it is the musician who comes towards me.

'There,' she says. 'I knew I'd find you.'

'You?' I rub my eyes. 'What are you doing here?'

'Practice,' she replies casually. 'You know – they let me practise here.'

'Ah—'

'I'm sure I told you.'

I wave my hand. 'I forget—'

'Well,' she begins awkwardly. 'If it wasn't for you—'

'Yes, yes – never mind that,' I break in. 'Come and sit down for a moment.'

We sit in silence. Though she is quite still, I can feel her energy thrumming. She glows like the Virginia creeper, shines like the elder leaves.

'*I* put the flowers there,' she says suddenly. 'I hope you don't mind? I thought that otherwise it looked – rather forlorn.' She shivers and stands up, reaching out her hand. 'Come on – I'll show you the angel. And then we'll go back.'

I suppose it is a simple thing to find peace in a graveyard. Simple, too, the act of laying flowers, visiting the stones, sitting beside the dead, talking or not talking to them. Simple that it should be so restful, so composing.

Sometimes it seems as though I can hardly get down here – I am old and tired, I ache, and it doesn't seem worth making the effort. But when I am here and especially now in the spring, with the leaves coming out and the sun so soft and welcome, I realize more and more that this is where I belong and that I am looking forward to lying in the ground next to them.

I have planted jonquils on Helen's and Marigold's grave. They dance in the sun and are bright against the white headstone. I still think Teddy went rather overboard with the angel but I can smile about it.

I doze a lot now, slipping from consciousness to sleep in seconds. Waking, I can be disoriented for whole minutes, confused not so much as to where I am but when and *who*? As if there are rows of costumes hanging in front of me and I must choose which to slip into . . .

Annie visits, Gregory is here, there is the coming and going of the Order. I try to practise my acerbity on the monks, but some of that acid has left me and I cannot be as sharp as I used to.

Celia is happy with the Annexe. I imagine her music fresh and new, purifying the rooms. She sends me tickets for her concerts but I give them away.

And Helen? I talk to the angel who stands poised with outstretched wings over her and Marigold's grave. She has a wry sense of humour, Helen, a characteristic I am only now coming to understand. She liked to puncture convention in the same way I did. She says of the angel: My name launched a thousand ships and now I'm celestial . . . She too can raise her eyebrow.

Oh, I suppose it is a strange thing to talk to the dead – and to talk not as if they are dead but as if they are living. To tell them not of one's regrets or sorrows or guilt – they aren't interested in any of that, they no longer need appeasing. But to joke with them in the afternoon sun as old friends joke, to have conversations, one butting into another, arguing, agreeing, changing our minds. To watch the seasons change, the leaves emerge and spread and fall. To look, not behind us into the past, not ahead into the future, but *now* – at the bird hopping from stone to stone, at the insects flying, at the grasses rippling in the wind.

Because the dead live in the now. And they try to elbow themselves in, to remind us when we aren't looking, when we're too busy, too preoccupied with yesterday and tomorrow, with what we did wrong then, what we mustn't do wrong next. Listen, they tell us, listen, look around, stay here. Don't miss it, don't let it fly past, because it will and one day you will look back and wonder where all the days went that made up the necklace of your life.

Stop, they say, just for a moment. Keep company with us now.